A Cornered Rat

Marty shouted, "Reed, give it up. We've got you cut off from the door, and the law is undoubtedly headed this way. I don't want to kill you, Reed. Throw out the shotgun and show me empty hands."

"Here's empty hands, you son of a bitch." Black Jack stood and fired at the center of the table as he spoke, busting the fractured wood to splinters.

Marty saw him coming and knew he could not depend on the tabletop to withstand another assault from the buckshot. He threw himself to the left, firing his pistol as he rolled away from the ugly menace of the shotgun. . . .

Ricochet

Thom Nicholson

A SIGNET BOOK

SIGNET
Published by New American Library, a division of
Penguin Group (USA) Inc., 375 Hudson Street,
New York, New York 10014, USA
Penguin Group (Canada), 90 Eglinton Avenue East, Suite 700, Toronto,
Ontario M4P 2Y3, Canada (a division of Pearson Penguin Canada Inc.)
Penguin Books Ltd., 80 Strand, London WC2R 0RL, England
Penguin Ireland, 25 St. Stephen's Green, Dublin 2,
Ireland (a division of Penguin Books Ltd.)
Penguin Group (Australia), 250 Camberwell Road, Camberwell, Victoria 3124,
Australia (a division of Pearson Australia Group Pty. Ltd.)
Penguin Books India Pvt. Ltd., 11 Community Centre, Panchsheel Park,
New Delhi - 110 017, India
Penguin Group (NZ), 67 Apollo Drive, Rosedale, North Shore 0632,
New Zealand (a division of Pearson New Zealand Ltd.)
Penguin Books (South Africa) (Pty.) Ltd., 24 Sturdee Avenue,
Rosebank, Johannesburg 2196, South Africa

Penguin Books Ltd., Registered Offices:
80 Strand, London WC2R 0RL, England

First published by Signet, an imprint of New American Library,
a division of Penguin Group (USA) Inc.

First Printing, November 2007
10 9 8 7 6 5 4 3 2 1

Copyright © Thomas Nicholson, 2007
All rights reserved

 REGISTERED TRADEMARK—MARCA REGISTRADA

Printed in the United States of America

To my wife, Sandy.
And to my editor at Penguin, Brent Howard.
Both helped make my character Marty come alive.

Chapter 1

Back-shooter

"I don't cotton to bounty hunters."

The harsh statement grated against Marty Keller's soul like fingernails on a schoolhouse slate board. His eyes narrowed as he coolly appraised the county marshal, a weather-beaten man of advanced middle age. The man's gut rolled over worn whipcord pants held up with soiled gallows. His boots were scuffed and dirty, the heels nearly worn away. His shirt was a dingy gray, no matter its original color, and was loosely stuffed in his pants. This country boob had the audacity to insult him just because he knew he could get away with it?

"Whatever you say, Marshal Willard. I'm just interested in your poster for a James Bennett. I saw it in Fort Smith last week. It still good?"

"Jim Bennett? Sure is. But I aim to catch him myself. I don't need no bounty hunter trying to back-shoot him like a mangy dog. The man needs to come back here and stand trial. I figger he's got another side to the story I got from the jaspers that put him on the dodge."

"How's that?"

"It's jus' that I know Jim and his wife, Julia. They're good folks. He's got a little spread a few miles east a'here, right at the Missouri border."

"How come you're handling the jurisdiction instead of a Missouri lawman?" Marty shifted his weight, wishing the grumpy lawdog would offer him a seat in the chair by the scarred desk. Be damned if he would ask to sit. Rather than ask anything of the rube sheriff, he would stand until his feet were bloody.

"The crime happened just outside of town a couple a'miles. Made it my problem, and I wish it weren't."

Marty kept quiet. He had learned that the best way to encourage others to talk was to keep his mouth shut. He looked intently at the marshal, patiently waiting for the lawman to continue.

An uneasy pause followed. The marshal shifted in his chair and picked at his teeth with a hoary fingernail. After inspecting the result, he looked back at Marty. "Seems Jim inherited some land in Wyoming Territory. Three fellas from Cheyenne came here and made him an offer fer the land. Jim apparently said no thanks, so the men left and were riding back here when Jim rode up after 'em, according to the two men who was there with the victim. Anyways, they said Jim asked fer more money and when they said no, he got mad and drew down, shootin' one of the three offa his hoss. Killed him deader than a stuffed turkey too. The other two hightailed it over here to me and swore out a murder warrant fer Jim."

"They the ones that gave you the three thousand dollars?"

"Yep, had it wired in from Wyoming Territory. The county wouldn'ta gone more'n three hunnerd otherwise."

"Someone must have some deep pockets in Wyoming."

"Well, yur the second bounty hunter to show up since the poster went out, so I guess it's a'workin' fer 'em. I still don't like it, though. It pears to me that Jim oughta have his say in court. You bounty hunters have a habit of bringin' yur prisoners back dead more often than not."

"Not my way, Marshal. I always give them the chance to come in peaceable with me." Marty nodded, growing weary of standing so long without moving around. "I do agree with you. If he'll let me, I'll try my best to bring him back so that he can make his case in court. You have any idea where he might have gone?"

"Shore do, but I ain't gonna share nothin' with a bounty hunter, that's fer damned certain. You wanna catch Jim Bennett, you gotta do it yurself."

"Whatever you say, Marshal. I'll be on my way. Thanks so much for your help." Marty turned on his heel and left the office, not bothering to see if his sarcasm registered with the unfriendly sheriff.

He walked out into the early April sunshine. It felt good on his back after the gray days of March. He slowly made his way up the packed-dirt sidewalk, looking in the wavy glass windows of the few stores open for business in the village. Fort Wayne had a long way to go before it would be worthy of being called a town. Marty stopped at the window of Hermann Volker, Gunsmith, if the painted sign over the door was correct. Leaned up against the corner of the display area was a telescopic sight, a slender brass tube nearly two feet long, with a leather cover over each end to protect the glass lenses.

"I saw one of them in Georgia, just before the war ended," he murmured to himself. "Might work just fine on my Sharps." Marty went to his horse and retrieved his .50-caliber Sharps buffalo rifle from the saddle holster. As he did, he mentally tallied up what money he had left from the reward he had earned when he'd killed Long Tom Carter at the shoot-out in Bixley, Kansas, nearly a year earlier. He had lived all this time on the reward for the notorious outlaw and his gang of cutthroats. Unfortunately, riding the bounty hunter trail took lots of money and Marty was nearly tapped out again. The reward for bringing in James Bennett would carry him through the summer and the fall, so he could continue to track Hulett and Sanchez without interruption. If the rifle scope was not too expensive, he'd add it to his arsenal of manhunter tools.

Marty stepped inside the shop, the familiar scent of gun oil, cleaning solvent, and black powder filling his nostrils. A heavyset man with powerful arms, more like those of a blacksmith than a gunsmith, glanced up at him from behind a workbench at the far end of the room. The man had a friendly, age-worn face, his dark hair turning silver at the temples and fast retreating from his forehead. His brown eyes were alert and inquisitive as he peered from under bushy brows at his potential customer.

"*Guten tag.* May I help ya?"

Marty handed over the Sharps rifle after checking to make certain it was unloaded. "I saw the telescopic sight in your window. Think it would work on this Sharps?"

The gunsmith took the rifle in his meaty hands and inspected it carefully. "Ya, it vill do jus' fine. You a buffer hunter?"

Marty grinned. He had been just that only a short while earlier. "I've shot my share, I suppose."

The shop owner grunted. "You haf der rifle fer it. Dis is one powerful veapon." He walked over and got the brass scope out of the window. Turning it in his hands, he nodded. "Ya, I can put der scope on. Cost you therdy dollars. I vill haf it fer ya by tomorrow afternoon. Ya?"

Marty took the scope and focused on a shingle hanging on a store across the street. The crosshairs framed a small knothole, magnifying it five times or more. He passed the scope back to the gunsmith. "It's a deal. I'll stop by tomorrow, right after lunch."

"Dat vill be fine. It vill be done."

Marty walked out, satisfied. He had a new and better sighting device for the heavy buffalo gun. He was already a dead shot with the big Sharps. With the scope, he should be even more accurate and deadly. For Marty, it was a pleasant afternoon. He cleaned up, had a good meal, and slept for two hours in a real bed at the hotel until just after the sun set.

Marty made his way to the only saloon in the town, at the corner of the crossroads of the town's two main streets. He pushed open the batwing doors and stepped inside, moving out of the doorway and pausing until his eyes adjusted to the gloom and tobacco smoke. The stench of stale beer and the odor of unwashed men permeated the dank interior.

A pile of cold cuts and thickly cut bread lay on a silver platter at the end of the bar. Marty slowly walked across the sawdust-covered floor to the end of the bar and made himself a massive sandwich, then chased it down with a mug of cool beer. As he chewed, his thoughts drifted to his family, as they did most evenings around supper time. Sweet Meg, happy little Matt, both dead and buried in quiet loneliness under the big oak tree at his old ranch in Texas. Five desperate, evil bastards had killed his family while he had been away, tracking Comancheros for the Texas Rangers. Of the quintet he had dedicated himself to tracking down and killing, two of the killers still lived and rode free. Hulett and Sanchez. Their names were burned into his brain. They dominated his every waking moment like the sun dominated the day, and the moon the night. It had been so long that he could not imagine what life would be like without their hated faces whirling across his mind's eye.

He sighed, wishing for his dead family a peaceful rest, and turned his attention to the five men sitting around a table filled with chips and cards. Marty eased over to the gamblers.

"Room for another, gents?"

"Sure, partner, grab yourself a seat. I'm Ray Lieske. This

here is Bob, Luke, and Sam, and the little guy there is called Ross."

Marty pulled out a chair and sat down. "Thanks. Call me Marty. Came to town looking for an old army buddy. What's the game?"

Chapter 2

Digging for Clues

"Dealer's choice," Ross interjected. "Nothin' funny, though. Draw, five- and seven-card stud, and that's 'bout it. What's the name of the fella yur looking fer?"

"Name's Bennett. Marshal told me about his misfortune, though, so I'm outa luck seeing him, I suppose."

"Yep, that's a fact," Ross replied. "Jim done stepped into the cow pile big-time."

"I'll say. Marshal Willard says he'll get a fair hearing once he stands trial against the charges. That's worth somethin', I suppose." Luke solemnly nodded at his own words.

Marty smiled at the other players. "Anyway, let's play cards. I need some travelin' money."

"You're liable to end up afoot if you think we're gonna roll over and play dead fer ya. You been warned." Luke gave a flinty smile.

"I suppose I can handle those terms." Marty threw twenty dollars onto the green felt. "Who's got the deal?"

"I do," Bob answered. "The deal is five-card stud. Ante's a dollar."

Marty pushed over a silver dollar and settled in for a spell of card-playing. He knew he could learn a lot about the area if he did not win too much or push too hard for answers. He played conservatively and lost more often than he won. After several hands, he casually commented, "Marshal told me about the big gunfight. Said it happened just outa town."

"Weren't all that big," Ray answered, shifting his cards from his right hand to his left so he could grab the half-empty glass of beer beside him. "Jim shot some jasper from Wyoming. He claimed they drew first. They claimed otherwise. Jim went on the run right after. I don't know why, 'cause he ain't that sort of fella. I've knowed him since he moved here after the war. I don't believe it's as cut and dried as those jaspers said."

Marty nodded. "When he stands trial, what really happened should come out." He looked over at Luke, who was sitting quietly beside him. "I raise your bet a dollar, Luke."

Luke stared at his cards for a minute, then sighed and tossed them down onto the table. "No use throwin' good money after bad. I fold." He paused to light a small cigar. "It's too bad Jim lit out. He's still on the run. I'll bet he wishes he weren't. He's got a nice little wife and boy."

"You knew him too, then?"

"The Bennetts are nice folk. Never let you go by without offerin' ya a hot meal. I reckon ole Jim is gettin' a raw deal fer a fact."

Ross spoke up as he dealt the next hand. "Well, some-one'll get him sooner or later. He might as well give hisself up and face the music, rather than stay on the dodge for who knows how long."

Bob shook his head. "He can stay out as long as he wants, I reckon. He ain't where everybody is a'lookin'."

Luke glanced crossly at Bob. "Bob, you talk too much. Someone who don't need to know might hear ya."

Bob glared back at Luke, angered by the rebuke. "I know when to stay shut and when not. 'Sides, most everyone in town knows Jim headed fer his sister's place in El Dorado, rather than into the Indian Territory."

"Well, not everybody knows Jim had a sister there, at least until you started blabbin' about it."

"Well, hell's bells. Didn't he sneak back jus' last week and say so to ole Sy here?"

"And didn't he say to keep our mouths shut about it? Marshal Willard has anyone after him headed into the territory, wastin' time and horseflesh while he tries to figger out a way to get Jim outa the mess he's in."

Marty threw a dollar onto the tabletop, eager to keep the talk going without appearing to be too interested. "I'll open for a dollar. I'd say that Jim Bennett's best chance is to surrender and face up to those that accused him."

Luke nodded. "I reckon that's Jim's plan, once the hubbub's died down a mite. He'll show up one of these days and get things straightened out."

"I'd bet on it," Marty murmured. "I raise your raise, Sam. That's two dollars to you, Luke. In or out?"

Marty excused himself an hour later. Although he had not gathered any more information, the fifty dollars he'd lost at the table was money well spent. He headed for his bed in the hotel, whistling aimlessly. His fitful sleep was no different from that of most other nights, filled with painful memories that kept him from a satifying rest.

The next morning, he commissioned the local blacksmith to replace all of Pacer's horseshoes. He had been riding the big gray for over six months now and was doubly satisfied with the deal he had made with the horse trader in Kentucky. The gelding had never failed him, was fast when it counted, and could go all day without breaking down. Marty felt like the two of them had formed a solid partnership. He rubbed the horse's velvety nose as the smithy got his tools ready for the shoeing.

"You rest up today, big fella. We'll be on the trail again tomorrow." The horse snorted softly and submitted to the work-hardened hands of the smithy, who expertly pulled the nails from the old shoes so he could file and measure Pacer's hooves for the new ones.

After his lunch at the only café in town, Marty ambled over to the gun shop. Mr. Volker looked up from a pistol he was working on as the jingling bell over the door announced Marty's arrival. "Ah, here ya are. Der rifle is ready. Vill ya vant to try it out?"

"You know a place?"

"Ya, two miles east on der border road. Der is a big bluff 'bout a half mile off der road. Ya can shoot at dat all ya vant."

Volker showed Marty how to adjust the elevation and windage knobs, and Marty left the shop, pleased with his new purchase. He'd also picked up an additional box of .50-caliber brass cartridges as well as a box of .44-40 rounds for his six-guns and saddle rifle. As soon as he purchased some food supplies, he would be ready to start after Bennett. He stopped just outside the doorway and then turned back into the shop.

"Mr. Volker, you know how to get to El Dorado?"

"Ya, it's 'bout one hunnerd fifty mile south, in Arkansas. Go east from here to Bentonville, den take der Shreveport Road south till ya git to Lewisville, near da Louisiana border. Den go east twenty miles to El Dorado."

"Sounds like a plan, Mr. Volker. Thank you very much."

"Bitte, ya kum back agin."

Marty forced the modified Sharps rifle into the saddle scabbard hanging on Pacer's left side. With the scope attached, it was a snug fit. "Probably better in the long run," he mumbled. "Keep the gun from bouncing around and jarring the sight off center."

Marty headed to the local general store and loaded up on

supplies for his trip. He casually passed the time with the store's owner, a tall, skinny man with only a sparse crown of graying hair over his ears. Marty noticed from a small sign on the wall that he was also the town postman.

"You know James Bennett, Mr. Blum?" Marty inquired.

"Only slightly. He shopped here now and then. He did use the post office, but mostly did his buyin' at Fletcher's trading post, north of here. Claimed he got a better deal from that ole skinflint. If he did, it was just so Fletcher could put the screws to me. We ain't exactly friends."

Marty took out the rangers badge he always carried. Though it was not legal for him to show it, it had proved useful in the past. "I'm lookin' for Bennett. I understand he's got a sister in Arkansas, place called El Dorado. You ever see any of his mail addressed to that town?"

"See here now, I can't be showing you any mail. That's agin federal law."

Marty reached into his shirt pocket and took out a twenty-dollar gold coin. He put it on the countertop, halfway between himself and Blum. The storekeeper's eyes grew wary and his hand fluttered around the coin like a moth around a flame. He wanted it badly. Licking his lips, he looked around. Nobody else was in the store. Finally, his hand swooped down on the coin and it was gone.

"I ain't certain, but it seems to me that Bennett mailed a few letters to a Liz. Liz . . . What was it? Liz Penny or something like that, over to El Dorado. That's all I can tell you, Ranger."

"It'll do. Thanks."

As the sun peeked over the horizon the next morning, Marty rode Pacer out of Fort Wayne, headed east to Bentonville, in western Arkansas. At the bluff described by Mr. Volker, he stopped and fired up thirty .50-caliber rounds at ranges from three hundred yards to more than twice that distance. He carefully cleaned the rifle, then practiced with his

pistols and saddle rifle until it was midmorning. He cleaned
the weapons and then proceeded toward Bentonville.

Five days of hard riding brought him to the little town of
El Dorado, in southwest Arkansas. Hardscrabble farms, in-
habited by tired people worn thin trying to scratch out a living from the rocky clay soil, surrounded the place. Marty
eased in after dark and stabled his animals at a ratty livery
located at the south end of town. A dour-looking woman
with her gray hair pulled back in a severe bun took Pacer
and Marty's pack mule from him.

"Give them both extra grain, ma'am. They've come a
long ways and deserve it."

"I'll do it and give 'em both a good rubdown. Cost ya
four bits a day."

"A deal. Your husband around?"

"Nope. Went off to war in 'sixty-two and didn't come
back. Fertilizin' the flowers in Tennessee—a place called
Franklin."

"I was there. My regrets, ma'am. That was a bad time."

"Well, he drank too much and liked to get rough when he
was in his cups, so I'm better off without him, I reckon. Still
miss the sumbitch, though. Funny, ain't it?" She took a corn-
cob pipe from her mouth and smiled at Marty, exposing a
row of rotting teeth. "How long ya want to leave yur animals?"

"Not long, I suppose. I'm looking for the sister of an old
friend of mine. Her name is Liz. Liz Penny, maybe?"

The stable lady shook her head. "Nope, don't know her.
There is a Pennington family that lives out on Turkey Ridge,
north of town a couple of miles. The wife's name may be
Liz. I ain't certain."

"Well, I reckon I'll favor the hotel for a bath and bed
tonight. Maybe tomorrow I'll swing out that way and pay
my respects."

"Yur animals'll be ready anytime, mister. The best hotel

in town is the Sawyer House, at the north end of Main Street. They got a brass bathtub fer inside bathin' too."

Marty took his leave, walking up the wooden sidewalk, carrying his saddlebags and saddle rifle. He checked into the hotel and bathed in hot water before partaking of a hearty meal of pork chops and boiled greens cooked with fatback and lots of salt. He leisurely had a beer and retired to a soft bed, where he spent another restless night dreaming of his deceased family and tossing in anguished slumber.

The next morning, he had flapjacks, a slab of ham, and two cups of bitter coffee before making his way back to the livery. The same woman was swamping out the stalls when he arrived. She pushed her hands against the small of her back, then put the pitchfork aside and walked over to him.

"You want yur hoss?"

"Yep."

"How 'bout the pack mule? Takin' him or leavin' him here?"

"I think both. Who knows, I just may keep on going, once I get started. Or, I may be back. Can't ever tell with me." He smiled at the woman. "I keep turning up, like a bad nickel."

"Yur the boss, mister. But you ain't no bad nickel or my name ain't Hattie Gathman. And that's sure what it is."

Marty smiled at her again. "Some folks might argue with you, Hattie, but not me. It's too nice a day for that. Come on, let's get my horses ready to go. Daylight's burning."

As Marty swung into the saddle, he put a five-dollar greenback in Hattie's hand. "That's for your trouble, Hattie. Maybe a little extra for the fund to get your husband back here. A man needs to be buried near folks that miss him, if you ask me." He paused. "Can you direct me out to the Pennington farm?"

Marty found the Pennington farm exactly where Hattie had told him it would be. He eased off Pacer while they were still hidden from view by the thick growth of trees covering the rolling hills surrounding the house and barn.

He carefully worked his way down to where he had an unobstructed view of the place, and settled in behind a clump of wild blackberries, content to watch and wait for the time being. He estimated that he was nearly three hundred yards away from the front door of the house. Too far for anything but his Sharps rifle, but he was not interested in shooting at anyone. For now, he waited to see what was going on at the farm. He stared through his captured Yankee binoculars, watching a solitary man furrow a nearby field with twin workhorses pulling an iron plow. A woman walked out of the house and headed for a chicken coop built along one side of the unpainted barn. She threw some grain around her, drawing a crowd of clucking chickens, then collected eggs from nests inside the coop before heading back to the house.

Marty surveyed the house through his binoculars, but he could see nothing inside the place, as the windows of the farm were covered not in glass but in some sort of oiled paper. The sun was halfway up the sky, in his face. Marty patiently waited and watched for thirty minutes without anything more happening. Then, the door opened and a man in trousers and a faded red undershirt walked outside. He stretched mightily, then slowly ambled over to the corral, where he patted and talked to his horse for several minutes before walking the animal into the barn.

Marty settled back and mumbled to himself. "That you, Bennett? Are you there? Wish I was a mite closer, so I could be more certain."

Jim Bennett was sure something was wrong. Once inside the barn, he quickly saddled his horse, then crept to a knothole in a board where he could see the wooded hillside from which the flash of sunlight against glass had originated. He strained to see the source of the flash but was unsuccessful. Still, he had seen it. Someone was definitely on the hill south of the farm, watching the place with a telescope.

After looking in vain for several minutes for any further indication of the watcher's presence, Bennett casually walked back to the house and entered, fighting the urge to stare back at the hill. "Liz, honey, someone's up on the south hill, watching the place with a telescope. I gotta go now."

"Oh, Jim. Are you sure?"

"Yep, I saw 'em, all right. Make me some grub for the trail, will you, Sis?"

"Let me go get Harvey. Maybe the two of you—"

Bennett held up his hand. "Don't even think of it, Sis. So far you two ain't done nothing illegal. Besides, if you leave, the fella out there might come on in. If he's the law, I don't want to fight with him."

"Why don't you just give up? You know you're innocent."

"It don't make no never mind. Once the court finds out I'm a deserter from the Union army, they're likely to hang me anyway. All I can do is keep runnin' till they quit lookin' fer me. Then I can send for Julia and Johnny and start over, maybe in Wyomin' Territory."

"Oh, Jim, I'm so scared for you and Julia. You know Sam was killed out there in Wyoming."

"Don't you fret. I've got away before. I can do it agin."

Chapter 3

Don't Fight a Bounty Hunter

Liz Pennington wrung her hands. "Oh, Jim, what'll we do?"

"Just make me some food and put it in a sack. Take it out to the barn. Don't let on anything's amiss. I'll wait in here. After a few minutes, you call for me. I'll come to the barn. I can sneak out the back and make it to the trees without being spotted by whoever is up on the hill. Once I get there, I'll hightail it to the Injun Territory and lay low. It'll be all right. Don't you fret."

Liz nodded, her face pinched in worry as she hastily put together some food and canned goods in a small flour sack. "What if he comes down here?"

"There's a shotgun in the barn. If he comes down, you put it on him and fire one barrel. That'll bring Harvey a'runnin'. You'll be okay; it's me they want, not you."

"Jim, I don't know if I can kill someone."

"You don't have to. Just fire it in his general direction as soon as he reaches the edge of the corral. That'll send him scurryin' fer cover while he's still far enough away that the shotgun won't cause him any damage. Once Harv is with you, you can decide how to handle him if he won't skedaddle."

Liz finished packing the food and tucked the filled sack under a shawl thrown over her shoulders. She squeezed Bennett's hand, then hurried out to the barn and went inside. Once hidden in the gloom of the barn, she looked intently for the man on the hill, but to no avail. Finally, she walked to the open door and shouted, "Jim, come out here. I need your help."

Bennett followed his sister's footsteps to the barn and entered the dim interior. He untied his horse and led him to the rear door, then looped a rein over the handle to keep the animal from wandering away. He joined Liz at the front of the barn, and peered through a gap in the raw wood siding toward the hill to the south of the ranch.

"You see anyone?" Liz whispered to him.

"Nope," Bennett answered. "But someone's up there— I'm certain of it. Keep your eyes peeled. I'm gonna fill a sack with grain for my hoss. It's liable to be a long time afore he gets the chance to laze around in a stable agin." Bennett filled an empty flour sack with nearly twenty pounds of oats and tied it to the saddle horn.

"I see him," Liz whispered loudly.

"Where is he?" Jim hurried to her side and peered out a gap in the boards.

"Over there, by the big oak tree that's got the top broke off by lightning. I saw the sunlight reflectin' offa his telescope."

"Good girl. I'm gonna go outside now and bring in a couple of those boards Harv has cut to make another stable. Then I'm gonna scoot. Hopefully the fella on the hill will think I'm working inside the barn. Maybe I can get a good head start on him. If he heads down here afore Harv comes in, shoot the shotgun at him and then run like blazes with it to Harv, unnerstand?"

"Oh, Jim, I'm so worried for you. Please, be very careful."

"I will. Don't worry. Well, here I go." Bennett slowly walked out of the barn and gathered up the boards lying against the outside wall. He carried them back inside and returned to the gap. "See anything?"

"No, nothing since that first time."

"Just the same, I'd better git a'goin'. Bye, Sis. I love you and thanks for takin' me in. Thank Harv fer puttin' me up, old gal. I'll write you once I figger out where I'm settlin'. You both have been just great. Write Julia and tell her that I'm movin' on and will write her once I git settled somewhere in Indian Territory."

Bennett hugged his older sister and kissed her on her weathered cheek. He slowly led his horse out of the barn and toward the woods to the north of the farmhouse, careful to keep the big structure of the barn between him and where the observer was hiding halfway up the hill to the south of the barn. Once he was fifty feet inside the tree line, he climbed into his saddle and rode away from the farm, pushing his horse as hard as he dared.

In an hour he would be on the Fulton Road and then he would be only a day's ride from the territory. He could hide in there until the searcher grew tired of chasing him. Then he'd head for his home and the loving warmth of Julia's embrace. They could light out together for parts unknown.

Marty shifted to relieve the strain on his legs. He'd had his sights on the barn for over half an hour and had seen absolutely nothing. At first he had caught glimpses of movement inside, but now nothing. He frowned. It seemed impossible that there would be so little movement, no matter what the man was working on inside the shielded interior. Marty moved to another position, where he could see inside the open door a little better.

He groaned to himself as he swept the scene with his binoculars. From where he now was, he could see light from an open door at the rear of the barn. He must have been spotted. "Dammit, just my luck. Five cents to a penny the jasper has ducked out the back and hightailed it into the woods," he muttered to himself.

He hurried to his horse and swung up, heading straight for the barn, leading his pack mule. As he rode out of the woods, he slid his pistol up and down in its holster, making certain it was loose and easily drawn if necessary. He had just reached the corner of the corral when a shotgun blast rent the air and buckshot whizzed by him like a cluster of hungry flies. He immediately slid off his horse and drew his pistol, taking what cover he could behind the corner post of the corral.

He spotted the woman streaking around the side of the barn, running like the wind toward her husband in the field, the smoking shotgun still in her hand. Carefully, Marty approached the barn and looked inside the cavernous front door. The interior was empty—not even a horse—but the back double doors were wide open. Marty led Pacer through to the back of the barn, spotting fresh droppings in the end stall. A horse had been stabled there not an hour earlier, he was certain.

As he exited the barn, he climbed back onto Pacer and led his pack mule toward the two people standing together in the field. The man now held the shotgun. Marty stopped Pacer fifty yards away from the pair, not wanting to get within effective range of the scattergun in the hands of the farmer.

Marty stayed mounted and kept his hand away from his weapons. "Howdy, folks. That was Jim Bennett that took off into the woods, wasn't it? He's wanted by the law, you know. It'd be the best thing if you told me where he was heading. I'll take him back so he can face the charges against him. The marshal in Fort Wayne talks like Jim's got a good chance of getting out of the mess he's in, if he'll only stand trial."

"You can see he ain't here no more, mister," the farmer shouted at Marty. "Git offa my land. We ain't gonna tell ya nothin'. Jim's gone now. You git too."

Marty bowed to the inevitable. "Okay, folks, I'm going. But if Bennett comes back here, tell him to give it up. I'm not gonna quit dogging him until he's caught. Better he does it quiet-like and not fight it." He reined Pacer toward the woods where Bennett had to have disappeared. "Come on, hoss. Let's go catch us that reward." He rode away without looking back.

Marty quickly found the tracks left by the fleeing man. They headed directly north and were easy to follow. "This fella knows where he's headed, Pacer. Come on, let's get after him. He's pushing his horse pretty hard. He'll have to slow up before long."

Marty crossed the Fulton Road before noon and rode into the small southwest Arkansas town of Lewisville, halfway to Fulton, just after dark. At the edge of town he stopped at the livery, the edge of town where the owner was sitting in an old rocker, smoking a pipe and monitoring the traffic traveling past him.

"Hello," Marty said.

"Howdy, stranger."

"See a man ride in an hour or so ago? Maybe in a bit of a hurry."

"Maybe. Why do you want to know?"

Marty flashed his ranger's badge, knowing that in the gloom of early evening it was barely decipherable. "He's on the dodge and I'm after him."

"Well now, I reckon I did see someone. A fella stopped and asked me where to grab a hot meal. I sent him on down to the Star Café. That's the last I saw of him."

"What can you tell me about his horse?"

"A bay gelding, two white stockings on the front legs, a blaze on the nose. Branded with a lazy *B* and a crossed-out *US*."

"Bought from the army, huh?"

"Bought or stolen, who knows?" He looked closely at Pacer. "Say, that's a mighty fine animal yur a'ridin'." The livery owner grinned. "In my business I notice things like that."

"Thanks. Pacer is a cross between Morgan and Tennessee walker. I've had him six months now and am mighty pleased with him. He's got speed and stamina. I just wish I could breed him someday. What colts he would have sired."

"Yeah, but if he weren't gelded, he'd be a lot harder to control and train, don't ya think?"

"I suppose. Well, I best get going." Marty thanked the observant man and rode on down the dusty street to the café sitting midway in the last block of buildings in the town. He climbed down and slapped dust from his pants with his stained hat before entering the café. Most of the evening customers had already eaten and departed by the time he arrived. A slight woman, brown hair stuck to her sweaty forehead, was wiping off tables when he walked in.

"Howdy, ma'am. Still got any grub in the pot?"

"Sure thing, mister. Pot roast or fried chicken. What's yur pleasure?"

"I think I'll try the chicken. Been a while. Coffee and pie, if you've got any."

"Rhubarb, fresh made this afternoon."

"Works for me. Bring on the coffee now, if you don't mind."

The woman headed for the kitchen at the rear of the café and Marty took a seat at the back of the room, where he could watch the front door. The woman delivered his coffee and returned to the kitchen. The next time Marty saw her, she was carrying a plate filled with food. He dug in with relish, hungry and tired from the long ride.

"Mighty good food, ma'am. Tell me, did a stranger eat here about an hour ago? Tall fella with dark hair?"

"I think so. Took his pie, said he'd eat it in the saddle. Said he was in a hurry to git to Fulton. I told him it was forty miles up the road. He'd have to ride all night to git there."

"That's him. Always in a hurry." Marty smiled at the woman. "I don't think I'm gonna catch up with him tonight, do you?"

"Not unless his hoss breaks down from ridin' him too hard." The woman sighed. "Leave four bits at the front counter when yur done, mister. I gotta finish them tables afore I can go home tonight." She returned to her table-washing, pushing a lock of hair away from her eyes with the back of a soapy hand.

Marty finished his meal and returned to the livery. The same man was still sitting in the rocker, still smoking his pipe in solitary splendor.

"Find yur man, Sheriff?"

Marty did not bother correcting him. "Yes and no. He was here, but rode on toward Fulton. I think I'll rest my horse for a spell and grab some sleep. I'll start after him tomorrow morning. He's liable to stop somewhere in the dark and I'd likely ride right past him."

The livery owner cackled. "That's a fact. Ain't much of a moon tonight. Want me to give yur hoss and mule some grain?"

"Yes, please. And a good rubdown as well, for both of them. I'll be over at the hotel, if you need me."

"Okeydokey. Cost ya four bits."

Marty put two half-dollar coins in the man's hand. "A bargain at twice the price. I'll pick them up tomorrow morning."

"I'm likely to still be asleep. Just be sure to shut the door on yur way out."

Marty threw his saddlebag over his shoulder and walked to the hotel, carrying his smaller rifle. He checked in and took a room on the third floor, where he slept until the dark sky was turning gray to the east.

Marty was on the road to Fulton as the first red sunbeam rose over the wooded hills of western Arkansas. A little while after noon, after six hours of hard riding, he saw the spires of the Methodist Church of Fulton as he crossed a small rise. He rode into the town, his eyes vainly searching for any sign that Bennett was still somewhere close, although he expected the wanted man to be long gone.

Marty stopped at the café and had a hearty lunch of pot roast and coffee, then headed to the general store. He replenished his supplies and packed them on his mule. He asked around but could not find anyone who would admit to having seen Bennett ride through. The man either had skipped the town or had ridden straight through without stopping. Marty was confident he would find the trail on the far side of town.

Within minutes of leaving Fulton, he located Bennett's sign and steadily dogged his tracks as the wanted man headed into Indian Territory. For two days Marty trailed Bennett ever deeper into the rugged badlands of eastern Oklahoma Territory. The fleeing man seemed to be working his way toward Tahlequah, the capital of the Western Cherokee Nation, the same tribe that had made the bitter march on the Trail of Tears from Alabama thirty years earlier.

"You know, Pacer," Marty said softly to his big gray horse, "I wonder if Bennett is making his way back toward his place in Fort Wayne. Maybe to pick up his wife and light out for good."

Pacer did not answer but plodded on along the narrow

game trail, following Bennett's tracks. Marty's gaze continually swept the rough terrain. He knew how easy it was for the hunter to be surprised by the hunted.

As darkness gradually fell, cloaking the rolling hills in inky blackness, Marty spotted a campfire burning up ahead. It looked to be a hundred yards off the trail, set back among some trees on the hillside. He slid the Winchester from its scabbard and jacked a shell into the chamber. "Easy, Pacer." He gently gigged his knees into the horse's sides. "Let's move up close and see if this is our man."

They had not gone far when Pacer walked over a flint outcropping several yards wide. Pacer's metal shoes immediately slipped on the slick rock. The agile horse recovered his footing, but with a clatter that would have awakened a deaf man. Marty groaned in disappointment.

As he reached the spot of the campfire, Marty slid off the saddle and quickly ran toward the small fire. He had not reached it when he heard the clomping of retreating hoofbeats. "Dammit," he groaned. "He's lit out on me." Marty ran up to the campfire but his instinct was right. The man he was tracking had ridden away.

Marty looked around. A saddle and a bedroll lay beside the fire. A blackened coffeepot sat on a rock near the tiny blaze, steam issuing from its spout. "Left his gear," Marty murmured. "Looks like he's gonna have an uncomfortable night ahead of him."

Marty returned to where Pacer and the pack mule were patiently awaiting him. He led them back to the burning campfire and gave them their nightly care before settling back and enjoying a cup of Bennett's coffee with his bread and dried salt pork.

As soon as he'd eaten, he piled a load of wood onto the fire and then moved back into the shadows, where he wrapped his bedroll around his shoulders and leaned against a thick tree trunk. He needed to be ready in case his quarry circled back and tried to surprise him. He dozed on and off until daylight, but all stayed quiet.

He had a quick breakfast and got back on the trail. He easily picked up Bennett's tracks, which he doggedly followed all morning. He found where the wanted man had stopped and rested his horse for a while next to a small stream, then continued on, always headed north by east.

He spotted his man for the first time around noon. He had just topped a rise when he saw the figure of a man riding bareback going over another rise about a half mile ahead of him. The man looked back just as he topped the rise, and Marty was certain the man saw him.

"Well, Pacer, the cat's outa the bag. Now he knows we're close. He'll be lookin' for a spot to hole up and ambush us. We'll have to be extra careful." He loped ahead, trying to close ground on the fleeing man. "No need to give any more time than necessary to get prepared for us, is there, ole hoss?"

They crossed the rise where Marty had spotted Bennett. Ahead of them a mile or so, a raw outcropping of flint boulders had piled up like pebbles washed up in a creek. "He'll be in there, Pacer. A perfect spot. We'll have to take it easy once we get close. I sure hope I can convince him to come in peaceable-like."

Chapter 4

A Fateful Decision

Marty took it nice and easy as he approached the jumble of boulders that his quarry was possibly using as an ambush site. He stopped three hundred yards away and sat looking at the massive stones, tumbled about like a sack of spilled potatoes. Pacer shifted, catching the scent of another horse hidden somewhere among the seemingly impenetrable rocks. Marty shouted, loudly enough for anyone hiding among the rocks to hear him.

"Bennett, I know you're in there. Come on out and let me take you in. The marshal at Fort Wayne says you've got a good chance of beating the charge against you. Come on out and let's talk about it."

The only answer was a rifle shot that skipped across the ground, twenty feet short and ten feet to his right, raising a small puff of dust. He gigged Pacer and moved quickly to the left. His eyes scanned the rocks and crevices, looking for Bennett or the telltale sign of gun smoke.

The second shot missed by more than the first, but it betrayed Bennett's location. He had holed up behind a hefty boulder that towered some twenty feet in the air, over all the others scattered around it. Bennett fired from behind the tall rock again, signifying his determination to fight it out. Marty kept moving farther to the left, until he had put a wall of large boulders between him and Bennett. Then he spurred the horse hard and rode quickly until he was at the periphery of the rock outcropping. He swung down, taking his Winchester with him, and moved into the edge of the rock field. Carefully, he eased around a boulder. Marty scanned the outline of the massive boulder against the blue sky background. He ducked and bobbed his way deeper into the field, moving ever closer to the big rock. He saw nothing of Bennett.

Suddenly, a bullet pinged off a boulder behind him, ricocheting away into the cloudless blue sky with a scream of tortured metal. Marty involuntarily ducked down, but not before seeing the gun smoke from Bennett's rifle. Bennett had moved farther up into the rock pile, headed for a sheer bluff from which the rocks had originally broken away.

Marty pushed on, careful to keep low and covered. Bennett was shooting to kill. "Damned jughead," Marty grumbled softly to himself. "Just determined to make it hard on me, isn't he?" His breath wheezing in and out like a field hand's, he continued darting from rock to rock, working his way closer to Bennett.

Finally he could go no farther; there was not enough cover between him and where he thought Bennett was hiding. He risked a quick glance around a man-sized rock and was rewarded with a bullet that showered stinging grit against his face. He did see Bennett's horse, patiently waiting for its master, tied to a small shrub. He could shoot it, if necessary, to keep Bennett afoot. "Hope it ain't necessary," he mumbled to himself. "Better the horse than Bennett, however." He inhaled deeply to slow his rapid breathing. As during every gunfight, his heart was beating like a jackhammer.

Marty carefully eased his head up. "Bennett," he shouted up toward the hidden outlaw. "Give it up, man. I've got you cornered. You can't get away. Make it easy on both of us."

Two quick shots fired his way was the only reply. Snorting in frustration, Marty shifted his position until he could see Bennett's horse without exposing himself to rifle fire, and settled back, willing to trade some time. "Maybe once he gets hot and thirsty, he'll listen to reason," Marty whispered to the breeze.

He patiently awaited Bennett's next move for twenty minutes, then caught a glimpse of the fugitive sneaking toward his horse. Marty snapped a quick shot that zinged by Bennett's head, driving him back. "Don't try it, Bennett," he shouted. "I've got a clear sight on your horse. Just put down your weapon and come out, hands where I can see 'em. We'll go back to Fort Wayne and get this all straightened out. You hear me, Bennett?"

He was answered by only silence. Marty shook his head at the stubbornness of the man. "It's gettin' pretty hot down here, Bennett. I can see your canteen still tied to your saddle. You getting a little thirsty up there? Give it up, man."

Marty slowly eased his head up until he could risk a quick look. A bullet fanned the air by his cheek so closely that it nearly singed his ear. "Damn you, Bennett!" Marty shouted, and fired three quick shots with his rifle in the general direction of Bennett's location. "Quit shootin' at me or I'm gonna do something we'll both regret."

As soon as the panicky Bennett had fired at Marty's head, Bennett turned to make a desperate dash for his horse. One of Marty's bullets hit a rock and skipped off, flattening out and slamming into Bennett's back, just below his right shoulder blade. Grunting in agony, Bennett sprawled in the dust, trying to get air into his lungs. Every breath brought a fresh explosion of white-hot pain. He could not move.

Marty rose at the sound of a man in agony. Bennett's

horse was crabbing away as far as it could from something Marty could not see, perhaps a body. Slowly, carefully, he eased around the rock and made his way toward the boulder Bennett had used for cover. He made a final rush around the far side, his pistol in one hand, the rifle in the other.

Bennett was sprawled out on his stomach, frothy blood bubbling out of a hole in his back, staining his faded blue shirt a shiny red. He knelt beside the wounded man.

"Bennett, hold still. I'll try to plug that hole in you. Why didn't you just give it up, man? Look what it's got you." He ripped open Bennett's shirt. A thin, bloody hole was gushing with every breath. Bloody bubbles grew and burst, spraying tiny droplets against Bennett's pale skin.

Marty pulled Bennett to a sitting position, with his back against the big rock, and let him slump forward. He had seen men bleeding frothy blood before and knew what it meant. Either the bullet or a busted rib had punctured a lung. Bennett was doomed; the only question for him now was how long it would take for him to die.

Marty wadded up Bennett's kerchief and pushed it against the slice in the man's back. The pressure of the bandage stopped the blood from streaming out like a red fountain. He settled Bennett with his back against the rock again. The wounded man groaned, then looked up at Marty, a tiny trickle of frothy blood leaking from the corner of his mouth.

"Thanks, mister. I'm hit bad, ain't I?"

"Bad as it can get, Bennett. I can try to take you to a doctor, but all that will do is cause you more pain and a quicker goin'."

"Damn, bad luck has dogged me lately."

"Why didn't you give it up, man? I told you what the marshal said. There was no need for this."

"It's not that. Those skunks that swore out the warrant on me would never been able to prove anything in a court of law. But I deserted the Union army in 'sixty-four. I'd have likely been hung fer that."

"Sorry. I didn't know."

"Ain't yur fault; it's mine. Lordy, I sure do hurt inside. Could I bother you fer a drink of water?"

Marty hurried back to his horse and led him to where Bennett had tied Bennett's animal. He carried his canteen back and cradled Bennett's head while he dripped water into Bennett's open mouth.

With every breath, more blood trickled out of the side of Bennett's mouth. Marty made the wounded man as comfortable as he could. He knew he was powerless to stop the inevitable filling of the man's lung with blood. Soon Bennett would drown in his own blood. Marty gently shook Bennett's shoulder. "Bennett, you want me to give your wife a message or anything?"

"Would you? That's decent of you, mister. Give her the money in my pocket. It's near two hundred dollars. And my hoss and saddle." The dying man coughed and spit out a clot of cherry red blood. "Do you have any paper? I'd like to write her a note while I still can."

"Sure, I'll get it for you."

Marty sat in the shade of the rock, next to Bennett, and watched as Bennett laboriously wrote out a page and a half. He signed it with a sigh and folded the letter in half before giving it to Marty. "Thanks agin fer your kindness, mister." Bennett's head lolled forward until his chin was resting on his chest, and his breath grew ever more labored and shallow. Finally, there was no sound or movement and Marty knew he had another man's soul chalked up against his in the Lord's tally book.

For several long minutes Marty sat motionless, looking at the dead body. Finally, he sighed and got to his feet, tucking the letter into his shirt pocket. It never occurred to him to read what the dying man had written. He would deliver it and the other items to Bennett's wife just as soon as he could. It was the least he could do for a man who had died so bravely. The man had had the decency to thank him for his kindness, even though Marty had been the cause of his death.

Marty wrapped Bennett in his own bedroll and tied him facedown on Bennett's horse. He mounted Pacer and, leading the animal with its grisly burden behind him, rode out of the rock outcropping and back onto the trail. They reached Tahlequah before sunset. Marty abruptly decided to ride around the city and on to Fort Wayne, only another day's journey beyond. Bennett could be buried with his family around him. The decision provided Marty's sodden spirit some reprieve, but in hindsight, it was a bad one.

His entrance into the fledgling town of Fort Wayne was cause for excitement. Marty stopped Pacer in front of the marshal's office and climbed down. He tied Bennett's horse next to Pacer before slapping at his dusty sleeves with a suntanned hand, then opened the door to the office. Several curious people trailed along, both on the sidewalk and in the street, as he stepped into the office.

The old, scruffy-looking marshal was behind his desk, as if he hadn't left since Marty had seen him last. He looked up in surprise as Marty entered the office.

"What the h . . . ?" He pushed back from the desk, scrutinizing Marty. "Yur the bounty hunter. Whatta ya want now?"

"I brought Bennett in, Marshal. He's outside."

"Well, hell. Bring him on in." The marshal hitched up his pants and glared at Marty. "You got him in chains?"

"Nope, he's slung over his horse. He's dead."

"What's that you say? Jim Bennett's dead? Look out!" The marshal pushed Marty aside and hurried out, ducking under the hitching post with more agility than Marty had thought him capable of exhibiting. He held up the head of the corpse and looked at the face. "Jim, it's you, all right. Jim, you fool. All you had to do was come back and we'd have worked something out." He glared at Marty. "Where was he?"

"I caught him in Indian Territory, south of Tahlequah. He tried to ambush me and got a slug for his troubles. I tried to convince him to give himself up, but he wouldn't." Marty thought of explaining why Bennett did not want to surrender, then decided it was better left unsaid.

"Damn, I never thought you'd catch up to ole Jim. LeRoy, you and Murph take Jim over to Doc Mitchell's. Tell him to get him fixed up proper-like fer Julia Bennett to see him. You"—he glared again at Marty—"git on back inside and tell me the full particulars."

Marty had just finished telling his story the first time when a wizened old man dressed like a prim New England schoolteacher rushed into the office. His rumpled suit was all in black, and bifocal glasses were perched on his long, slender, and heavily veined nose. His watery blue eyes were magnified by the glasses, giving him the appearance of a frog. He gave Marty a disinterested look and leaned over to whisper into the marshal's ear.

"What! In the back?" the marshal shouted.

The marshal turned on Marty, his eyes flint hard and cold. "Jim's been shot in the back. You shot him in the back?"

"By accident. I assure you I was not trying to shoot him at all. I fired to keep his head down and one of the bullets must have ricocheted into Bennett." Marty looked at the old man. "You Doc Mitchell?"

At the man's nod, Marty continued. "Dig out the bullet in Bennett. You'll see it's all flattened out where it hit a rock."

Marty looked back at the marshal, his face defiant. "Even so, he was wanted and on the dodge. It's not the same as shooting some innocent person in the back and takin' their pocket watch."

A worn but deadly .44 Army Colt pistol suddenly appeared in the marshal's hand, pointing straight at Marty's stomach. "I don't give a what fer, back-shooter. Yur going to sit in my jail cell till I get this thing figgered out. Drop yur pistols on the desk, right now."

"Now look here, Marshal. This isn't right. I was within the law."

The marshal wiggled the barrel of the pistol back and forth like he was shaking his head. "I don't give a damn. Yur goin' inna cell till we have an inquest and this here thing is straightened out. Now, march!"

Frustrated at his inability to talk his way out of it, Marty submitted, and allowed himself to be locked in a dirty cell behind the marshal's office. He had a rope-harness bed with a thin straw-filled mattress, and a three-legged stool. Next door was a smelly half-breed drunk sleeping off a two-day toot.

Marty threw himself down on the bed and laced his fingers behind his head. He steamed for a while and then drifted off into a restless sleep, not to awaken until the marshal came back into the holding room and unlocked the cell door of his neighbor.

"Git outa here, Little Horse. Try to stay sober fer a spell, why don't ya?"

"Marshal, when are you going to let me outa here? Did the doctor get back to you?"

"Yeah, he did, back-shooter. He said the bullet what killed poor ole Jim was deformed like it had hit a rock, but he couldn't say fer certain that's what happened. All we got is yur word on the subject."

"That mean you're gonna keep me locked up?"

"Yep. I talked it over with the magistrate. He's callin' a inquiry fer day after tomorrow. I think I'll leave you right here where I can keep an eye on ya till then."

"What about the reward money?"

"It's coming in by wire from Wyomin'. I suspect it'll be here in a few days. You don't wanna leave without yur blood money, I reckon."

"Marshal, you folks put out the wanted paper on Bennett, not me. You didn't say that he had to be brought in alive."

"Yeah, but it don't say he was to git plugged in the back, either. Now, hush up or I'll forget to bring you any supper." The marshal stalked out of the room and slammed the door behind him.

Marty tried to sleep but finally gave it up and restlessly paced the narrow confines of his cell until a broken-down old mule skinner delivered his supper, courtesy of the local hotel dining room. "Lordy, but this is bad," Marty growled. "Do folks actually pay for this slop?"

The old-timer cackled, showing a mouth almost devoid of teeth. "Naw, they give prisoners what's left after the payin' customers has ett." He collected the tin plate and the wooden spoon Marty had used. "The regular food ain't all bad. Don't complain too much. Marshal Willard has been known to fergit to order meals fer prisoners who gives him a hard time."

After a breakfast of cold porridge the next morning, Marty made a request of the marshal. "Marshal Willard, can I get cleaned up? I haven't had a bath for a week now. I can't stand being in the same cell with me."

"Ain't likely, Keller. You jus' gonna have to handle it until after the inquest tomorrow."

"I'm gonna look and smell like a wild man, Marshal. It'll

just make my case that much harder to get across at the inquest."

"Tough, but that's the way it's gonna be."

"A person would think you want me to go on trial for killing Bennett."

"Nothin' would suit me better, back-shooter. Nothin' a'tall."

Chapter 5

The Inquest

Marty was chagrined to discover that he would go to the inquest in chains, like a convicted criminal. "Marshal, you don't have to do this. I'm not gonna give you any trouble. The last thing on my mind is any idea of running away. I'm anxious to tell my story at the inquest and get everything cleared up."

"Tough, back-shooter. I make it a point to be safe rather than sorry, so jus' hush up."

"Don't call me that, please."

"I'll call you what I want, back-shooter. Give me any more sass and you'll stand in front of the inquest with yur nose layin' 'side yur ear."

Marty swallowed his bile and meekly followed the marshal and a deputy out the door and down the sidewalk to a small room in back of the general store, where the inquest was to be held. Several townspeople stood aside and stared unabashedly at Marty, increasing his feeling of shame and humiliation. The store owner, the man Marty had dealt with when he had bought his supplies before starting out on his manhunt, was also the town's magistrate. Marty hoped that his essentially bribing the proprietor/postmaster with twenty dollars in gold to tell him the name of Bennett's sister in Arkansas would not work against him.

The magistrate, Mr. Blum, commanded the assembled crowd to come to order and quickly ran through the formalities, swearing in six townsmen as jury, before calling the marshal as the first witness. Marshal Willard swiftly recounted the circumstances as they had unfolded, trying his best to paint the dead man, Jim Bennett, as a paragon of good citizenship and decency. He dwelt at length on the fact that the bullet hole was in Bennett's back, then sat down, casting a sly, indicting look at Marty.

Blum scribbled some notes on a tablet, then turned his attention to Marty. "Ya got anyone who ya want to have speak at this inquest?"

"Yes, sir, I do. First, I'd like to make a statement, then I'd like to call Doc Mitchell to the stand."

Blum nodded. "Marshal, you go git Doc Mitchell. We'll have a recess till you git back." He pointed to Marty. "Keller, you jus' stay where ya are. The deputy'll stay with ya. The rest of you folks clear out until the marshal gits back with the doc." Blum smacked the table with a small gavel and walked out of the room.

Marty pulled Marshal Willard's arm and whispered in his ear, "Sheriff, please ask Dr. Mitchell to come and bring the bullet he took out of Jim Bennett's body. I'll need his testimony to prove my case." He then sat glumly in his seat, waiting for the sheriff to return and mulling over what he wanted to say. He quickly reviewed the entire chain of events leading up to Bennett's death. Willard returned with the old doctor in tow. The inquiry was quickly brought to order and Blum swore Marty in. "Okay, Keller. Tell us yur side of the story."

Marty carefully and completely outlined the events leading up to the shooting. He omitted the bribe to Blum, instead saying he had overheard some men talking about Bennett's hiding place in Arkansas. He glanced at Blum to gauge his reaction, but the magistrate/postmaster had his head down, as he made some notes. Marty wondered if the magistrate was relieved that Marty had omitted the postmaster's part in violating postal regulations.

"I assure the inquest that I gave Bennett every opportunity to surrender. I didn't want to shoot him and did not even aim at him when he shot at me. The bullet that killed him was a ricochet and hit him entirely by accident." He turned to the magistrate. "Now, I'd like to call Doctor Mitchell to the stand."

The old doctor took the stand. Marty walked to the witness chair. "Doc, did you bring the bullet you took out of James Bennett?"

"Yep, here it is." He handed the misshapen slug to Marty. Marty glanced at the lead bullet. The nose was flattened away from the front to nearly the end, deep scratches showing where the rock it had bounced off had gouged away metal. Marty handed the evidence to the magistrate. "Doctor Mitchell, did the bullet get that way from hitting a bone in Bennett's body?"

"Nope, it sliced twixt two ribs and right into the deceased's right lung. The poor fella was doomed from that instant on. He bled till his lungs filled and he drowned in his own blood. There weren't nothin' anyone coulda done, once he was hit."

"Thank you, Doctor. I'm done with this witness." Marty returned to his seat.

"You got anything to ask him, Marshal Willard?" The magistrate looked at the marshal, an eyebrow cocked.

"Yep." The marshal heaved himself out of his chair. "Doc Mitchell, you know fer a fact that Jim Bennett was kilt by a ricochet bullet? Couldn't a bone have flattened out the bullet?"

"Nope, Sam. Ain't likely. A bone just ain't hard enough. But I can't say it were or weren't a ricochet. It sure looks like it, but I just got the defendant's word on that."

"Thanks, Doc. That's all I got. We just got Keller's word on that. And what is he? A back-shootin' man-killin' bounty hunter, don't fergit. That's all I got to say about that."

Marty stood up and faced the jury. "I would like to point out to this inquest that Bennett was a wanted outlaw on the dodge. I had a valid warrant signed by Marshal Willard to hunt him down and bring him in. I did not want to kill the man, and I did nothing that warrants this inquest. I was within the law that you made. Thank you." Marty bowed slightly to the jury and returned to his seat.

The magistrate led the jury out of the room. In ten minutes they returned and Blum rapped his gavel for order. "In consultation with the jury, we find that James Bennett's death was the result of a lawful action by the defendant and no criminal charges can be filed against Martin Keller. However, we recommend that he be held as a material witness in the city jail until his reward money comes. How long will that be, Marshal?"

"I reckon a day or two more," Marshal Willard replied.

"Good. Then we suggest that as soon as you pay him his blood money, you escort Mr. Keller to the city limits and send him on his way. Fort Wayne don't need nor want his kind in our town."

"You got it, Judge."

Marty stood. "Your Honor, may I ask a word of you?"

"Sure, Keller. What do you want?"

Marty moved to the desk. "Your Honor, Marshal Willard wants to stomp my face pretty badly. I'd like to leave Fort Wayne looking like I do right now. Would you make sure that happens?"

"I guess. Marshal, I don't want nothin' happenin' to the witness. Make sure he don't fall down or nothin' like that."

Willard sullenly answered, "Okay, Judge."

"And," Marty continued, "I've got twenty dollars left. If you'll allow me, I'll get a bath and shave and buy some new clothes from the general store? There's blood, sweat, and dirt all over the things I'm wearing now."

"I reckon that's fair. It will cost ya twenty dollars for the lot. Marshal, you make sure Keller here gets all that before you lock him up."

"Yessir, Judge."

Disgusted with the whole rotten setup, Marty dropped the twenty-dollar gold piece on the table. "Thanks, Your Honor." The sarcasm in his voice resonated across the desk, but Blum paid it no attention; he was too preoccupied with scooping up the money and putting it into his pocket.

It was nearly dark by the time Marty finished cleaning up and changing into his new duds. He felt much better as he followed the quiet deputy back to the jail, where he ate another sorry meal, hardly fit for a stray mutt, much less a human being.

Three days later the reward money finally arrived, and as soon as it did, Marty was paid and escorted out of town by the same morose deputy, who warned him to stay away from Fort Wayne or suffer the consequences. "Don't worry; it's the last place I'd ever want to come back to, let me assure you," Marty replied. He rode toward the east, now burdened with the promise of delivering the letter and the money Bennett had given to him in the last moments of the dying man's life. He patted the hidden pocket he had sewn into the lining of his boot. The two hundred dollars Bennett had given him was still there.

"Pacer, old pal, being a manhunter ain't much satisfaction at all, let me tell you." The two of them rode on in silence for a few minutes, then Marty continued. "Still, it's given me three of the scum that killed Meg and little Matt. I don't plan on stopping anytime soon, so I might as well quit my bellyaching."

Pacer snorted, as if in agreement. The two rode on in silence, rapidly putting miles behind them. About an hour later, Marty encountered a passing rider heading toward Fort Wayne. "Howdy, mister. Can you tell me the way to the Bennett farm?"

"Shore can, stranger. But if yur lookin' fer Jim Bennett, it won't do ya no good. He recently passed on to his heavenly reward."

"I'm aware of that, thanks. I'm actually delivering a letter from Jim to his wife, Julia."

"Julia's a fine gal. You ain't far from the Bennett farm now. I wish I could take you over there, but I'm headed to Fort Wayne. I got a fearsome toothache, what's damn near killin' me. I got to get to the doc's right quick and get it pulled."

"Doc Mitchell?"

"Yeah. You know the ole reprobate?"

"I was talking with him just yesterday. He pulls teeth as well as mending folks and healing horses, does he?"

The man laughed. "Ow, don't make me laugh. It hurts too much." He'd relaxed after Marty had mentioned the doctor's name. "Well, I reckon yur on the up and up. Follow this road until you come to a creek, 'bout five miles on down. Right after you cross the creek, there'll be a road goes off to the north and east. Follow that fer a couple of miles and you'll run plumb onto the Bennett place. Tell Julia that Sal Bender said hello, will ya?"

"Be my pleasure, Mr. Bender. Thanks for the directions." Marty gave Pacer a nudge with his knees. "Let's go, boy. Time's a wastin'."

Marty paused at the creek, allowing his horse and the mule to drink their fill, then rested awhile in the shade of the trees growing alongside the creek bottom. He sat on a

downed log and threw pebbles into the trickling water while
he talked to himself, as lonely men on long trails are apt to
do. "What am I gonna say to the poor woman? Howdy,
ma'am. I shot your husband and I'm delivering a letter he
wrote to you while he was dying. Oh, by the way, can I stay
for supper?"

Shaking his head at the absurdity of it all, Marty
stretched out in the shade of a lone oak tree, then dozed for
a few minutes. Finally, realizing that all he was doing was
postponing the inevitable, he sighed, got up and tightened
the cinch on Pacer's saddle, and then headed on down the
road toward the Bennett homestead.

The place was neat and clean yet showed the lack of
money evident on most farms in the area. The house was in
need of some minor repairs and the barn needed twin doors
at the front. A pair of sturdy mules stood in the corral, and a
small farm wagon was drawn up next to the front porch, the
two horses hitched to it waiting patiently in the afternoon
sun for their owner.

Marty pulled up Pacer and warily climbed down, wondering what the wagon meant. A ruddy-faced woman came
out of the house, as if in answer to his unspoken question,
and looked at him, her face showing neither welcome nor
alarm.

"Howdy, mister. Can I do you for somethin'?"

"Hello. Mrs. Bennett?"

"No, I'm Elsie May Whitaker. I'm a neighbor of Julia's.
She lost her husband recently and ain't receiving guests. We
only buried Jim yesterday at the Mt. Union Church Ceme-
tery. Can I give Julia a message?"

"No thanks, Mrs. Whitaker. I can appreciate what you're
doing, but I promised Jim Bennett that I'd deliver this letter
into his wife's hands, so I reckon I'd best do it that way. I
can come back later if she wants."

"You say you've got a letter for her?" Now the woman's face was clouded with suspicion.

"Yes, ma'am."

"And how is it that Jim gave you a letter?"

"I reckon I'd better answer those questions to Mrs. Bennett, ma'am. Please, just tell her that I've got it and let me know what she wants me to do."

The woman scrutinized Marty, seeming to wonder if she could trust the stranger before her. Finally, she decided. "All right, mister. I'll ask Julia what she wants. What's yur name?"

"Keller, ma'am."

"You wait right here, Mister Keller." The woman returned to the house, shutting the door firmly behind her. Marty stood waiting by the side of his horse; the only sound Marty could hear was Pacer's tail swishing away flies from his flanks. The time seemed to drag, until the door opened and the Whitaker woman returned to the front porch.

"Julia'll speak with you, Mr. Keller. But please remember that she's in bereavement."

"Believe me, ma'am, that fact has not left my mind for some time now."

Chapter 6

Lassoed by Tears

Marty took off his hat as he entered the house, remembering to stomp the dust off his boots just outside the doorjamb. On a chair at the dining table sat a woman dressed in a plain black mourning dress, her eyes red and swollen from crying. She would have been attractive under better circumstances. Her hair was drawn into a bun, secured at the nape of her neck. Marty's heart skipped a beat as he looked at the widow. She had hair the same color of light brown as his Meg.

He nervously walked over to the table and reached into his pocket for the letter. "Mrs. Bennett, my deepest sympathies for your loss. I brought you a letter from your husband. He wrote it very shortly before he . . ." Marty paused out of respect. He hated to say *died*. "Before he passed on," he lamely finished.

The woman looked at him with her red-rimmed eyes, not saying anything. Marty held out the letter, which she took eagerly and opened immediately. "Pardon me," she hoarsely whispered. "I'll read this right now, if you don't mind."

"Not at all, ma'am." Marty turned away to allow her

some small privacy and looked around the house. He had no idea what Bennett had said in the letter. He hoped it was not a command to blow his head off with the shotgun Marty saw hanging over the fireplace in the tiny living room, next to the kitchen.

Marty's eyes drifted over the interior of the place. There was not much in the way of luxuries in the simple house, but it was clean and cheerful, with lacy cotton curtains framing the windows. The kitchen smelled of freshly brewed coffee, and a blackened iron pot of something was simmering on the cookstove. In the corner of the kitchen, a barefooted boy about five sat quietly playing with a small toy train, which he slowly ran in a semicircle around his legs. A big dog, a cross between a hound and a collie, lay beside the boy. He looked at Marty with thoughtful brown eyes but did not leave his place by the lad.

The woman's friend had kept her stern gaze on Marty, causing him to shift nervously from foot to foot. The crying woman looked up at Marty, then turned to her friend. "Elsie, would you get Mr. . . . ?" She looked back at Marty, the question in her eyes.

"Keller, ma'am. Marty Keller."

"Give Mr. Keller some fresh coffee if he would like some."

"Thank you, Mrs. Bennett. That'd be just fine."

The new widow returned her attention to the letter she held like a fragile flower, and laboriously started to read her husband's last words, slowly forming them with her lips as she read.

The Whitaker woman poured Marty a cup of coffee in a small tin cup, which was worn and beaten up but as clean as everything else in the kitchen. He slowly sipped the hot brew as Mrs. Bennett reread the letter, bitter tears coursing down her pale cheeks. Occasionally, she would sniff and wipe her eyes and nose. Marty completely finished the coffee before she looked up at him again.

Finally, she carefully folded the letter into thirds and put it on a worn hutch sitting next to the table. She wiped her eyes and gave Marty a slight smile. "Thank you for bringing me the letter from my Jim, Mr. Keller. Would you please stay for supper? Please?"

"Why, I hadn't planned on staying that long, ma'am, but if you want, sure, thanks. I'll go put my animals in the corral, if you'll excuse me for a moment. Mrs. Whitaker, nice meeting you." Marty bowed his head toward the other woman and left the house, trying to decide what was on the bereaved widow's mind. While he led Pacer and his pack mule to the corral and unsaddled them, he spoke out loud to the horse, as he was wont to do when trying to puzzle through some question. "Pacer, old chum, I don't get it. Do you suppose Bennett didn't say I was the one that shot him? I wonder how Mrs. Bennett thinks I came by the letter? Reckon she's gonna poison me while she feeds me supper? Damn, I sure wish I was on the road. Why on earth did I agree to stay for supper? Just because that stew smelled so good, I reckon."

As usual, Pacer just shook his mane and buried his nose in a bundle of fresh hay that Marty threw into the corral from a pile next to the twin gates. The big gelding ignored the two strange mules standing meekly in the far corner of the corral. He did share his hay with the mule that had accompanied him on the trail for so long. Marty watched as Pacer chewed on his hay; then Marty slowly walked back to the cabin, still berating himself for not riding on.

As he headed for the front porch, Mrs. Whitaker came out, wrapping a green wool shawl around her shoulders. She spotted Marty walking toward her, and swiftly scrambled into the wagon without his help.

"Julia says fer me to go on home, Mr. Keller, so I'm

a'goin'. You take care to see she don't git too upset. I'll drop by tomorrow, after I finish my chores. I sure hope yur gone by then."

Marty tipped his hat to the feisty farm woman. "Me too, Mrs. Whitaker. Me too." He watched her drive off, turning his hat in his hands until she was out of sight. Then he knocked on the door and walked inside the house at Julia's invitation. Julia Bennett was about to ladle some of the stew onto a blue ceramic plate. She shot Marty a quick glance, then returned to the business of getting the supper on the table. "Johnny, git yur hands washed and come to supper. Hurry up now; we've got company."

"Lead the way, Johnny. I'll wash my hands as well," Marty added. He followed the quiet boy out the back door of the cabin. On a roughly hewn table rested a tin bowl and a chipped ceramic pitcher filled with water. Marty poured some fresh water into the bowl, grabbed a slab of homemade soap from a small platter, and lathered up his hands. The boy followed suit, shyly looking at Marty out of the corner of his eye.

They wiped their hands on a clean rag hanging from a nail next to the door and returned to the table. A plate filled with steaming stew was sitting at Marty's spot, the fragrance making Marty nearly drool in anticipation. The food tasted as good as it smelled. Marty wolfed down a couple of mouthfuls and then complimented the chef. "Mighty good vittles, Mrs. Bennett. Best food I've tasted in a long while." Marty smiled at the boy, who was silently nibbling at his food, a big spoon clutched in his small hand. "Eat up, boy. Your ma's a mighty fine cook." Marty grinned at Julia Bennett. "I sure thank you for the meal, Mrs. Bennett. It's mighty tasty."

"I'm glad you liked it. Elsie brought over some fresh beef, so I had the right fixin's." She looked at Marty. "Tell me, Mr. Keller. Did you read the letter my husband sent me?"

"No, ma'am. It was for your eyes only, to my way of thinking."

She looked at Marty, her face solemn. "Did you shoot Jim, like he said in the letter?"

Marty gulped. "Yes, ma'am. I swear to you, I didn't mean to hurt him. I was only trying to drive him back under cover. His shots at me were beginning to get too close. I'm terribly sorry it ended the way it did. I wish there was something I could do to make it up to you, but I know that can't ever happen." Marty shifted uncomfortably. "I lost my wife and son to senseless violence, so I know something of the pain you're going through. I'm sure sorry." He passed over the money Jim Bennett had given him. "He said to give you this."

"Thank you, Mr. Keller." She put the money aside without looking at it. "My husband said that he considered you to be a man of principle and honor. Are you?"

"Why . . . why, I would like to think that I am, Mrs. Bennett. Your husband said that? How 'bout that? I think I would have liked to know your husband, Mrs. Bennett."

"He was a good man, Mr. Keller. He's the only man I'll ever love and he's gone. Just because of his brother's land in Wyoming Territory. He was framed for a killing that was really self-defense. Someone in Wyoming used the law and used you to do his dirty work. It cost me my husband and Johnny his daddy."

Marty did not know how to respond, so he sopped up the last of the gravy on his plate with a chunk of bread and slowly chewed, trying to collect his thoughts. "Ma'am, are you sure your husband was framed? Many a man has sworn up and down that he didn't do something, when all along, he had done just what he was accused of."

Julia Bennett vigorously shook her head and got up to

freshen Marty's cup of coffee. As she poured, she continued. "Jim told me that when he was stopped by the three men, they demanded that he sell them Samuel's land in Wyoming at the price they named or they would kill him. One drew and shot at Jim. The bullet barely grazed Jim's side, but it knocked him off his horse. The men tried to shoot him where he lay, but the commotion spooked their horses so that they had to struggle to stay in the saddle. Jim drew his pistol and shot one of the men, just as the man's horse was spinning him around. He said his shot hit the man right between the shoulder blades, knocking him out of the saddle. The other two ran off, shouting that Jim would pay for killing their friend."

She wiped at her eyes with the edge of her apron and looked up at Marty. The misery on her face was so grievous that he winced in sympathy. "Jim came back here and decided to go hide with his sister in Arkansas until the furor died down. We never imagined that someone would put a bounty on him for murder." She looked down at her lap, where she was twisting her hands around each other. "Jim had a reason he felt like he had to run, or we would have fought the charges till kingdom come."

Marty nodded. "The army thing, you mean."

She looked sharply at him. "Jim told you?"

"Yeah, he was explaining to me why he had run, even though he felt he could have beaten the murder charge."

"It was the winter of 'sixty-four. Little Johnny was coming. I was sick and didn't have nobody to help me. Jim had been in nearly two years without a furlough. He meant to go back, but his regiment was in a big fight at Franklin, in Tennessee. He was afraid after that. So many of his friends got killed there."

Marty nodded again. "Yeah, that was a bad one. I was there too, only on the other side."

She looked at Marty, a sudden blaze of hatred flashing

across her eyes, only for an instant. "I wish to God you had died there, Mr. Keller."

"I'm sorry you have to feel that way, ma'am, but I surely understand your feelings."

Julia ruefully shook her head. "I'm sorry I said that, Mr. Keller. I guess I should be satisfied that you killed my Jim instead of some cold-blooded killer, who would not give a damn about me and my Johnny." She sniffed and put her hands back in her lap. "My Jim said you were a man of principle and that I was to get your help. I'm asking you for it right now. In fact, I'm demanding it."

"What help can I be for you, ma'am?"

"You can get me and Johnny to our land in Wyoming. Samuel's land, before someone killed him. Jim inherited it when Sam was killed two months ago."

"Why, Mrs. Bennett, what on earth makes you think I will take you and your boy to Wyoming?"

"Because you owe me, Mr. Keller. Because Jim says you're a man of honor and I need your help. Because you took Jim from me and Johnny. Because . . ." She pulled a .41-caliber derringer out of the pocket in her apron and pointed it at Marty's chest, the twin bores of the deadly little pistol looking as wide as fence gates. "Because, if you won't swear to get me and Johnny there right now, I'm gonna kill you where you sit and that's a promise."

Marty looked into eyes as cold as death itself and gulped. "Mrs. Bennett, I wish your stew had not smelled so good and that I had just ridden on after giving you your husband's letter." He cocked his head. "What makes you think I won't promise to do whatever you ask and then just clear out at the first opportunity?"

"Because you and Jim both say that you're a man of your word. Jim said to get you to agree any way I could. I think he had another way in mind, but I'm not able to share my bed with the man who killed my husband, not just yet. This gun and your word will have to do for the time being. Will you give me your word, Mr. Keller?"

Marty looked in frustration at the determined woman and her handgun, which she held as steady as a rock, directed toward his midsection. "I must be crazy, but all right, Mrs. Bennett. I'll do it. You have my word, for what it's worth."

Tears began leaking from the corners of Julia's eyes. "Thank you, Mr. Keller."

"Now, don't be hitting me with your tears, ma'am. You can't have it both ways. A loaded gun at my stomach and tears as well. One's enough."

Julia Bennett angrily brushed back her tears. "It will have to be the gun, at least for a while, Mr. Keller. I know it will get your attention."

"If we're gonna travel to Wyoming Territory together, you may as well call me Marty."

"I cannot, Mr. Keller, at least not yet. My anger at you is too strong. I may never feel that kindly toward you."

Marty's jaw clinched in anger. "You'll forgive me if I try and convince you to give up this foolishness. You have no business going to Wyoming Territory with someone you hate, and I'm crazy for agreeing to help you."

Julia Bennett sniffed again. "Be that as it may, I'm selling my place to Elsie's husband tomorrow. He'll give me a thousand dollars for the property and I can keep the mules and Jim's horse and prize bull to take with us to Wyoming. With that money, if you run out on me, I'll simply hire some gunslinger to hunt you down, don't you see?"

Marty shook his head and turned to the boy, who sat quietly at the table, watching the interplay between his mother and the strange man. "Well, Johnny, we'd better get to bed. Sounds like tomorrow is gonna be a busy day. We have to put together a wagonload of supplies to get us across Kansas and Colorado." He looked at Julia. "Where are we going, exactly?"

She turned in her chair and pulled a folded map out of a drawer in the hutch. Carefully, she placed it before Marty. "Here." She put a finger on the map. "Southern part of the territory, northeast of a place called Warm Springs, about fifty miles west of a town called Laramie, which is on the Union Pacific Railroad right of way. The land is in a valley of the Medicine Bow Mountains. Sam said it's a lovely place, surrounded on three sides by snowcapped mountains. According to my brother-in-law, the land has a special feature, which will someday make it worth twenty times what he paid for it."

"What does he mean by that?"

"I don't know. Sam wrote to Jim about a month before Sam was killed and said that he had discovered something that made the land more valuable than gold, whatever that means. Sam was a smart man, smartest I ever knew. He knew farming and land like nobody I ever saw."

"And you don't know what he was talkin' about?"

"Jim and I discussed it over and over, but we never really knew. We supposed it meant gold or silver or something like that."

"Yet he said the land would be worth more than gold, don't forget."

Julia Bennett wanly smiled. "I guess we'll have to jus' go there and find out for ourselves."

"They never caught whoever killed Sam?"

"No."

Marty nodded thoughtfully. "Mrs. Bennett, Julia, starting up a new spread is tough work. Believe me—I know. You certain you want to take something like this on? Maybe you ought to sell it and go back to your family. They can help you raise the boy."

"No, I want to go to the land. Once we find out what Sam thought made it so valuable, maybe then I'll sell. It would be worth a lot more then than it is now. The men who saw Jim only offered three dollars an acre for the place. There's over four thousand acres in Sam's ranch. Fifty dollars an acre would set Johnny and me up for the rest of our lives."

"They offered you three dollars an acre and you plan to sell it for fifty dollars an acre? That's quite a difference."

"That's my plan, Mr. Keller."

Julia looked down at the derringer she still held in her hand. "Can I put this thing away now?"

Marty nodded glumly. "I reckon. I gave you my word and I'll stick to it. I'll take you and your boy to Wyoming. After that, you're on your own."

"After that I'll be happy to be on my own, Mr. Keller. Believe it."

Chapter 7

Preparations for the Trail

Marty made his bed in the hayloft of the barn, on some sweet-scented scattered hay. As he settled down in his bedroll, he cussed himself once again for saying yes to the distraught widow's demands. "My only hope is that she gets discouraged on the way and agrees to turn back," he mumbled to himself. "I suppose that even if she insists on going the whole dang way, I could visit my friends working on the Union Pacific, then check out that part of the territory again. Now that the railroad has reached Laramie, the scum I'm huntin' might be in the area, lookin' to pick up some easy money."

Marty rolled deeper into his bedroll and tried to get some sleep. He did fretfully, haunted by the dreams, the never-ending, brutal dreams of his past.

He awoke to the new day, shaved, and washed his face before currying Pacer's sleek gray coat. It was a pleasurable ritual he never tired of. As soon as he saw smoke issuing from the cookstove chimney, he knocked on the door of the farmhouse. He nodded at Julia Bennett after she bade him to enter, and he walked into the kitchen. "Good morning, ma'am."

"Good morning, Mr. Keller. Did you sleep well?"

"Good enough, I reckon. Better than some nights."

"Guilty conscience?" She flashed a quick glance at him from her place by the stove.

Marty refused the bait. "No. ma'am. Just the opposite." He changed the subject. "That coffee sure smells good."

"Ready for a cup?"

"Yes, ma'am."

Marty polished off a plate stacked with buttermilk flap-jacks lathered with fresh honey and home-churned butter, and drank two hot cups of coffee. Sighing in satisfaction, he pushed back from the table, wishing he had a cigar to savor after such a fine meal. "Mighty good, ma'am."

Julia barely nodded, then sat down across from him. "As soon as I get Johnny dressed and fed, I'm headed to Elsie's place. I'll sell the farm and then go on to town and buy some supplies. What do you think it'll take?"

"How far is it to your new land?"

"Jim said he figgered it to be just short of seven hundred miles."

"We can average about twelve to fifteen miles a day, I reckon. Say fifty days, sixty at the most. Besides the trip, we'll need enough grub to sustain us once we get there until we can get resupplied. Get enough to carry us ninety days. Count on four adults and little Johnny."

"What?"

Marty nodded emphatically. "Yep, I said four. I plan to hire two dependable men to accompany us."

"What on earth for?"

"We're going on a dangerous journey, across a lot of wild territory. There're Indians and outlaws all over the places we're going to travel. We're late for most of the wagon trains; they're long gone from Missouri by now. We might hook up with a supply train carrying goods to a trading post, or to one of the western towns, but we might have to go some of the way alone. I want some help in case we have to fight off anyone."

"Where do you plan to find help like that?"

"I don't know, ma'am. You have any suggestions?"

Julia Bennett furrowed her brow in thought. "Elsie's oldest boy, Thomas. He's been lookin' for work among the farms around here. Maybe he'd be interested. I'll ask while I'm over there sellin' the farm."

"I want someone who's dependable and able to handle a gun. If you think he's capable, have him come over and talk to me. I'll make the final decision."

"How much will he make?"

"I'll pay him myself. Twenty-five a month for at least three months."

"Very well, I'll get myself ready if you'll excuse me. I'll send Johnny out to the barn when he's up and fed. You'll watch him while I'm gone?"

"You trust me with your boy?"

"I don't know why, Mr. Keller, but yes, I do. Besides"— she smiled smugly—"I've still got my derringer, if I need it."

Marty stared her down. Finally, he spoke. "I'll get the wagon ready for you. Do you want me to accompany you?"

"I'm surprised you'd want to. If you do, I'd be happy for the company."

"I was just thinking that you'll be carrying a lot of money once you sell your place. No need to take chances, I reckon. I'll get the mules hitched up to the wagon and be standing by."

"I won't be long."

Marty sat on the wagon seat, mulling over the most direct and still safest route to Wyoming. The faster he got her there, the faster he could be about his business. Julia Bennett and Johnny stepped out of the house, ready to travel. Marty jumped down to help them into the wagon. Julia wore a black dress, a sign of her bereavement, and the boy was dressed in a linen shirt, dark knickers with long socks, and button-down shoes. A child-sized straw hat framed his freckled face. Shyly grinning at Marty, he scrambled into the bed of the wagon and made himself a cushion out of several empty sacks. Holding on to the side, he eagerly looked over the railing and gave a sharp whistle, then shouted loudly, "Pawpaw, come on."

A dog bounded out of the doorway and leaped into the wagon as effortlessly as if he were leaping up the front steps of the house. The dog sat beside Johnny, panting with his tongue flopping against his furry chin.

"Ma, I can take ole Pawpaw, can't I?" the boy asked.

"Ask Mr. Keller, son."

"Can I, Mr. Keller? Can I? He'll be good. He minds me real good, don't he, Ma?"

Marty smiled. They were the first words he had heard the boy speak to him. "Sure, Johnny, you can take him. He's got to be good when we're in town, though. We don't want him causing a ruckus."

"He will be. Won't you, Pawpaw?"

Julia Bennett looked lovingly at her son with an expression that only a mother can give her child, and then softly asked Marty, "You sure you don't mind? He is an awfully good dog and Johnny loves him to pieces."

"Not at all. I'm happy to have a dog on our trip, as a matter of fact."

"Oh?"

"They're better than any person at guarding our camps. They'll alert us to the presence of any varmints long before a man would. Human or critter." Marty chucked the reins, and the two big mules jerked the wagon forward. They rumbled out of the farmyard in the general direction provided by Julia Bennett.

The mules held to an easy pace that slowly ate up miles. Marty knew that it would not be worth the trouble to try to get more speed out of them, so he settled in and made small talk with Julia Bennett to pass the time.

"I've been thinking about the route we should take to get to Wyoming."

"Oh, what did you decide?"

"First, we'll head for Kansas City, then follow the railroad right of way to Denver. The Union Pacific is building a line from Kansas City to Denver. The rails might not be down yet, but the roadway the surveyors and the suppliers made is there. We'll find a supply trail to join up with. Safety in numbers, you know."

"Whatever you think, Mr. Keller."

"Well, that's what I think. Then, we'll head north to Cheyenne. I've been there before. It's about a hundred miles, straight shot, from Denver. Then, we'll cut west until we reach this place you're lookin' for, Warm Springs. It appears to be about a hundred miles west, another straight shot. If we have to, we can follow the railroad tracks west out of Cheyenne. The tracks have to run close to Warm Springs, according to what your map shows."

"I don't know. I've never been farther west than right here. Jim and I moved here from Indiana after . . ." She paused and then continued. "After his time in the army."

Marty nodded. "Well, that's the way to go, as far as I can figger. Is that the Whitaker place up ahead?"

"Yes, that's it. Johnny, don't you run off with Robert and Silas. We won't be here long. Then we're going over to Joplin City to visit the store to get our supplies. I don't want to be lookin' all over for you when we're ready to go."

"I won't, Mama. I promise."

Marty helped Julia Bennett off the wagon and grinned as

Johnny and Pawpaw leaped out and streaked across the raked dirt front yard toward the barn, where two little tykes stood by the door, eagerly waving at Johnny. Elsie Whitaker opened the front door as Julia and Marty stepped onto the first stair of the porch.

"Hello, dear. What a surprise. And Mr. Keller, wasn't it? What are you doing out, Julia? I coulda come to you."

"It's all right, Elsie. Is Sy around? I need to talk to him about business."

"Oh, Julia! You're not gonna sell Sy your place, are you?" She gave Julia a quick hug. "I'll miss you, honey." Elsie frowned. "You don't have to be in no hurry, dear. Why not wait a spell before makin' any decision?"

"Well, Elsie, I am in a hurry. Mr. Keller has agreed to take Johnny and me out to our land in Wyoming Territory. It was always Jim's and my plan. I'm gonna take advantage of Mr. Keller's kind offer."

Elsie Whitaker glared sternly at Marty. "You make sure Julia gets there safe and sound, Mr. Keller, you hear me?"

"I promise I'll try my best, Mrs. Whitaker."

"Well, Julia, if you're sure. I'll run and get Sy; he's forkin' hay in the barn. You two wait right here. There's coffee on the stove iffen you want some."

She darted out the door before another word could be spoken. Marty looked at Julia. "A kind offer, huh?"

She smiled sweetly at him. "You don't want me tellin' folks I held you to account with a little ole popgun, do you?"

Sy Whitaker walked in before Marty responded. He wiped his hands on a rag and introduced himself to Marty. He was lanky and worn, his face creased by numerous sun wrinkles. He looked ten years older than he was, a by-product of the hard work of making a living from the soil. A long, slender nose seemed to spring out of a single dark eyebrow. His grip was evidence of the many hours he had spent behind the plow. Marty knew he would lose in a handshake contest. He sat silently while Julia explained her purpose for the visit. In a few minutes, Julia Bennett had sold her farm for twelve hundred dollars.

Marty accompanied Sy Whitaker to the barn while the women said their good-byes to each other. "Sy, I need to buy a better wagon than that ole farm wagon Mrs. Bennett has. You have any ideas?"

"You two goin' to Joplin City to cash that check I gave Julia?"

"I imagine. We gotta stock up on food and other supplies for the trip."

"There's several lead mines opening up around Joplin. Bound to be some folks there that come in by wagon to work the mines and might want to sell their wagons, I reckon."

"Thanks for the tip. I've got another question. I want to hire two men to ride along with Mrs. Bennett and me. Just in case we don't hook up with a wagon train before we start across the plains. Julia said your boy Tom might be interested."

Whitaker looked hard at Marty before he answered. "Tom's just turned eighteen. He's a good boy, dependable and hardworkin'. It would be a good way fer him to spread his wings. I ain't anxious fer him to get scalped or anything bad, though."

"I can certainly agree with that."

"My sister's boy, Walt Paxton, lives just a few miles north of here. He's a year older than Tom, and they're good chums. I'll bet his pa would agree to let Walt go iffen he knew Tom was going."

"I intend to pay them. Twenty-five dollars a month for three months minimum. Why don't you talk it over with your wife? If you folks are willing, send the two boys over tomorrow and I'll speak to them. I want to size them up and lay out the trip so they know what it's all about."

"Hell, fer seventy-five dollars, I'll come as well."

Marty chuckled. "I imagine you'll have your hands full putting the Bennett farm together with yours."

"Yeah, I suppose so. I think you'll find that Tom and Walt are good boys. Both of them are used to a day's work and neither's too wild fer his own good. We got the spring plantin' done, so three months away from here on the trail would be a nice adventure fer 'em without causin' me no hardship. I'll talk with the wife and Lute Paxton and send Tom and Walt both over to see ya tomorrow."

"Wonderful." Marty shook Sy's hand on it just as Julia and Elsie walked out of the house. "Well, it looks like it's time to go. Thanks, Sy. Hope to see you again, someday. Don't you worry if I take your boy on the trail. I'll take good care of him for you."

"I'll hold you to that, Keller. Tom's got a nice pony and Walt's pa'll let him have one of his horses, I reckon."

"Good. I'll pick up a couple of saddle rifles in Joplin City for them. Just in case."

"They'll appreciate that. Well, good luck to you and to Julia. She deserves it, especially after some yellow-livered bounty hunter done went and killed her husband."

Marty swallowed an angry retort and walked quickly to the wagon, where Julia and Johnny were already waiting, ready to go. Marty headed the team toward the road and Joplin City, some ten miles east and north. In the new, busy mining town, he quickly found at the local livery a hefty Studebaker freight wagon that would serve his purpose on the trip. It was not as sturdy as a Pennsylvania-built Conestoga wagon, but it was made along the same lines. Marty picked up a pair of mules and traces for them at the same livery at a price that was less than he had paid for his pack mule in Arkansas six months earlier.

He hitched up the team to the wagon and drove to the store where Julia was purchasing supplies with some of the money she had received from the Whitakers' check. Marty walked in and began his own shopping.

He motioned the store owner over and pointed at two Henry .44-40 carbines in a gun case behind the counter. "How much for the Henrys?"

"Oh, them's two fine guns, no doubt about it. A couple of cowboys sold 'em to me to git money fer a grubstake. Eighteen dollars apiece." He passed the two rifles over to Marty. Marty checked to ensure both were empty, then carefully examined the breech action, the inside of the barrel, and the tip of the firing pin.

"Not too bad. I'll give you forty dollars for the rifles and a hundred cartridges. You throw in some cleaning solvent and grease."

"You got a deal, mister. Say, ya interested in these two Navy .36s bored out to fit the new brass thirty-eight cartridges? Ten bucks apiece and I'll throw in a used belt and holster fer each."

Marty looked over the two pistols. They were Civil War issue but still in fair condition. The boring out of the barrel to .38 caliber made the pistols slightly less accurate than before, but they would work for two men who didn't make a living off their guns. "Same deal. Throw in a hundred rounds of ammo and I'll give you twenty-five dollars. Also"—he thought of the shotgun over the fireplace at the Bennett house—"fifty rounds of ten-gauge double-ought buckshot and a hundred of bird shot."

"Done. Anything else?"

"Yep. I'll need some shirts, pants, and underalls. Maybe another pair of boots."

"Right this way, sir. I got a fine selection of duds fer men, just in from St. Louis."

Marty finished up his shopping and waited for Julia to make the last of her purchases. She outfitted Johnny in new clothes and shoes and bought several linen and muslin day dresses for herself. At Marty's urging, she also bought a pair of sturdy walking boots a wee bit larger than her regular shoe size.

"You'll be doing a lot of walking, believe me. Your feet will swell up a mite over time and the shoes will fit just fine. You just can't sit on a wagon seat all day. Your butt . . . you're a—well, you'll get mighty sore in spots if you don't get out and walk from time to time."

"I get your meaning, Mr. Keller." Julia chuckled, appearing more relaxed than Marty had seen her since they had met. The impending move had put something on her mind besides the loss of her husband.

Julia admired the fine wagon Marty had purchased, "Where did you get the money for that?" she asked. Then her expression grew grim as she realized where it had indeed come from. It put a damper on the trip back to her farm, but she did not break down, to Marty's relief.

Marty turned the two new mules out in the corral with the Bennett mules and his animals. The little corral was filling up; Marty hoped the close quarters would speed the introductions among the animals.

Marty returned to his bedroll in the hayloft after another tasty meal from Julia's kitchen and slept better than he had the night before, by a long shot.

Chapter 8

The First Step

Marty was currycombing Pacer when two young men rode into the yard the next morning. Both were on a rangy mule, and they looked enough alike to be brothers rather than cousins. Marty figured they were still working off the last of their baby fat. He smiled as he walked out of the barn to greet them. "Lordy, have I ever been that young?" he muttered to himself. Both were lanky and blue-eyed, with the characteristic sharp nose he had seen on Sy Whitaker.

"Howdy, boys," he said to the two as they slid off the mule.

"Hello," the two replied shyly, almost as one.

The more slender of the two, with black hair just like Sy Whitaker and brown eyes under a dark, almost single eyebrow, spoke out. "I'm Tom Whitaker," he said as he tied the reins of the mule he had ridden to the top rail of the corral. "This here's my cousin, Walt Paxton. My pa said you was lookin' fer two men to ride to Wyoming Territory with ya. We're up fer that."

Marty grinned at Walt. He was fairer than his cousin. His young face had reddened skin pulled tight across his cheeks along with a heavy sprinkling of freckles. His hair was rusty red, as were his eyebrows. He had long arms but wide, strong wrists, like most farmers Marty had known.

"Hello. I'm Martin Keller. You can call me Marty. You two given some thought to what you're taking on? We might run into Indians or owlhoots before we get there. A lot of graves along the trail, make no mistake. It's not gonna be all fun and games."

"We know," Walt answered. "My pa says it'll finish up makin' a man of me. And I've been hankerin' to see some of the country afore I start settlin' down."

"I promise you that you'll see sights that'll take your breath away." Marty nodded at the mule. "What's with the mule?"

Walt answered. "My pa says I can have him, Marty. I thought I'd rent him to ya fer the trip. Twenty dollars a month. He can help your mules pull the wagon. Tom's pa is puttin' new shoes on Tom's mare as a goin' away present." He grinned. "That's why we're a'ridin' double right now."

"Twenty a month, huh? That's fair, I reckon. It's a deal. If I agree to take you two on, I'll rent your mule as part of the bargain."

The faces of the young men fell. "You mean you ain't fer certain yet?" Tom asked.

"Nope." Marty smiled. "Come on, let's put four mules in harness and hitch 'em to the wagon. I want to see you two drive a four-in-hand."

The boys took a lot longer than they should have to get the four mules hitched to the wagon, but Marty knew that would smooth itself out as they got used to their jobs. He climbed up and motioned the boys to join him. "Now," he said. "Tom, drive these critters out to the main road."

Tom was willing and, in truth, not too bad a teamster. Walt was better but had a tendency to cuss the mules as he probably did when plowing the field with them. "Walt, you can't be talking like that on the trail," Marty admonished. "Mrs. Bennett and Johnny will be riding with you."

"Dang, you're right, Mr. Keller. I'm obliged to ya. I'll watch it."

"Marty."

"Right, Marty. I'll watch it; honest I will." He turned the mules toward the barn again, then looked back at Marty. "Say, I know who you are. It just come to me."

"If you do know, Walt, let's just keep it to ourselves. You can tell Tom on the way home tonight, but then let's not talk any more about it."

"Good enough by me," Walt answered.

As they reached the farmyard, Marty nodded his approval. "You both will do as teamsters. Just remember, with a four-in-hand, you have to always be looking out ahead. It takes longer to stop 'em or turn 'em. You can't go to sleep when you have the reins. Clear?"

Both mumbled their understanding. After they unhitched the mules and took care of the animals, Marty led the way out of the rear of the barn, carrying a saddle blanket wrapped around the guns he had bought in Joplin City.

The boys' eyes grew wide when they saw the pile of weapons. Tom was the first to speak. "You git these guns for us, Mr. Keller?"

"Yes I did. You fellows know how to shoot, I suppose?"

Tom Whitaker was quick to answer. "Me and Walt's put many a rabbit on the table, ain't we, Walt?"

"What do you usually use, Walt?"

"I got a single-barrel four-ten shotgun."

"And you, Tom?"

"I use my twenty-two rifle. I can knock the eye outa a squirrel at thirty yards with it."

"Well, bring 'em both. However, if we run into Indians, you'll need a little more stopping power. That's why I got these rifles and six-guns for you."

Both young men watched intently as Marty checked the rifles to ensure they were empty of cartridges before handing one to each of them. "You boys bear with me. I'm gonna start as if you knew nothing about a rifle. Once you've proven that you can take care of it properly, we'll shoot a few targets"—he smiled at them—"just to see if you can hit what you aim at."

Marty carefully explained the workings of the Henry repeating rifles and the Colt pistols. He broke the guns down and had the boys clean and oil the parts before reassembling their new shooters. Finally, he recognized that the boys were going to blow their corks if they did not get a chance to shoot up the place, so he grabbed a couple of boxes of cartridges and headed for the far end of the pasture, followed by Walt and Tom, who were both excitedly describing just how deadly they would be with their new weapons.

"You gonna show us how to fast draw, Marty?" Walt asked.

"It won't be a requirement for our trip, Walt. We'll need to be able to hit what we aim at. But I doubt that we'll be in any kind of fast-draw situation."

"We can practice it, though, can't we?" Walt asked.

"You two are grown men. You can do what you want, on your own time. However, if you want to play fast-draw, you have to make certain your weapon is unloaded, at least until I can work with you some. Right now, I want to see you shoot your rifles."

Marty pointed toward a decayed tree stump sticking up about five feet, a couple of hundred yards away. "How far is that stump?"

Walt squinted and quickly answered. "About two hunnerd yards, I reckon."

"Naw," Tom challenged. "It ain't but one eighty."

"Go step it off. I want a firm answer when you two get back."

Marty smiled as his two young recruiters strode away, each carefully counting his steps. They quickly reached the stump and hurried back.

"Two hunnerd and one yards," Walt announced, casting a smug look Tom's way as they walked up to Marty.

"You agree, Tom?"

"Yessir. I counted exactly two hundred yards."

"It's important you both learn to accurately estimate distances. While we're on the trail, spot things out and challenge each other to guess the distance. Now, let's talk about your Henry rifles. The maker sets the sights so that what you aim at one hundred yards away, you should hit. See that rock out yonder?" He pointed at a large stone maybe twenty inches in diameter sitting at the end of a plowed furrow.

The boys nodded.

"I walked it off last night. It's one hundred yards from here. I'm going to aim right at the middle of it. See if I hit it." He quickly placed six bullets into the feeding tube under one of the Henry rifles and jacked a round into the firing chamber.

Marty fired off two rounds in less than a second. Both hit the center of the rock, kicking a spray of dust into the still air.

"Now, I'm gonna take the same sight at the stump. What's gonna happen?"

"You'll be short," Tom answered.

Marty quickly fired two more rounds. Dust kicked up a good thirty feet in front of the stump.

"Ya gotta aim high when you shoot out a long ways," Walt announced.

"Exactly," Marty answered. "When I was in college in Virginia, I had to study cannoneering. It was taught by Stonewall Jackson. You've heard of him?"

"Shore have," Tom answered. "You in the war with 'im?"

"No, I rode with Nathan Bedford Forrest. Ole Stonewall was killed before I could ever serve with him."

"Well, we shore enough heard of Nathan Bedford Forrest, ain't we, Tom?"

"Anyway, we had to study how a cannonball, or a rifle bullet, for that matter, travels when it comes out the barrel of a weapon. It's called ballistics. I don't know if you know this, but a bullet starts to fall to the ground the instant it leaves the barrel of the gun. When you were in school, did you hear the story of the Englishman named Newton, who fell asleep under an apple tree and got hit on the head by a falling apple?"

"Yeah, we did," Walt answered. "We figgered some fellas ain't too bright what fall asleep under a tree full of ripe apples."

Marty continued, ignoring the levity. "When his head quit aching, he came up with the idea of gravity. One of his proofs was that when something falls, it starts at zero and accelerates to thirty-two feet per second. In the first second, it will fall one-half of thirty-two feet. Trust me on that. So that means that a .44-40 bullet that comes out the end of your rifle at fifteen hundred feet per second will go that far in one second and fall sixteen feet. If you aimed at the very top of a sixteen-foot-tall fence post fifteen hundred feet away from you, your bullet would hit the ground at the foot of the post one second later. Are you both still with me?"

The two boys nodded their understanding of the simplified explanation. Marty took a stick and drew in the dust at their feet a crude representation of the route a bullet took as it went toward a target. He then moved the angle of the rifle up until the arc of the bullet went out to the figure of the rock. "We have to aim higher to hit something farther out."

He drew the outline of the notched *V* rear sight and the front sight post. "You heard the story of the pumpkin on a fence post and the picket line along the top of the rear sight going between the post and pumpkin?"

Both nodded again, watching as Marty drew a bigger *V* in the dust with the front sight centered in the *V*, the round ball just above the top of the rear blade. "At one hundred yards, where your pumpkin is, is where the bullet will strike." He looked up from his crude drawing. "Walt, let's see you hit the stone out there. Load up five bullets."

Walt grabbed one of the Henry rifles and dropped five bullets into the feed tube. He took aim and fired a single shot, hitting the stone square in the middle. Grinning at Tom and Marty, he proceeded to hit the stone with each of his next four shots.

Marty nodded. "Good shooting. Okay, Tom, you're next. Load five rounds in the other rifle."

Tom did and put four rounds square in the middle of the rock, the fifth round clipping the right edge of the stone and pinging away.

"Always squeeze the trigger gently, Tom; don't jerk it. Just like you're stroking the cheek of a pretty gal. Now, let's talk about hitting the stump. I've got it figured out so it's gonna be easy. Your rifle round will drop three feet for every one hundred yards out your target is. Three feet at one hundred, six feet at two hundred, nine feet at three hundred, and so on. Since the bullet isn't much good out past three hundred yards, we'll confine our discussion to that distance or closer. So"—he grinned at the two—"what's the height above the stump we need to aim at to hit it at two hundred yards?"

"Six feet," they answered in unison.

"Nope, if you were aiming at your target's belt buckle, all you'd do is part his hair. Don't forget, the manufacturer has put in a three-foot correction for the first one hundred yards, so you only need to aim three feet above your intended target. For three hundred yards, you would put six feet of correction. Understand?"

Again, both nodded.

"So." Marty smoothed out a flat spot in the dirt and drew the outline of the rear blade sight of the Henry rifle. "You have two choices. One, simply hold your aim at three feet over the targeted spot that you want to hit, or"—he drew the image of the front sight post—"you can raise the pumpkin a small amount." He drew the image of the pumpkin. "Like this, and keep your pumpkin on the spot you want the bullet to hit." Marty took Tom's rifle and loaded four rounds into it. "Let me demonstrate."

Marty stood upright, took aim, and quickly fired all four shots. The boys' eyes were wide with admiration; every shot had hit the target dead center, sending wood slivers flying. He lowered the smoking gun and nodded, satisfied. "I put the pumpkin about an eighth of an inch above the picket line. For me, that gives me another one hundred yards. I want you two to lay down here and experiment until you can put the pumpkin on the target and hit it at two hundred yards. Then we'll walk back another hundred yards and try it from three hundred."

Tom and Walt were naturally good shots, and within an hour, Marty knew they would be able to hold their own shooting any distance between zero and three hundred yards. Then they practiced shooting their new pistols, until Marty told them, "Well, I'm fairly satisfied you won't shoot your toes off if you have to use your pistol. You both need to work some more on hasty aiming and standoff. If you'll come by tomorrow afternoon and bring your clothing, we'll load the wagon and then practice some more. We'll leave at dawn Thursday morning. First stop: Kansas City."

Walt and Tom thanked Marty profusely for the instruction and headed back for the house. Walt finally blurted out what he could not hold in another minute.

"Yur him, ain't ya, Marty? Yur the famous bounty hunter that killed Jim Bennett over in Injun Territory. My pa said you was."

"Yes, I am, but like I said before, don't dwell on it."

"I'm sorry, Marty, but Pa says I gotta know afore I can go with ya. Does Mrs. Bennett know who ya are?"

"Yes."

"And she don't mind?"

Marty looked hard at Walt. "She minds. But she's strong enough to see what I can do for her now, rather than lament the fact that I shot her husband, which I can't undo."

Walt mumbled something that Marty could not catch. "You have a problem with who I am, Walt?"

"No, Mr. Keller. Honest, I don't. If Mrs. Bennett is all right with things like they are, so am I."

"How 'bout you, Tom?"

"Not me, Marty."

"Good enough. I'd be obliged if you both don't say any more about it, then. Fair enough?"

The two boys rode off, talking animatedly. Marty walked over to the house, where Julia Bennett stood by the front door, her arms folded. "The boys'll be back tomorrow to help start loading the wagon. I reckon we can start on Thursday at first light. That'll put us in Kansas City before the first of the month. We might get lucky and find a late-starting wagon train headed for Denver. With the gold strike going on that way, we oughta find someone to share the trail with."

"Johnny and I will be ready, Mr. Keller."

"Have you sorted out your furniture and such? We can't get it all on the wagon as well as the supplies we'll need to get to Wyoming. You'll have to leave some behind."

"I want to take our own wagon as well, Mr. Keller. Jim and I rode it from Indiana to here four years ago. He got it all fixed up just before the trouble. New wheels and axles, new tack; he even replaced the bottom. I want to take it. With it, we'll be able to take everything necessary."

"It's a hard trip to Wyoming Territory, Mrs. Bennett. It might not make it."

"If we have to leave it partway, I don't care. But I want to try to get it there. I've got my mind made up on this."

Marty sighed. "All right. As long as you know it may break down anytime. If we can't fix it, we'll have to leave it."

"I agree. Now, get washed up. Supper'll be on the table in a minute."

"I'll load the light stuff on your wagon—the food, personal belongings, and small furniture. Thank goodness we have enough mules to pull both. Your pair are used to your wagon, so I'll put the pair I bought plus my pack mule and the mule I hired from Walt to pull the big wagon. I was planning on rotating the mules to rest them during the trip. But we can take it easy and stop from time to time if they get too worn out. They're not as good as oxen on a long journey, but they'll still beat any team of horses I ever saw."

"Whatever you think best, Mr. Keller. Now, how did the boys do—shootin', I mean?"

"They'll be just fine. We'll be able to defend ourselves, unless things get way out of hand."

Julia Bennett pressed her lips together in a firm line. "Damned guns. I hate 'em. I could tell the boys were excited about their new toys. I'm certain you felt it necessary to arm them like soldiers."

"Where we're headed, the only law is what you pack on your hip, Mrs. Bennett. I aim to get you to Wyoming and get on with my life. I've got things need doing."

"You mean kill more wanted men?"

"Exactly. Two in particular." He gave her as hard a look as she gave him, and stomped away to wash up.

Chapter 9

Headin' for Kansas City

Marty had just finished brushing Pacer's gray coat to a glossy sheen when Tom and Walt rode in, Tom on a small bay mare with four white stockings on her lower legs. Tom handed Marty a gunnysack filled with horseshoes and nails. "A good-bye present from my pa," Tom explained.

"Mighty thoughtful of him. I found some horseshoes for the mules in the barn. We'll be able to shoe on the trail if necessary." Marty knew it was unlikely they could make the entire trip without some emergency shoeing. He ran his hands over Tom's mare. "She seems pretty sturdy. I reckon she'll do. Unfortunately, you'll be drivin' a team most of the time. Mrs. Bennett wants to take both wagons."

Both boys shrugged off the news and put their packed personal belongings next to the barn door. The adventure was about to begin; it did not matter to them how they traveled, in a saddle or on a wagon seat.

"What'll we do first, Marty?" Tom asked.

"Hitch up the wagons and put 'em by the front door. We got a lot of loadin' to do before sundown. And I want to watch you two shoot some more, if we have the time later."

"Come on, Walt," Tom whooped. "Let's get crackin'. I want to shoot that rifle again. I'm betting my foldin' knife against your fancy belt buckle that I can outshoot you from any distance."

"Yur on, cuz. Come on, lend me a hand with the four-up tack. We'll hitch them up first, then the little wagon last."

Marty held up his hand. "Slow down a mite. Put the Bennett mules on the little wagon, Walt, and the two I bought in Joplin City in the lead on the four-up team. Put your mule and mine on wheel. I don't trust them in front yet. After a few days pulling the wagon, I'd be more comfortable with them up there if it becomes necessary."

"You got it, Marty. Won't be but just a minute now."

Marty enjoyed their enthusiasm. The entire trip would be more fun than work for the two young men. He hoped their enthusiasm would rub off on Julia. Sharing the trip's close quarters with the bitter widow in her current mood would be taxing enough.

Julia supervised the loading of both wagons. By late afternoon she was satisfied they would get her household items to Wyoming Territory undamaged. Marty put the small anvil and the portable forge found among Jim Bennett's farm implements in the bigger wagon. He made certain the useful tool was where it could be easily accessed if needed on the trail. As soon as everything was secured, Marty had the boys put the canvas top on the big wagon and then took them to the back pasture to practice shooting. Both remembered to use Marty's tips from the day before. Marty continually moved them around, to avoid shooting at a known distance.

At the end of the practice session, Marty was satisfied that the two were reasonably proficient in accurately firing their rifles. He agreed to be the judge on the shooting contest between them.

"What'll we shoot at?" Tom asked.

Marty walked to a place he estimated was 140 yards from the dead tree stump. "Look at the stump. See that branch sticking out to the right? The first one of you that knocks it off wins. Fair enough?"

Both boys agreed and Marty flipped a silver cartwheel to see who fired first. "Walt," he announced, looking down at the silver dollar. "It's heads. You win. You go first, Tom, second. If you both miss the first shot, Tom will go first on the second round. What position are you going to shoot from?"

"Standin'," Walt announced smugly. "Get out that foldin' knife of yurs, Tom. It'll be mine in a minute."

"Brave talk from a cross-eyed houn dawg," Tom answered. "Hit the branch first, then howl."

Both missed from the standing position. "Dang," Walt grumbled. "I thought sure I had that branch dead to rights."

"You're next, Tom. What position do you choose?"

"Kneeling."

Both missed again. Marty watched the impact of the bullets behind the stump. "Walt, you jerked your trigger. Tom, you were just a mite high." He nodded at Walt. "Okay, your turn. What position?"

"Laying down."

Marty watched while the two took up a prone position. Walt fired first and Marty thought he saw a fine spray of wood slivers fly off the branch, but the branch still bravely stuck out.

"It's your turn, Tom."

Tom aimed and squeezed off a shot. The branch exploded, a large piece flying twenty feet away from the stump. "Yahoo," he shouted. "I hit it. I won, I won."

Marty laughed as Walt pulled his belt and fancy buckle off. "Walt, you gonna need some rope to hold your pants up?"

"I'll do jus' fine, thank you very much. Tom, you cheated, dang ya."

"Yur just burned 'cause I got your fancy belt buckle. Well, you can keep it till we git to someplace where you can buy another. Fair enough?"

Marty chuckled. He was going to enjoy the banter between the two cousins. "Come on, I want you both to fire a few rounds from your pistols. We'll not have as much time to practice once we get on the trail."

They pulled out at sunrise the next morning, Walt driving the big wagon and Tom the small. Julia Bennett had her prize bull tied behind the lead wagon and her husband's pony tied next to Tom's mare, behind his wagon. She sat next to Walt, and Johnny rode next to Tom. Pawpaw trotted along beside Johnny's wagon. Marty rode Pacer at the head of the little column. They followed the road that ran from Fort Wayne through Lamar and then Harrisonville and on into Kansas City, eight days up the road.

By the end of the first week, each day had evolved into a familiar routine. They got up at first light, ate a hearty breakfast, and hitched the mules to the wagons. They were on the road an hour after awakening. They took a long lunch hour at noon, where dried pork and cold biscuits were the standard fare, then rode on until late afternoon. When they found a place where the animals had grass and water, they set up their night camp. After caring for the animals, the boys helped Julia prepare the evening meal, or assisted Marty in repairing whatever minor damage the wagons or tack incurred, and then went to bed early. The road was well enough traveled that they saw people several times a day and shared evening camp with some of the fellow visitors.

Marty was happy when they shared the evening camp with others. Julia Bennett grew more withdrawn the farther away they traveled from her home. He figured she would snap out of her melancholy eventually, but he dreaded spending time in her company while waiting for a swing in her mood. He was satisfied with the two boys. Both worked hard and cheerfully accepted the hardships of the road without complaint. In their free time they practiced fast-drawing their pistols or plinking at targets. Every day they became more confident in their ability to hit what they aimed at. Marty wanted them as proficient as possible by the time they ran into trouble on the trail or when they reached their final destination in Wyoming.

Marty considered how he would introduce himself to people they might meet on the trail or in Wyoming Territory. He finally made up his mind as the full darkness fell on their campsite about thirty miles south of Kansas City. He saw Julia Bennett sitting with her back to him, staring into the small fire burning down after their supper meal. He glanced over at the two boys, who were sleeping head to foot near the small wagon. There had been some lightning earlier, just after dark, and they were ready to duck under the wagon if it came. Little Johnny was asleep under the Studebaker.

Marty crossed over to stand beside Julia. "Julia, may I talk with you?"

Julia snuffed and wiped the back of her hand across her eyes. "Sure, sit down. I was lost in memories there for a minute."

"I'm sorry to intrude, Julia, but we need to talk. You up to it?"

"Of course. I was remembering the plans Jim and I had made for this journey."

Marty nodded. "You can still make them happen, Julia. I'll help you get started before I go on my way. I owe you that much."

She turned her gaze toward Marty and looked at him intently, her expression neutral. "Yes, I guess so. Without Jim it won't be the same, I'm afraid."

"It won't be. Not in the least. I've told you already and I'm tellin' you again, for the last time, I promise. I'm sorry about Jim. I sure didn't mean to kill him, but I did. He's gone on now and you're left here with your boy, Jim's boy. You've gotta do what will be best for the two of you."

Julia stirred the dying fire with a small stick, sending up glowing red embers into the dark night. "Johnny will be my only child. I sensed it even before he was born. I had an awful time of it. I begged and begged Jim to come home, to be with me. That's why he ran away from the army. It was the only reason. He wasn't a coward or such."

"I sort of figured that out when I talked with him that day. I think I would have been proud to call him my friend, if circumstances would have let us."

Her voice was soft. "Instead, you killed him."

"And I'm sorry as hell, Julia. But dwellin' on it until my guts tie up in knots won't bring him back. I'd give just about anything if I could, but I can't. All I can do is try to help you get started with a new life in Wyoming. I've pledged to do that and I will. Now, I came over here to talk about how we explain our situation and had a thought. I'm gonna be your brother, taking you out to your land because of your loss. What was your maiden name?"

"Turner. Julia Ann Turner."

"Good. From now on, I'm Marty Turner. Make it a point not to call me Keller. Understand?"

"Yes, if you say so."

"I think it's the best way. Now, get some sleep. We'll be in Kansas City in two more days. The first leg of the trip will be over."

They rode into the booming town of Kansas City by midafternoon on the second day, just as Marty had predicted. The place was in a frenzy of activity, mainly because a railroad was being built across Kansas that would head toward Denver and the high Rockies.

Marty parked the wagons in a field outside the town, next

to several other wagons all filled with men and women headed for the goldfields outside Colorado Springs. He put Julia and little Johnny next to him on the wagon seat. "I'm taking Julia and Johnny into town to get them a room for the night. Tomorrow, we'll make plans for the next step of the journey. Tonight, we'll have to sleep with the stock and wagons. Too many people roaming around here need transportation to the gold strike. If we all leave at once, our stock and wagons will likely be gone when we return."

Marty left Tom and Walt strict instructions. "I'm going to get a bath and a shave while I'm in town. As soon as I eat supper, I'll return and relieve you two. You can go into town and get yourself cleaned up, have a good meal and one—I repeat, one—glass of beer before you come on back. Fair enough?"

At their nods, he continued. "Don't let anyone get ahold of our animals. Don't be afraid to draw down on anyone who won't keep his hands off our stock."

Both assured him they were ready to fight to the death to protect the animals and the wagons. Convinced they would stay vigilant, Marty chucked the reins against the rumps of Julia's mules and headed for the center of town.

The place was indeed raucous, with men and women milling up and down the sidewalks, weaving in and out of crowded stores, saloons operating at full blast. As Marty pulled up in front of a clapboard hotel, two drunks came rolling out of a saloon across the street, fighting like alley cats, trailed by onlookers cheering one brawler or the other.

The two men pounded each other as they lurched across the muddy street, right up to the wagon. Marty leaped off and grabbed the reins of the mules, which were spooked by the commotion going on beside them. He quickly tied off the mules to a nearby hitching post and pushed one of the drunks away from the animals. "Take your fight somewhere else, boys. You're scarin' my animals."

The second drunk immediately stopped swinging at his opponent and glared at Marty. "To hell with you, buddy. I'd just as soon knock yur block off as look at ya. In fact, I think I will." He stepped forward and took a mighty swing at Marty.

Marty easily dodged the balled fist, drew his pistol, and smacked it down hard on the man's balding head, laying open a deep cut two inches long and dropping the man like he'd been kicked by one of Julia's Missouri mules. The other fighter turned and snarled angrily, "Hold on there. You can't pistol-whip my friend. . . ."

He got no farther as Marty poleaxed his noggin with his pistol as well, laying him in the dust beside the man he had been fighting only moments earlier. Marty turned to the crowd, who grumbled at his interference and the harsh treatment of the two brawlers. He turned his pistol their way and spoke softly but clearly. "I don't like men who take their drunken disagreements into the streets. Those things are best kept out back of the saloon, where they belong. Any of you got any objection to that?" He waved the pistol in a menacing manner, not quite pointing at any one person but covering them all.

There was loud grumbling but no overt action directed against him as the crowd dissipated away from the wagon. Friends helped the dazed and bloody fighters back to the sanctuary of the saloon from which they had burst forth. Marty turned to help Julia Bennett from her seat and saw the contempt in her eyes. There was no sign of gratitude for stopping the fighters from possibly injuring her or her son, only scorn for Marty using his pistol to restore order. Knowing he could presently do nothing to change her opinion, he simply helped her off the wagon seat, then escorted her and her boy into the lobby of the hotel.

Marty registered Julia for the only room left and followed her up the stairs to the door. "Get cleaned up and eat in the hotel dining room. I'll come by and check in before I go back to the wagons."

"Thank you, Mr. Keller."

"Please, Julia. I'm supposed to be your brother. You must call me Marty, or Martin."

"Very well." She turned away from him and busied herself with unpacking the small valise that she had brought from the wagon.

In two hours Marty had done all his chores. He checked Julia, and satisfied that she was secure, he got himself shaved, bathed, and well fed, then rode back to the wagon and the boys. He sent them off whooping to enjoy the sights and sounds of the biggest town either boy had seen. Marty checked the stock and settled under the smaller wagon, taking his ease until they returned several hours later, cleaned up but smelling like they had downed a gallon jug of beer apiece for their one drink.

Early the next morning, Marty walked to the circled wagons parked across the field from where his group was, and asked for the wagon master. A grizzled man, short, stout, with a big nose over a bushy red beard and long rusty hair falling to his shoulders, stuck out a hand. "Shamus McCreed at yur service, stranger. What can I do ye fer?"

Marty shook the offered hand. "Marty Turner, Mr. Mc-Creed. I'm takin' my widowed sister to Wyoming by way of Denver. You folks headed out that way?"

"Nope, sorry. We're all goin southwest, to Santa Fe. I reckon we're 'bout the onliest folks here'bouts that ain't headed fer Colorada."

"You know of any wagon trains forming up to head Colorado way?"

"Ya jus' missed a big 'un, left last Monday. There'll be another in a week or so. Just like hawkin', they build up till finally they got to git spit out and off they go, headed fer

Colorada or Californ-i-a." He scratched the mangled fur under his chin and gave Marty a shrewd look. "Ya got any money, Mr. Turner?"

"I might, Mr. McCreed. Why do you ask?"

Chapter 10

Riding the Rails

"Well," the crusty wagon train leader answered, grinning at Marty with a sly look, "I know a way you can get better'n halfway across Kansas in about a day, instead of taking two weeks."

"I'm listenin'."

"It's somethin' I was thinkin' about tryin' myself, till I calculated up the total cost fer my entire train. I was talkin' to Ed Kendall, the line boss fer the Kansas and Denver Railroad. They got the line laid out clear past the center of the state. That's over a hunnerd and eighty miles. Eighteen days a' trailing covered in about a day's time. Ride the rails, boy, that's my advice. Kendall'll put yur wagons on a flatcar, the hosses in a stock car, and yur family in the passenger coach. In twenty-four hours, he'll deliver ya to the end of track and unload ya. If that ain't a piece of cake, I don't know what is."

Marty nodded, calculating how many days it would take him to trek the same one hundred eighty miles with his party. At least two weeks travel time, plus the wear and tear on the wagons and the livestock. It sounded very tempting.

"How much does Mr. Kendall charge to provide us with this train ride?"

"I reckon I oughta let him and you work that out iffen yur interested. Want to go over and meet him?"

"I reckon so. It sure won't hurt to hear what he has to say, will it?" Marty trailed after the wagon master as they walked over to the rail yard, where several men were busy loading iron rails onto a flatcar with a boom and a pulley.

McCreed pointed out a slender man who had a dark beard covering the bottom half of his face. He was supervising the loading operation, moving back and forth as the rails swung across the gap from the freight wagon to the flatcar. "Easy, there. We don't want to drop any. Easy, dammit! Take it easy."

Marty and McCreed watched as the last of the rails were deposited on the flatcar and the men started strapping them down with chains and ratchets. Kendall turned toward them. "Howdy there, McCreed. Change your mind about my offer?"

"Nope, sorry, Ed. I got more time than money. However, this here is Martin Turner. He's takin' his family to Denver. I told 'im 'bout yur offer and he's interested."

The slender man held out his hand. Marty felt the hard grip and realized that the fellow was stronger than he appeared. "Hello, Mr. Kendall. Marty Turner, from down Joplin City way."

"Mr. Turner. Can I interest you in saving a good deal of time on your journey?" Kendall motioned to the siding yard, just beyond the main line. "I've got the ability to transport your wagons and stock, along with you, all the way to end of track, near to Fort Garland, nearly two hundred miles west of here. From there, it's only a three-week trip on into Denver or Colorado Springs. You headed for the gold-fields?"

"No, I'm taking my widowed sister and her boy out to

their land in Wyoming Territory. How much you charge to ride the train like you said?"

Kendall appraised Marty, as if to judge the amount of money he might be carrying. "What's your load?"

"I've got two wagons, six mules, two horses, and a bull. Plus myself and four others, one a youngster of five with his dog."

"Um, let's see. I'll take your rolling stock and animals for fifty dollars and you and your family members for fifty more. I'll let the dog ride free." He flashed a warm grin at Marty. "You'll save that much on food and wear and tear. What do you say?"

"I like it. When do we leave?"

Kendall scratched the fuzzy beard covering his chin and looked at the men tying down the load of rails. "I reckon we'll be ready to leave by noon tomorrow. Bring your goods over tomorrow morning and I'll get them loaded for you. You can stay and watch so you'll feel comfortable that they'll make the trip all right."

"Can I pay for the ride then as well?"

"Sure, that'll be just fine. Well, I got six more wagons of rails to load, so if you'll excuse me, I'll see you tomorrow. Thanks to you both. I think you'll find you made a good decision, Mr. Turner." Kendall hurried off and Marty returned to the field where he was parked, along with Mr. McCreed. He thanked the wagon train boss and strolled into town to tell Julia Bennett about the change in plans.

He bumped into her coming out of the hotel door just as he was about to enter. He quickly told her about his plan to ride the train the next morning.

"I certainly don't agree that it's such a good idea, Mr. Keller. That's money I can use once I reach Wyoming to buy food for the winter or cattle to stock the ranch."

"Please, Mrs. Bennett. You have to start calling me Marty. I'm supposed to be your brother, remember. As to the money, don't worry. I'm using my own funds. The sooner I get you and Johnny there, the sooner I can go about my business."

"Well, be certain that it is," she whispered as they reached the dry goods store. "I'm picking up some things I may need on the trail, if you'll excuse me." She went inside. Marty was left to steam on the sidewalk by himself, not certain if he needed to cuss first or get a stiff drink. Knowing he had to stay clear of the liquor, he ambled back to the wagons, cursing a blue streak under his breath. "Damned woman is gonna be the death of me, I swear," he grumbled as he walked over to the wagons. "Fellas, we've got to get the wagons over to the rail yard tomorrow morning first thing."

"How come, Marty?" Walt asked, a puzzled look on his freckled face.

"We're gonna take the train to the end of track before we start trekin' on to Denver. It'll save us two weeks or better."

"Wow," Tom said. "I ain't never been on a train before. Have you, Walt?"

"Nope. It'll be a first fer me, too."

"How long will it be, Marty?" Tom was as eager as a kid waiting for his first pony ride.

"About two hundred miles, the track boss said. A place called Fort Garland."

"How long will it take, Marty?" Walt questioned.

"The track boss said about a day."

"Whooee, we're gonna go two hunnerd miles in only a day? Wait till I tell my pa. He won't believe it." Walt danced a little jig, he was so excited.

Marty held up his hand. "First we gotta check everything out in both wagons. I don't want anything to spill or fall while we're on the train. Come on, let's get at it. Then I think we oughta shoot the pistols again, just to keep our hands in."

Both boys raced away to the wagons, eager to get started and get done. They both were excited about their upcoming target practice with Marty.

Marty rode Pacer to the rail yard the next morning to meet Kendall and pay the fare the train manager demanded. Kendall assigned a salty railroader named McClure to show him where to put the wagons and the stock. Marty sent Tom into town to pick up Julia and little Johnny while he and Walt drove the bull and then the horses into a stock car hooked just ahead of an empty flatcar that was to hold the wagons. By the time they had the big Studebaker wagon tied down, Tom arrived with Julia Bennett and her son in the smaller farm wagon. Marty escorted Julia and her son to the last passenger coach while the small wagon was loaded on and tied down behind the big wagon.

Marty returned in time to watch the mules and Pacer be placed in the stock car. Each animal was securely tied in a stall so small that it could scarcely move once enclosed. Marty liked the design. He did not want any of the animals trying to move around and getting thrown down by the movement of the train over the tracks. Pacer seemed troubled as Marty backed him into his stall. He pawed and snorted his discomfort, but Marty stayed with him, talking softly and soothingly to the big animal until Pacer settled down. After filling the grain rack and making sure there was a filled bucket of water in the corner of the stall, Marty left Pacer and headed for the stock car door. "Pawpaw, you stay here," he ordered the dog.

Whining but obedient, the dog lay down on the straw-covered floor, his head between his front paws.

As Marty walked down the loading ramp, he pointed toward the first passenger car with a forefinger. "Walt, Tom, I want you both to be with the wagons every time we stop, no matter what the reason. Our stuff is just lying there, inviting any passerby that wants an opportunity to pick it up. Got me?"

"You bet, Marty," Walt answered. "You want me and Tom to ride in the first car? We'll have a clear view of the wagons from the front windows."

Marty glanced in the windows of the car as they walked past. It was filled with rough, work-hardened men, probably people headed for the goldfields or new workers for the railroad. He paused, then shrugged. The boys were nearly men; they could probably take care of themselves. "Fair enough. I'll ride with Julia and Johnny in the other passenger car. You two ride close to the front, so you can keep your eyes on the wagons. And put your pistols in your bags. I don't want anyone mistaking you for hardened gunslingers."

"Aw, Marty. You know we won't cause no trouble," Tom grumbled.

"And I aim to keep it that way. Your rifles under the wagon seats?"

Both nodded. "Sure are," Tom answered.

"Stay close to 'em when you're watching the wagons. Otherwise, don't get them out either. You don't know how it is. Some men just wait for the chance to show everyone how fast they are with a gun or how quick they can kill some poor fool."

Marty waited until Tom and Walt entered the first passenger car. Heavy smoke was boiling out of the elaborate stack at the front of the black engine. They would be under way any moment.

Marty escorted Julia and Johnny to a seat near the back of the second car, opened the window so they could catch a breeze, and then sat down in a seat across from them. Julia looked away from him, and that suited Marty just fine. He sat silently as the train lurched, slowly inched forward, then picked up speed until they were going twenty or more miles an hour.

Though the day was hot, the breeze from the train flowed through the open windows, making the passenger car quite comfortable. The train sliced through man-high prairie grass flowing and undulating in the breeze like ocean waves. The peaceful view suddenly and inexplicably brought Marty's dead wife and son into his mind. That snapped him out of his reverie, and he bolted out of his seat and hurried to the rear of the train. For a long time he stood on the outside transom while he smoked a small cigar purchased in Kansas City.

Marty saw an occasional farm or cow, but for the most part, the landscape was barren of human pollution. Birds and small animals were his only companions, which suited him at the moment. Marty stood watching the landscape slip past long after he had finished the small cigar and flipped the glowing butt off the train. Finally, he returned to his seat.

Julia was looking out her window, her child asleep with his head on her shoulder. It was apparent she did not want any conversation, so Marty slumped in his own seat, listening to the clickity-clack of the wheels rolling over the gaps between rails. In another hour, the train slowed and then stopped at a small village, where the water and wood was replaced. Marty hurried to check the animals, noting that Walt and Tom were alert as they stood beside the two wagons, watching vigilantly.

"Everything all right?" Marty queried as he walked past the two.

"Yep," Tom answered. "You gonna look at the mules?"

Marty simply nodded and continued on his way. He climbed into the musty interior of the stock car and carefully checked the animals pinned inside. They had made the first leg with no incidents. Marty petted both Pacer and the dog, making certain they understood his approval of their conduct. Satisfied that Pacer and the other animals were all right, he returned to Walt and Tom.

"I'm going to take Mrs. Bennett and Johnny into the

town and get them a hot meal. I'll bring you fellas something if you want."

"Yep," Walt replied. "Bring us some food if you can find any. Me and Tom'll be right here when you git back."

Marty walked Julia and Johnny to a tiny café, next to the only hotel in the town. He ate with them and then purchased two box meals for the boys. Julia was quiet, saying very little and replying to Marty's attempts at small talk with single word answers, mostly yes and no. Finally he quit trying.

"You sure don't have much to say. Something botherin' you?"

Julia shook her head, a resigned look of sadness on her face. "Just thinking that Jim and I were supposed to be making this trip together. I guess I'm a little blue."

"A little? That's an understatement. Well, come on, Johnny. How about we go get some hard rock candy to eat while we're on the train?"

Julia wiped her mouth with the tiny cloth provided by their waiter, and pushed back her chair. "I'll go with you. I want to buy some hairpins, if they have any."

"Whatever you say. Ready, Johnny?"

"Say yes to Mr. Keller, Son."

"Julia. You have to call me Marty. I'm supposed to be your brother."

"Of course, Brother dear." Her sarcasm fairly dripped from the last two words.

"Dammit, Julia Bennett. You sure don't make it easy, do you?"

"You're damned right, Mr. Keller. Don't forget what brought us together in the first place."

"I haven't, Julia. Don't you forget how important it is that we appear to be brother and sister if I'm to get to the bottom of what started all your troubles."

Her silence was louder than words.

Marty walked in silence with Julia and Johnny to the dry

goods store. He bought the small boy two bits' worth of
sugar candy and waited until Julia had purchased her hairpins. As he walked back to the train with the pair, he was
glad he had accompanied them. The streets were crowded
with riders from the train, some staggering around, obnox-
ious and obviously drunk. He knew he would have to stay
close to Julia and Johnny for the rest of the night.

His threatening looks and determined carriage discouraged the milling men from bothering Julia. Marty helped
Julia onto the train without incident and, with a sigh of relief, settled back into his seat. The loud blasts from the
steam whistle brought the men in town running to catch
the train before it moved on west. As the men struggled on
the train, it slowly started up and then chugged out of the
town, leaving a void in its wake.

The village slumbered, awaiting the arrival of its next
trainload of visitors due the next day, headed the opposite
direction.

Chapter 11

Deadly Encounter

The train clickity-clacked along uneventfully through the rolling countryside. Every three or four hours it would stop for water and fuel, either at a small town or at a lonely water station beside the tracks. Marty used the stops to check on the wagons, Pacer, and the other animals. He was relieved at how well the animals took to riding on the train. "You'd rather ride than pull us along, is that right?" he asked the mules just before dark. "You've just got out of two weeks' work, so why not be happy?" The brindle male snorted as if in agreement.

Later on, the train stopped at a remote outpost. Marty stretched his legs beside the tracks, not interested in walking through the tiny village. He allowed Walt to run to the only saloon in the town and buy a small bucket of beer for him and Tom to enjoy. He waited by the rear transom until Walt returned, to make certain the boy was back aboard before the train left. The train chugged out, and Marty scrambled onto the rear transom as the train rolled past him. He felt like a brakeman must, swinging up onto the moving iron horse. He walked in and sat down in his seat, ready to endure still more hours of monotonous swaying as the train moved on into the darkness of central Kansas.

Marty drifted off to sleep. Sometime later, Tom Whitaker, insistently shaking him on the shoulder, rudely awakened him. "Marty, Marty, wake up. Walt's in trouble."

Marty jerked up, rubbing the sleep out of his eyes with the heels of his hands. "What's the problem, Tom?"

"Walt got into a game of poker with some fellas a while ago. He's been winning big. There's one guy, he's drunk and mean, won't let Walt leave. Says Walt has to lose back all the money he's won or he's gonna shoot Walt down like a dog."

Marty stood and glanced over at Julia. She and Johnny were both asleep in their seat. He shifted his gun belt and motioned with his head. "Lead the way, Tom."

Marty followed Tom up the aisle toward the forward passenger car. He swayed with the rocking of the train, alternating handholds on the backs of all the seats as he headed toward the front door.

Marty blinked as he and Tom entered the forward car. It was smoky and stuffy and it stunk of unwashed bodies and spilt liquor. Marty wrinkled his nose and murmured to Tom, "You fellas be better off riding outside on the flatcar with the wagons rather than put up with this."

"There's Walt," Tom whispered, pointing toward the front of the car.

Several men had cobbled together a makeshift table by placing some boards between two seats. Five rough-looking men and Walt were clustered around the table, playing poker. Someone had come up with a couple of chairs, so some were seated in the aisle as they played. Walt was backed up against the window side of the car, flanked by two men and facing three men across from him. Marty stepped behind the players and casually put his hand on Walt's shoulder.

"How's it going, pard?"

Walt glanced up, his face tense with concern. "Hi, Marty. I'm doin' okay. The thing is, Mr. McGuire here says I can't leave until I've lost all the money I won from him. He won't even let me just give back to the pot. I have to lose it. The thing is, he's so drunk I can't even lose to him when I want to. He's playin' too recklessly."

"You watch what yur sayin', boy. I'll slap a knot on yur thick head bigger'n a horse turd."

Marty carefully sized up McGuire. He was a mean-looking, bull-necked fellow, his face marred from many fistfights. Thick lips, rough and scarred from numerous cuts, curled in a sneer. Greasy blond hair cascaded over broad shoulders and a wispy handlebar mustache showed the effects of long years of chewing tobacco.

"And who are you, sir, if I may ask?" Marty inquired.

"I'm Devin McGuire and I'm the meanest, toughest pile driver you ever met. This here boy has decided to sit in on a man's game, and by God, he'll play till I say he's done, or I'll break his neck fer him." The man took a swallow from a pint bottle of whiskey, finishing it off. He wiped his hand across the back of his lips and snarled. "Deal, Harry. I'm feelin' lucky now."

"Just a moment, Harry." Marty held up a warning hand. "Mr. McGuire, is it? Just how much have you lost to my young friend?"

"Better'n seventy dollars to this little jerkwad, and I aim to win it all back. Deal, Harry."

Marty stepped back and watched the hand. Walt drew a pair of queens and bet ten dollars. McGuire called and the rest of the players folded. Walt took three cards while the drunken McGuire drew two. Walt bet ten more dollars and McGuire raised twenty more. Walt called and lay down queens and sixes. McGuire had a busted flush or straight—

three clubs, the king, the queen, and the jack, along with a three and a seven of spades.

"You lucky little stiff; you won another. I'm beginning to think yur holding kickers on me." McGuire's face grew even darker as he glared at Walt.

Marty leaned over the table and coldly stared into McGuire's bloodshot eyes. "You drunken pig. You're mad at Walt for winning when you raised a busted flush. Are you stupid as well as ugly?" Marty's gun appeared in his hand faster than McGuire could blink his eye. Marty ground the barrel into the scared man's mouth until it looked as if the suddenly cowed drunk was trying to swallow it.

McGuire was as quiet as a mouse stalked by a barn cat. He looked up at Marty, the blood draining from his face. He kept both hands visible and still, his body tense and frozen. He fearfully waited for what was to come next, scarcely daring to breath and not taking his wide eyes off Marty's face.

Marty's eyes were as cold as a January night as he glared down at the ridiculous sight of a man with a gun barrel shoved halfway down his throat. "You got a decision, you pig-faced sumbitch. You can nod yes that you'll go sit down in your regular seat and be a good boy. You do that, I'll put my gun away and you can live to see the sun rise tomorrow. Or, you can shake your head no and I'll blow that pile of cow shit you call brains out the back of your head. You'll be watchin' grass grow tomorrow, from the bottom up. You need to know, just as certain as tomorrow's sunrise, that I'll kill you as dead as a stepped-on cockroach and with just as little hesitation. You understand me, you loudmouth blowhard?"

McGuire gingerly nodded, his eyes crossing as he watched Marty ease the hammer down on his pistol. Marty glanced over at Walt. "Walt, you're outa the game. Take your winnings and go back and sit with Julia and Johnny.

Stay away from McGuire here for the rest of the trip. Go on, boy."

Walt scooped the money into his hat and headed for the rear exit of the car. Marty slowly eased the gun barrel out of McGuire's mouth and motioned with it. "Get over to your seat and relax. Don't even look back my way while I leave. Now, move!"

Marty watched McGuire get up and move to his seat. Slipping his pistol back into his holster, he nodded at Tom. "Okay, Tom. Head on back and join Walt. I'll be right behind you." As Marty opened the rear door, he called out loudly enough for everyone in the room to hear him. "Don't none of you step through the door of the car behind this one. If you do, I'll shoot you dead before you can blink."

As the door closed, McGuire swung around and glared at the form through the streaked window. "I'll kill that son of a bitch just as soon as the train stops, by God. You see iffin I don't."

The man sitting across from him shook his head. "I don't know, Devin. Did you see that fella's eyes? They was cold as winter ice. He surely ain't nobody to mess with lightly."

"I don't give a good gosh damn. He's crow bait just as soon as we stop this here train. You still got that Greener?"

"Yep, it's up there with my luggage."

"Get it fer me. And half a dozen shells."

"You think this thing through, Devin. He don't look like one to mess with."

"Jus' do as I say, Slim. Don't give me none of yur lip."

"Yur funeral, Devin. Here's the shotgun. I only got five shells."

"That'll be enough."

McGuire loaded the shotgun and held it cradled in his arms, like a little baby, nursing his hatred and shame. He smiled as he envisioned hitting the smart guy in the guts, so he would hurt for a while before he died. Slim sadly shook his head. He would not give a spent cigar butt for Devin's chances against the stranger head to head. Maybe if Devin could get behind the fellow, come up on his blind side, he might just have a chance. He leaned over and whispered in McGuire's ear. A deadly smile creased the drunken man's features and he nodded in agreement.

"How'd you end up, Walt?" Marty asked.

"I came out a hundred and thirty dollars to the good."

"Well, it damn near ended your life. Pay attention to what kind of folks you sit down to play cards with from now on."

"You bet, Marty. Thanks fer gettin' me outa that jam. I didn't know what to do."

Marty chuckled. "I wasn't too certain myself. I reckon we slipped outa trouble, at least for the time being." He settled himself down in his seat and tried to go back to sleep, hoping the rhythmic clicking of the wheels would lull him off to dreamland. He could hear Walt telling Tom that he was going to buy a horse and a good saddle with his winnings, just as soon as they reached Wyoming.

The train chugged on, eating up miles at a monotonous fifteen miles an hour. Just as the sun peeked over the grass-covered plains, the train slowed at the end of track, a few miles outside the fort named after General Hosa Graham. Marty swung down the rear steps and checked the crowd of men climbing down from the first car. McGuire was not among them. Marty hoped the bully was sleeping off the liquor he had consumed.

As he grabbed the valise passed to him by Walt, a stranger walked past and whispered out of the corner of his mouth. "I ain't one to git involved, mister, but it looks like a certain fella took a shotgun and got off on the other side of the train. Could be he plans on shootin' another certain fella in the back as soon as the train moves on. Me, I can't abide a back-shooter." The man moved on and rejoined a cluster of others headed for the railroad's hiring tent, set up among a group of tents located just beyond the tracks. A big sign proclaimed the need for both graders and layers, three dollars a day plus room and board for any man hired.

Marty handed the bag to Tom. "Walt, you and Tom escort Julia over to the shade of that cottonwood over yonder. I'll be joining you directly."

"Anything wrong, Marty?" Tom asked.

"Nothing I can't take care of. If something does happen, I'll depend on you two fellas to get Julia and her boy to Wyoming Territory. Understand?"

"Sure, Marty. You can depend on Walt and me. Where you goin'?"

"I've got to see a fellow behind the train. Go on, take Julia over to the tree. I'll be along directly." Marty waited until they were well away from the train before he moved.

He slowly eased around the end of the train, staying close to the car and in its shadow. As he moved toward the first passenger car, he spotted McGuire hiding in the space between the car and the flatcar to its front. A lethal short-barreled shotgun was pointed at the milling crowd on the other side of the train.

Marty carefully moved closer to the hidden McGuire, until only twenty steps separated them. "You looking for me, McGuire?" Marty called out, squaring himself to face the threat head-on.

Mcguire jerked in surprise, looking at Marty with a blank expression on his face. He did not speak but quickly stepped out of the opening, swinging the shotgun toward Marty as he did. Marty's move was smooth and quick. His first bullet was on its way toward the ambusher's chest before McGuire's racing heart completed another beat.

As fate would have it, McGuire swung up his hand holding the deadly scattergun just as Marty's bullet arrived. The lead pill directed toward the coward's heart hit his fist instead, busting a knuckle, then passing on through the hand to shatter the bones in McGuire's wrist before lodging in the fleshy biceps of his right arm.

Marty knew that he had not killed the man and instantly shifted the aim of his second shot to smash into McGuire's left knee, dropping him like a sack of potatoes. The big man screamed like a stuck pig, a keening wail that caused people on the far side of the train to stop and turn toward the sound.

Marty cautiously moved up to McGuire, his gun never wavering from the man's beefy chest. Mcguire was too busy hurting and screaming to pay any attention to anyone. His face was contorted with pain and he shouted and moaned continuously, trying to grab first his knee, then his arm, with his one good hand. Marty picked up the shotgun and looked down at the writhing man without remorse. "You were lucky, bub. I was aiming at your heart. I suspect you'll not be dancing the fandango for a spell, nor hitting anyone with your fist again, for that matter. I told you before, and now I'm tellin' you for the last time. Stay away from me and mine. I'll kill you the next time I see you."

Marty walked back around the end of the train and toward the tree where his people awaited him. He didn't bother to look back.

Chapter 12

Back on the Trail

Julia was curious. Giving Marty an inquisitive look, she asked, "What's going on?"

"Nothing. Just a misunderstanding I had to set straight," Marty answered. He directed a sharp glance at Walt and Tom, and the two knew enough to keep their mouths shut.

"Well, I thought I heard gunfire," Julia sniffed.

"I didn't," Marty replied. "It must have come from over in the tent area somewhere."

"Then who's that those men are carrying toward the hospital tent? And where did that gun come from that you're carrying?"

"Someone must have fallen down and got hurt or something." Marty held up the shotgun. "As for this, some fellow just now gave it to me. He thought we might need it, going through Injun territory and all." He held out his hand toward Tom and Walt, who were lying in the shade of the big tree. "Come on, fellas. Let's get the wagons and stock unloaded." He pulled Tom and Walt up and they returned to the train. The experienced train crew quickly unloaded the wagons and the stock from the train. Julia's prize bull docilely moved to his spot behind the small wagon, as if ready to get under way again. Marty and the boys laughed at the sight. "Ole Victor sure knows his place in the line of march," Marty said, chuckling.

As soon as the mules were hitched to the wagons, Marty led them away from the end-of-track campsite. "Too many rowdies around," he explained to Julia as they slowly made their way north, headed for the wagon train trail, located about ten miles from the railroad tracks according to directions Marty had received from McCreed back in Kansas City. Marty planned to camp along the trail until a wagon train headed for Denver came along, then join up with it. He presumed it would not be a very long wait before one came past.

As they topped a small hill, Marty looked back. The train they had ridden in on was already almost completely unloaded. Within a couple of hours it would be headed back to the East to pick up more supplies for the crawling monster that was a railroad system under construction.

Suddenly a revelation hit Marty like a thunderclap. He slapped his head with the palm of his hand. "Well, if I'm not the most dumbest, slab-sided, cream-sucking, thick-headed cigar-store dummy in six states."

"What on earth are you talkin' about, Marty?" Tom asked.

"Look back there, Tom, and learn from a dunderheaded fool. What did we just do?"

"Rode a train?"

"Rode a train and saved us two hundred miles. Right?"

"Right."

"Well, why in hell didn't I save us all of it by just driving on up to Omaha and getting on the Union Pacific, all the way to Cheyenne or even farther. What the heck was I thinking?"

"Say, you're right. Why, I never even thought about it."

"Me either. I could have saved us thirty days on the trail. What a dummy I am." Marty shook his head in exasperation. "I don't think we dare try to cut across northern Kansas to the rail line in Nebraska. Too many bad Indians up that way. We'll just have to make the best of my mistake and keep on goin' the way we've started. I guess I've got to get used to having a railroad figure in any travel plans from now on." Marty chucked the reins. "Come on, Pacer. Let's work the kinks outa your legs. Giddyap."

They rode north across the rolling prairie for three hours. Almost without warning they came upon the rutted road known as the Santa Fe Trail. Farther to the west it would split, one leg of the famous route headed toward Denver, and the other toward Santa Fe, in New Mexico Territory. Marty turned west and they rode for another hour until they came to a small river meandering across the prairie. Though it was just a few feet in width, numerous cottonwood trees grew along its banks. Marty held up his hand.

"This looks like a good place to make camp. Let's get the stock picketed and make ourselves comfortable. We'll wait here until a wagon train that we want to join up with comes along. Walt, you see that dead tree? How about you get us some firewood? Tom, help Julia set up camp. I think I'll take a look around, just to be on the safe side."

He looked at Julia, who was busy unloading cooking utensils from the farm wagon. "You and the boy'll be all right with Tom and Walt. I'll be back before supper."

She paused in untying the tub and the washboard from their place on the side of the outside wall of the wagon. "While we've got the time, I plan to do some washing. Leave me that shirt and anything else you need cleaned."

"You sure?"

"Of course. While you're out, keep your eyes peeled for some fresh meat. We can save the bacon and dried beef for later."

Marty walked over to the wagon and got a fresh shirt and socks. He skinned out of his dirty clothing and bundled it for Julia to wash. In short order he was riding away from the camp. Julia already had Tom toting water up from the stream to the washtub, which sat on an iron grate over the fire Walt had started. Marty grinned. "Well, Pacer, it appears that Julia Bennett has plenty of work for the boys. Let's get outa here before she finds something for us to do." Marty followed the creek bottom as it meandered toward the east and north. He had been riding for half an hour without seeing anything of interest when a slight movement caught his eye. He saw the dusky image of two deer, who trotted into some brushy cover along the bank of the creek

Marty took out his Winchester rifle and swung down off Pacer's back. He tied the horse to a small bush and walked toward the place where the deer had taken cover. Marty moved slowly, taking advantage of what concealment he could, hopeful of supplementing their supper with some fresh venison. His patience was rewarded when he spotted one of the deer, a sleek, young doe, munching some grass right beside the running water. He dropped to one knee and took quick aim. The shot scattered a covey of quail and other small birds, but the doe dropped where she stood, a clean kill.

Marty returned to where Pacer was tied and led him to the dead animal. He quickly field-dressed the deer and took what parts he felt Julia would be able to use. As he loaded the fresh venison onto Pacer's back, movement farther down the creek caught his eye. Three horses were standing quietly, taking their fill of the cool water.

Marty put the meat aside and mounted Pacer. Walking his horse slowly, Marty moved down to the three loose animals. Talking softly, he was able to put a loop on a dark bay with white markings on its nose and forelegs while a slightly smaller buckskin and a sturdy paint watched, almost in calm

curiosity. They all followed along when Marty turned back
to pick up his meat. As he crossed the stream, followed by
the horses he had found, he spotted the remains of a small
campfire, long cold, maybe since the last rain. "What
the . . . ?" he murmured. "Looks like Indian sign. Sure hope
they've moved on a ways."

When Marty led the three animals into the camp, Walt
and Tom hurried over, eager to see what he had found.
"Walt, put the hobbles on these three. I suspect they're Indian ponies, although they must have belonged to white men
at one time. They weren't spooked by my smell when I rode
up on them."

"Whatta we gonna do with 'em, Marty?" Walt asked.

"We'll see, Walt. If nobody puts a claim on them, we'll
keep 'em for ourselves. They certainly look like solid animals. However, they can't have been running wild very
long; they're still tame. Their owners might show up and
want them back."

"If they belonged to Injuns and they show up, we'll just
run 'em off and keep 'em fer ourselves, right?"

"Don't be in too big a hurry to tangle with redskins, Walt.
Ever since that bluecoat General Custer wiped out a bunch
of Southern Cheyenne Indians on the Washita River a couple of winters ago, there's been bad blood between the tribes
and the white man. We've got a long way to go before we're
where we're headed. I'd like to avoid any confrontation with
Indians if I can."

"Hell, the way me and Tom can shoot and with you back-
ing us, we're likely to wipe out anybody who gits in our
way."

"Don't go getting bloodthirsty on me, Walt. You've not
seen just how bad a determined war party of Indians can be.
Believe me, we don't want to mess with them." Marty
pulled a raincoat filled with venison from behind his saddle.
"Tom, give this meat to Julia. I got us a deer for supper.

Then take my slicker down to the creek and wash the blood off it, if you would, please."

"Sure thing, Marty." Tom slung the venison over a shoulder and deposited it next to Julia, who was busy boiling some beans in a small cast iron kettle.

"Walt, put the three strays in our corral. Be sure and hobble 'em good. I don't want them wandering off during the night."

Marty unsaddled Pacer, wiped him down with handfuls of dried bunchgrass, and turned him loose in the small enclosure the boys had made for the animals. Old Victor was in a far corner all alone, not caring to mingle with the mules and the horses.

Marty looked at the animals for a moment, then returned to where Julia was starting to fry strips of fresh venison. "Julia, when was the last time someone rode your husband's horse?"

She looked up at Marty, pushing back a wisp of brown hair that had fallen over her eyes. "Nobody since it was returned to me."

"You want to ride in a saddle tomorrow? He needs to feel someone on his back again."

"I don't think so. Let one of the boys ride him. It's all right with me."

"I reckon I will. I'll take one of the boys and scout to the north and west tomorrow. I'll leave one here to help out. The next day I'll take the other."

She stirred the cooking meat, then turned her face back up. "Do you think we'll run into any Indians?"

"I'm hoping they're all farther north, chasing the summer buffalo migration up toward the Dakotas. You never know about Indians, though. They'll as likely show up where you least expect to see 'em as not. I know that we're going on watches during the night from now on."

"Give me a watch as well as the boys, then, please."

"You don't have to do that, Julia."

"I want to. I'm not having much luck sleeping anyway. It won't hurt for me to stand a watch. I'll take the watch until midnight. I'm up that late anyway."

"All right, if you say so. Do you think you could shoot that short barreled shotgun?"

"I don't see why not."

"We'll try it tonight and see how it goes."

"Boys, come and get it," Julia called to Walt and Tom, who were chasing Johnny down by the creek.

Marty smiled at the sight. He was tempted to get involved in the horseplay, maybe get a little closer to Johnny, but was stopped by the searing pain of the loss of little Matt that still ripped his heart. However, his loss was not Johnny's fault. The little tyke did not have a pa of his own, thanks to Marty. "Reckon I ought to step up more than I have been," Marty mumbled to himself as he got in line for his serving of the hot food.

"What's that, Marty?" Tom asked.

"Nothing, boy. Eat up, then get some sleep. You've got the midnight to two watch. Morning will come awfully early after that."

The first night's guard duty was uneventful. Marty had Julia sit on a chair next to where he had laid out his bedroll so he would be close to her if needed. His silver pocket watch was passed around to keep track of time. Marty took the four-to-morning watch and rousted everyone as the sun peeked over the plains.

By the time breakfast was over, the day was already getting hot. Not a blade of prairie grass stirred in the windless air. Marty ordered that Jim Bennett's horse be saddled, then watched while Tom and Walt flipped a coin to see who would accompany him and who would stay behind in camp with Julia and Johnny.

Tom won and excitedly strapped on his pistol and checked his saddle rifle to make certain it was ready for use. "Walt, why don't you take some good-sized rocks and make us a bathtub out there next to where the stream cuts around the bank? Don't forget to keep your rifle close by all the time. Don't relax a second while Tom and I are gone. Anybody comes along the trail, you watch 'em close. Understand?" said Marty.

"Sure will, Marty. Tomorrow I get to ride with you, don't I?"

"You bet." Marty smiled at Johnny, who was standing close to his mother. "Johnny, you watch out for your ma. We'll be back before supper." The boy shyly ducked his head into the folds of his mama's dress.

Marty and Walt cheered on Tom while the young man fought to stay in the saddle as Jim Bennett's horse made a halfhearted attempt to buck him off. The animal quickly surrendered to Tom's control and meekly followed Pacer as Marty led out, headed toward the northwest, from the camp.

They saw no sign, man, or animal until after they had consumed their midday sandwiches. As they topped a small hill, a rolling mass of brown furry beasts dotted the countryside to their front. They ambled along, docilely munching on the brown grass.

"Lookie there, will ya?" Tom exclaimed. "A herd of buffalo. I never saw a buffalo before. Can I shoot me one, Marty? Please?"

"All right, just one. Come on, get your rifle and follow me."

Marty slipped his big Sharps rifle from its saddle holster and slowly walked to the crest of the hill. He knelt down, Tom right beside him, and looked over the herd. Marty finally pointed at a yearling bull eating slightly off to the rear of the herd.

"See that bull to the rear there?" Marty pointed. "I guess

he's about a hundred and seventy-five yards away. See if you can bring him down."

Tom lay down and took aim. The report of his rifle caused a few of the buffalo to trot ten or twenty yards farther away from where the two men lay, but most ignored it and simply kept on munching the prairie grass. The target staggered forward a few steps, then collapsed on his folded front legs like he was kneeling down to sleep. The animal shuddered and then was still.

Marty slapped Tom's shoulder. "I do believe you got him good, Tom. Great shot, right through the heart. Let's go skin him out and head on back with fresh meat. Maybe Julia will make us a stew with the hump."

Marty showed Tom how to skin out the buffalo, a job he had learned when he had hunted buffalo for the railroad the previous year. Tom listened eagerly as Marty recalled his time hunting with Buffalo Bill Cody and Big Mick O'Rourke from the Union Pacific Railroad. After they finished, Marty cut some of the choice meat away from the carcass and wrapped it in the fresh hide.

They returned with their prize to the campsite, where a welcomed meal of biscuits, beans, and venison awaited. After they ate, Marty tried out the bathtub Walt had fashioned by stacking a ring of large rocks around the sandy bottom of the creek. He took a leisurely scrub-down, relaxing in the cool water. After he finished, he rousted both Tom and Walt, then helped the two young men tote enough water to fill up the washtub for Julia to bathe Johnny and then herself in behind a canvas screen tied off between the two wagons. Marty watched the boys brush down the mules and the horses, making certain they did not try to slip around the front and sneak a peek at the bathing woman, but Tom and Walt stayed respectful young gentlemen.

After Julia finished her bath, she washed the men's pants in the used water and hung them out on the clothesline that had held the canvas screen. Marty took the midnight-shift guard duty that night, so he tried to talk to Julia until his shift started. He smiled at the young widow sitting on the log, the Greener shotgun lying across her lap, and a fierce, determined expression on her face. She took her guard duty seriously. He stirred the fire, shooting a shower of sparks into the night sky.

"There's bound to be a wagon train come along soon. As long as we're not threatened by anyone or anything, I'm for sitting right here until we find one that suits us. You agree?"

"What do you mean, 'suits us'?"

"I don't want to be on any train that doesn't have a goodly number of women and children, for example. Nor a supply train of goods headed for Santa Fe or Denver. Those teamsters can be pretty raw and reckless around a gentle-woman."

"I'll be just fine. I don't want to spend too long lolly-gagging in the middle of Kansas. I need to get to my land before the summer's over."

"I agree, but we're ahead of our original timetable, thanks to the railroad. I doubt we'll be here much longer."

Julia sniffed and primly pressed her lips together, as if she was holding something back, but said nothing. The silence stretched between the two, and finally, Marty pulled his bedroll up under his chin. "Well, I'm going to get some shut-eye until it's my turn on guard. Call out if you need me."

"I will, Mr. Keller."

"You're just not gonna call me Marty, are you, Julia?"

"And I think you understand why, Mr. Keller. Good night."

Chapter 13

The Big Hunt

After they finished their coffee the next morning, Walt and Tom approached Marty, who was saddling Pacer.

"Marty," Walt asked, "can me and Tom go see that buffalo herd? I ain't never seen a buffalo either and I'd like to shoot me one. I'd like to git me a nice hide same as Tom's got. Could we, please?"

Marty pulled the cinch tight and rubbed Pacer's velvety nose as he considered the request. There was no reason why the two boys should not return to the buffalo herd. There had been no sign of Indians around the herd. It might be good for them to get away from him and Julia for a few hours. Finally, Marty nodded. "All right. I guess that would be okay. Why not get four more hides? When we get to Denver, I'll have them made into winter coats for all of us. Nothing beats a buffalo-hide coat when the snow's falling like there's no tomorrow."

"Oh boy!" Walt fairly shouted. "Tom, we can kill four buffalo. Grab yur rifle, Cuz, and let's git a'goin'."

Marty held up his hand. "Listen to me, both of you. Don't do anything foolish out there. If you see any sign of Indians or buffalo hunters, you skedaddle back here to camp, pronto. Tom, you remember what I said about sneaking up on the herd from down wind and such?"

"Sure do, Marty."

"Think you can skin a buffalo?"

"Sure. I watched how you did it."

"All right then, go on. Have a good time, be careful, and don't dawdle around once you got the hides. Get on back here so I don't have to ride out looking for you. I don't want to leave Julia and Johnny here alone."

"We will, Marty," Tom promised. "Come on, Walt. I'll let you ride my horse and I'll take Mr. Bennett's. If that's okay with you, ma'am." Tom looked at Julia.

"Certainly, Tom," she replied. "Just you two be careful. We're a long ways from any help, if something were to happen."

She stood beside Marty as the two boys trotted off, leading one of the mules to serve as a pack animal on the return trip. A worried frown crossed her brow. "Do you think we should let them go off like that? They're so young and full of themselves."

"Well, they're near enough grown men to be given the benefit of the doubt, I reckon. Maybe now's a good time to find out if they can be responsible for themselves."

She watched the two youngsters ride over a hill, then wiped her hands on her apron. "I hope so, for their sakes."

Marty spent the morning shoeing the new horses and one of the mules. With only enough horseshoes for two more replacements, he reminded himself to stop by a farrier's shop and pick up some more blanks when they reached Denver. He still had several extra shoes for the mules, which took a narrower shoe than the horses did.

The three horses he had found were all easily shod, reinforcing Marty's belief that they had once belonged to a white man before the Indians had obtained possession of them. He brushed all the stock with a stiff brush and turned them back into the rope corral that Walt and Tom had constructed.

Julia spent the morning mending various articles of clothing and preparing a pot of buffalo stew for the evening's meal.

From time to time one or the other of them would stop and look toward the north, an unconscious act to allay their worry about the two young men.

Tom and Walt trotted their animals until they were out of sight of the camp, then gradually slowed down until they were riding at a more moderate pace. Walt was jabbering about the opportunity to shoot buffalo. Tom, who considered himself more the professional hunter because of his lesson from Marty the day before, limited his responses to single syllables.

The trail that led from the herd back to camp was still clearly visible in the waist-high prairie grass, which was turning a golden brown in the baking hot sun. Within an hour they crested the same small hill where Marty and Tom had shot the buffalo the day before. The herd was nowhere in sight, but the barren swath of churned-up land the grazing herd had cut in the dark soil was easily followed. Carrion-eaters scattered from the carcass of the dead buffalo as they rode past. Several ravens and hawks circled in the blue sky above the remains, a sure sign the something dead was right below.

The two followed the trail across the small valley. As they crested the rise, the herd spread out below them, slowly eating its way toward the north.

Tom swung off his horse. "Come on, Walt. We're close enough now." Tom led the way as they crept up to a satisfactory shooting location. Relying on the meager knowledge that he had obtained from Marty's instruction the day before, Tom got Walt properly positioned, then let him have the first shot. It was a clean kill. Tom's was as well. In short order the required four animals were down and the herd had moved a short distance away from the carcasses of their companions.

Laughing and enjoying the novel experience of buffalo-hunting, the boys soon had the animals skinned and the hides wrapped around several choice pieces of meat. After tying the hides and meat on the pack mule, the two boys re-traced their ride back to the campsite.

As they topped a low rise, Tom reined up his horse and pointed to the east. "Walt, look over there. See all them crows circlin' around the sky? There must be somethin' mighty interestin' on the ground for them to gather up like that. Let's go take a look."

As they crossed over another rise, the butchered bodies of two dozen buffalo littered the ground to their front. Drawing their rifles, they slowly moved on down until they were among the leavings, scaring away several coyotes and a red fox that were feasting on the largess. At each remains, the twin marks of the trailing edge of a travois, with the hoof-prints of the horse that pulled it in between, led off to the northeast.

"Injuns?" Walt exclaimed.

"It has to be. A lot of 'em. I see twenty or more different hoofprints headed over thataway, besides the travois tracks." Tom pointed in the direction of the travois trails, which crossed a high spot and disappeared. "Come on, we'd better tell Marty."

"If they jump us, I'll make 'em sorry they was ever born," Walt boasted.

"Yeah, well, they just might have the same ideer about us. Come on, let's git going. All of a sudden, my scalp is gettin' a mite itchy."

Both boys talked at once as soon as they reached camp.

Marty listened intently and waited until they both ran out of steam. "You certain you weren't spotted or trailed back here?"

"I'm positive, Marty. They'd been gone a couple of hours when we found their huntin' site."

"You fellas get all the animals roped and hobbled. I'm going to ride out a ways and see if I see anything unusual."

"You be careful, Marty. There's too many for just you to take on."

"I don't plan to. I believe they'll head on back to their summer camp with the meat they took. I just want to be sure none of them dropped off to do a little mischief before headin' home. If I spot any and they spot me, I'll head back here faster than a scalded cat, believe me. If you see me coming in on the run, get to your guns and be ready to give me cover fire."

"You bet we will, Marty," Walt said confidently. "I'm anxious to get me a Injun scalp to go with my buffalo robe."

"Just be certain it's not the other way around. You fellas keep a sharp eye out till I get back."

Marty followed Walt and Tom's trail back to where they had found the Indian sign. He carefully examined the ground. "Sure enough, Pacer. About two dozen braves and that many more pack animals. Let's follow along and see if we can figure where they're going, shall we?"

Marty had followed the sign for more than a mile when he spotted the hoofprints of a single rider joining the group. The entire party had stopped and palavered for a time. Then six riders had peeled off from the group and headed back toward the south and east, back toward the Santa Fe Trail, some miles to the south. "Hello, looks like we may have a few who are up to no good, old pard. Let's follow after them."

The Indians had not bothered to hide their trail, conveniently making it easy for Marty to follow. It led directly to the immigrant trail to the American Southwest.

Marty slowed as he crested one of the many small hillocks that dotted the central-Kansas prairie. He peered over the top and immediately jerked Pacer to a quick halt. Down below, hidden behind a fold of the earth, the six Indians were watching a wagon train slowly making its way along the Santa Fe Trail.

There were over thirty wagons in the train, plus a hundred or more cattle and about thirty horses in two separate herds, which followed along at the rear of the snaking column of canvas-covered wagons. Several riders were attempting to herd the animals, but they were scattered around the entire herd, so their defense of the animals would be limited. Marty was certain the horses were the target of the Indians, as their numbers were far too few for any type of attack against the main column of wagons.

Marty eased off Pacer and securely tied him to a small bush just over the hill from the waiting Indians. He took both his rifles, the big Sharps and the multishot Winchester, then moved back to the top of the hill, looking down upon the waiting Indians.

Taking a comfortable firing position on his stomach, he aimed with the Winchester. Letting out half a breath, Marty sprayed a dozen shots around the surprised Indians. Rattled by the angry buzz of passing bullets and unsure how many hidden gunmen were firing at them, the panicked braves leaped aboard their ponies and galloped away, yipping and howling like angry coyotes. Marty put two bullets from the Sharps in their dust as they galloped over the far hill and out of sight.

Chuckling at their hasty exit from their ambush site, Marty replaced his rifles in their saddle scabbards and rode down the hill toward the wagon train, which had stopped and circled in a defensive position in case they were being attacked.

Marty rode confidently up to where several men, holding their rifles at the ready, were standing, cautiously watching both him and the surrounding countryside. Stopping Pacer, he smiled and thumbed back over his shoulder. "You had a small war party hidden behind that fold there, looking for a chance to swoop down and pick off some of your horses, if I don't miss my guess."

A gray-haired man, wearing farmer's overalls and armed with a double-barreled shotgun in his hands, stepped out a pace. "You the fella doin' all the shootin'?"

Marty nodded. "Yep. I think I put the fear of God into 'em. They headed out across the plains like the devil himself was chasing them."

A darker man, taller, harder, and ill kept, spoke up. "How many of 'em did you kill?"

"Why, none. I scattered bullets all around them. Scared 'em good. There was no need to kill any of them. Besides, I was afraid that if I did shoot some of them and the others got away, they might return with their friends. Signs point to twenty or thirty braves passing this way yesterday."

The dark-haired man sneered at Marty. "We can take care of thirty just as easy as not."

"True, but chances are you would suffer some loss. Why chance it when you don't have to? Those fellows are taking fresh buffalo back to their village. They won't want to drop it and come back to fight us without provocation."

The older man licked his lips, then nodded and spoke up. "Makes sense to me, Black Jack. Better to leave well enough alone, I say. Thanks, mister. I'm Gabriel Laderman, from French Lick, Indiana. I'm sort of the captain of this here wagon train. Who might you be?"

"Howdy. I'm Marty Turner. I'm taking my sister and her

family out to Wyoming Territory. Where you folks heading?"

"There's thirty-two families of us headed for the Pike's Peak area in Colorado. We've all purchased land from the government, near a place called Fountain. That's near Colorado Springs."

"You aiming to dig for gold?"

"Land's sake no. We're farmers. We've bought land to farm. We'll sell produce and cattle to the miners to get our gold."

"A wise plan, if you ask me, Mr. Laderman."

"Please, call me Gabe. Can I call you Marty?"

"Sure can, Gabe." Marty held out his hand to the scowling, darker man. "Hello, I'm Marty Turner."

"Sorry, Marty. This here is our scout, Monty Reed. Everyone calls him Black Jack, though."

Reed reluctantly took Marty's offered hand and mumbled a weak hello. Reed turned back to Gabe. "Gabe, we need to push on. I want us to get to the Cottonwood Bottoms ford afore dark." He mounted his horse and rode off without another word, leaving Marty and Gabe where they stood.

"Sorry 'bout Black Jack there, Marty. We got a sickness in our company just afore we was to leave St. Joe and missed out on jinin' up with the big trains. We was lucky to find anyone to guide us. He's surly, but so far he's took us right where he should."

"Whatever you say, Gabe. He acts like his face would break if he ever smiled, but I guess that's his worry."

"Whatta ya doin' out here, Marty?"

"Two of my boys went out this morning to shoot some buffalo and spotted the tracks of the Indians I told you about. I was just taking a look when I came upon them getting ready to hit your train."

"Where ya parked?"

"About three hours down the trail at a ford across the

river. I'll bet it's the very same Cottonwood Bottoms your
man Black Jack was talkin' about."

"Well, we'll jine ya fer supper iffen ya don't mind. Ya say
ya know where some buffalo are? Would you mind tellin'
me? We could use some fresh meat."

"Gabe, I'd be happy to get you some, if you can loan me
some pack animals to carry the meat. I'll take a few of your
men and meet you back at the bottoms with all the fresh buffalo you can use. When you get there, please tell my hired
men, Tom or Walt, that I'll be along directly."

"Well, by gobs, that's mighty nice of ya, Marty. I'll let
your men know as to where ya are and I'll put together a
huntin' party right now, if ya'll excuse me."

"My pleasure, Gabe."

"Hey, Sam. You and the missus git this fella something to
drink, would ya?"

Gabe rode away, shouting for men to volunteer to join a
buffalo-hunting party, while Marty moved over to where
Sam and his wife were dipping a ladle of cool water from a
barrel tied to the side of their wagon, a massive Conestoga
so commonly used as the prime carrier of the pioneers
across the Great Plains.

"Thanks, folks," Marty sighed after taking a long drink.
"Tastes mighty fine on a hot day like this."

"I hear you say you're gonna take some men out to get
some buffalo?" Sam asked.

"That's right," Marty answered.

"I ain't never seen a buffalo afore. Marsha, would you
mind drivin' the wagon a spell so's I can go along?"

"Go ahead. I'll make out."

Marty took one look at the raw-boned Marsha, her work-
hardened hands as big as some men's, and smiled. She
would have made two of the skinny Sam, and Marty had no
doubt that she could hold her own behind a team of four-up.

Gabe returned with six men leading two dozen horses

and motioned to the blond young man in front, who was riding easily even though he was missing most of his left arm. "Marty, this here is my son, Dan. He'll lead up the men from our train. Ya goin' along, Sam?"

"You bet, Gabe."

"Watch ole Sam here, Marty. He's 'bout a cross twixt a mule and a monkey. I ain't never certain just how he's gonna jump."

"Why, Gabe, don't take on so. You'll have this nice fella thinkin' I'm a regular no-account coot."

"Nope, yur the man I'd want at my back any day, Sam. It's just that ya can git into the dangest situations I ever did know of."

"Well," Sam sniffed, "I'll be careful and do what Marty here says. Fair enough?"

"Fair enough, old friend. Be seein' you boys at the campsite. Bring us back some good, fresh buffalo meat."

Marty shook hands with Dan, who was in his middle twenties. He was a younger copy of his father, with the same sandy hair and broad shoulders. "Pleased to meet you, Dan. You fellas ready to go?" Marty did not comment on the empty sleeve hanging from Dan's shirt. There were many men who had left an arm on some lonely Civil War battlefield.

At their nod, Marty led the party away from the wagons and returned to the trail he had followed toward the buffalo herd. Marty glanced over at Dan riding beside him. The manner in which the younger Laderman rode his horse seemed familiar. Marty asked casually, "You a cavalryman during the war, Dan?"

"Still shows, uh?" Dan answered with a faint smile.

"I was too. It's easy to see by the way you ride."

"Yeah, I rode with Gen'ral John Buford. Caught a Reb musket ball at Gettysburg and lost my arm. With your accent, I'd guess you rode for the South?"

"Yes, with Nathan Bedford Forrest. We stayed mostly in Tennessee, Mississippi, and Alabama. Never made it back east."

"Well, that's all behind us now. I made out a lot better than a lot of my bunkies, so I can't complain."

"I agree wholeheartedly. Hello, here's where the Indians made their kills. See the tracks, leading away to the north-east?"

The lighthearted banter of the hunters dried up as they saw the stripped carcasses of the buffalo and the sign the Indians had left with their ponies and travois. In another half hour they passed the spot where Marty and Tom had killed their animals. They trotted on in the churned-up trail left by the grazing buffalo, easily a quarter mile wide. In a short period of time, they saw the tail end of the herd, which was slowly grazing its way to the north.

Marty led the party in a loop around the herd, pulling up in a small gully just behind a hill from where buffalo were feeding. Even from where they were, the noise of the grazing buffalo was audible. Marty led the men with their rifles to the top of the hill. They were only a hundred yards or less from the edge of the massive brown spill that was several thousands of buffalo.

Marty quickly instructed the men and placed them in a line along the hilltop. Satisfied that everyone was ready, he smiled at Dan, who had declined a chance to shoot at an animal. "Time to get some fresh meat." He pointed at the first man in the line. "First man, fire when ready."

Chapter 14

Faieren

Marty led his hunting party down the slope and into the ring of wagons set up by Gabe just across the creek from where Marty had placed his wagons. The husky Indiana farmer turned wagon-train captain walked over to Marty.

"How'd you boys do?"

Marty pointed at the pack mules, each carrying a heavy bundle wrapped in buffalo hide. "We brought back about a ton and a half of fresh buffalo and thirty-six prime buffalo hides. They'll make mighty nice winter coats for your folks, if that's something you might want."

"My goodness. Mama, gather up the womenfolk and let's parcel out this here meat right away. My mouth's a waterin' for some good buffalo roast. How 'bout you, Dan?"

"Same fer me, Pa. Marty's asked me to join him fer supper, iffen that's all right with you."

"Sure, that's fine. Marty, why don't you and yours come over after supper? I'll have Ma bake up a dried apricot pie fer our dessert."

"My thanks, Gabe. We'll stop by, you can count on it."

After they finished the warm pie later that evening, all of

Marty's party sitting around the Laderman campfire, Marty pulled out three cigars and passed two over to Gabe and Dan. "Cigars?"

Both men eagerly grabbed the offered smoke. Gabe sniffed his appreciatively. "Thankee kindly, Marty. Ain't had a decent smoke in a couple a'weeks. We're savin' our money for necessities on the other end of the trip, so I didn't regulate myself enough to have tobacco fer the entire way." Gabe puffed his from a lighted branch Marty held out. Sighing in satisfaction, he blew out a long stream of rolling smoke and settled back. "Mighty good smoke, Marty."

Marty watched as Julia and Mrs. Laderman cleaned up the dishes. "How was your buffalo, Gabe?" Marty inquired.

"Wonderful. Shore hit the spot." He turned to his son, who sat silently, smoking and staring into the fire. "You full, boy? We had some left over iffen you want."

"No thanks, Pa. Julia is a fine cook, almost as good as Ma."

"Umm. Oh, there's Black Jack. Hey, Black Jack. Come over and have yurself a piece of Ma's apricot pie. It'll top off yur buffalo steak jus' fine."

"Thanks, Gabe." Black Jack stepped into the circle of light from the fire. He saw Julia approaching with Mrs. Laderman and quickly took off his hat. "Howdy, Mrs. Laderman. Howdy, ma'am. I'm Black Jack Reed, the wagon train guide." He offered his hand to Julia. After a long pause, she withdrew her hand, when it became apparent that Black Jack was not going to withdraw his.

"Mr. Reed. Pleased to meet you." Julia slightly turned away from Reed to indicate that she did not want any further attention from him.

Frowning, Reed turned his attention back to Marty and Gabe. "I just wanted to check, Gabe. What time do you want to take off tomorrow?"

Gabe pondered for a moment, then answered. "Let's take

a day off, Black Jack. We've been pushing hard for two weeks. We'll let the womenfolk smoke some of the meat Marty here got fer us and let the animals git a day of rest and good grazin'. As dry as it is, their vittles might not be so good once we leave the riverbed."

"Well, I don't think it's necessary, but whatever you say. It's just another day we won't be in Colorado afore the snows come."

Marty touched Gabe on the arm. "Gabe, I've been meaning to ask you. We'd like to join up with your train, the rest of the way into Colorado. We're headed for Denver, so when you cut south to Colorado Springs, we'll split away. Would that be all right with you?"

Before Gabe could answer, Black Jack Reed jumped in. "We don't need no more pilgrims with us, Gabe. I'm agin lettin' these folks tag along. We don't know nuthin' about 'em, don't forget."

"Damn, Black Jack, but you're surly tonight. I reckon we'll git along jus' fine with these nice folks. Shore, Marty, you can come along. Maybe we'll run into another herd of buffalo afore we git there. You're too good a hunter not to have along."

Black Jack stood and scowled at Marty and Gabe. "You're the captain, Gabe. But I still think it's a mistake." He stalked away, leaving a bemused Marty wondering why the guide would have so much hostility toward his presence in the train.

Shrugging, Marty turned his attention to Gabe and Dan. The three men talked, as did the women, until the fire burned low; then Marty walked back to his camp, carrying Julia across the shallow ford that bisected the two sides of the river.

Tom and Walt made certain everything was ready to resume the journey the following day. Dan Laderman stopped by, supposedly to inform Marty and Julia about their place in the line of march, but perhaps more so to say hello to Julia.

Marty listened to Dan's instructions, then called his group together. "Dan here says we'll fall in at the rear of the train for the time being, and that's fine with me. Tom, you tie one of the horses we found to Pacer and another to Jim Bennett's horse—what's his name, Buck? We'll let them travel with the horse herd. Julia, you'd better keep Victor tied to your wagon for a while. There's bound to be some bulls in the cattle herd and we don't want him getting hurt in a scrape with one of them."

"What about the third horse, Marty?" Walt asked.

"I'll ride the paint and let Pacer have a day off. I want to make certain those three don't try to run off the first time we free them up on their own." He took a sip of water, then pulled his work gloves back on. "Come on, Tom. I think we need to change a shoe on the gray mule. He seems to be stepping gingerly on that hoof."

Marty saddled the paint pony the next morning, relieved to see that the animal remembered the feel of a Western saddle on its back. After a few halfhearted bucks, the resigned horse settled down and responded to Marty's use of the reins. As the wagon train left the bottoms, Marty signaled for Walt and Tom to fall in behind the last wagon in the line. He introduced himself to the middle-aged farmer driving it, a balding, nondescript fellow named Sam Driggs, whose plain, sturdy wife, Rose, was slowly going to fat as she aged.

Both were cheery and kind in their comments and actions, for which Marty was grateful. Julia and Rose spent the morning gabbing back and forth. As the day slowly wore on, the wagon train crossed the river and proceeded west deeper into the rolling prairie of western Kansas.

The third day out, the area grew even drier, and the fine

dust accumulating in the air behind the wagon train became even more aggravating. Marty pulled his two wagons out until they were far to the side of the wagons directly in front. He was riding the most promising of the found horses, the big bay, with its cream-colored mane and tail. He had spent a lot of time with Pacer that morning, because he knew that the faithful horse was edgy that Marty was not riding him.

The train was traversing the shallow slope of a long narrow valley, with the leading wagon already deep in the natural bowl while Marty's wagons were just entering it. His position was higher on the slope than any of the other wagons in the train. He looked at the front of the wagon train. There was no sign of Black Jack Reed or the so-called assistant scout, an undersized bandy rooster of a man called Junior. Marty speculated as to where they might be instead of their assigned position. Neither Black Jack nor Junior had spoken to him since he had joined the train, and that suited Marty just fine. He had not liked the way Black Jack had stared at Julia the night he had been introduced to her. He had seen barflies stare at a crib gal the very same way too many times not to recognize Black Jack's base intention with the comely widow.

Marty viewed the rim at the far end of the valley. He would hate to top it and find a few hundred painted Indians awaiting them. He spurred the bay he had found into a light canter. He wanted to be at the top well before the first wagon. As he rode, he admired the gait of the animal he was on. "You're a pretty good horse, old fellow. I wonder who used to own you." Marty patted the animal's neck as they ate up ground toward the top of the valley.

Ta-a-naka, or Crooked Teeth, was one mad Cheyenne Indian. He had discovered a wagon train of whites with five hands of horses trailing along in a herd guarded by only three men. It would have been an easy coup to lead his fellow braves down on a fast attack of the herd, once the wagons had passed the ambush site he had chosen, and steal all of it. He would have been honored at many council fires after that.

The abrupt rifle fire that had poured down on them from their rear from the unseen whites had spooked the braves with him and they had run for their camp, many miles to the north, without stopping. By the time the story had been told over and over, the other braves had become minor heroes at the campfires, but Crooked Teeth knew better. Only one or two men, none of whom could shoot straight, as none of his party had even been scratched by a bullet, had routed them.

As soon as he was able to obtain the permission of Walks Alone, the Indian chief, he had returned to shadow the wagon train, even though only Little Dog, a boy of fifteen winters, had agreed to accompany him. He had easily found the wagons and had skirted the edge of their number without being seen for most of the day. He desperately tried to develop a plan that would allow him to return in triumph to his village with some of the horses. His village was angry that three of their captive horses stolen from an earlier wagon train had wandered away the previous week. A return to camp with new replacements would give him valuable prestige among his peers.

The Cheyenne brave worried on his problem as he rode his pony ahead of the wagon trail, searching for the perfect ambush site. He looked down from the back of his pony. The ground was covered belly-high to his horse with dry *Kia-hi* grass, what the white man called bluestem. Poking their heads up in dense patches were the purple flowers of fireweed, whose blossoms were shaped like clusters of flames. The sight gave Crooked Teeth an idea. "Little Dog, we will start a great fire. The wind blows toward the white eyes' wagons. The horse herd will run back to the river for safety. They will scatter over many miles. It will be easy to gather up many horses. The white eyes cannot make it to the river before the fire reaches their wagons, so they will die. This is a good plan. Come, we must find the right place to begin."

The two Indians galloped their ponies until they had out-paced the slower wagon train by a couple of miles. The land slowly rose and the grass thinned out to rock-covered sand. Crooked Teeth quickly started a small fire. He took two dried mesquite bushes and tied a length of braided rawhide rope to each. He threw them into the blaze, waited until the bushes were burning hotly, then galloped away from Little Dog, dragging a burning bush behind him. Little Dog rode in the opposite direction, dragging his own burning bush in the same manner. In ten minutes, a mile of fire was burning, growing with every passing moment, and being driven by the prevailing winds directly toward the wagon train.

As his bush burned out, Crooked Teeth halted his sweat-ing pony and slid off. He looked back with a sly smile across his face as the fire burned over the hill to his front and moved on, devouring every flammable thing in its path. Seeing Lit-tle Dog riding toward him, he turned and looked for a place to wait out the fire in safety. As he was upwind, the fire was moving very slowly in his direction. He had time to find a rocky outcropping on a distant hillside and lead his compan-ion there. Securing their ponies, the two Indians settled back to wait for the fire to do its mischief with the uninvited white man that was crossing their land.

Marty rode over the top of the valley and saw still an-other rolling hill exactly the same about a mile ahead of him. He trotted on until he topped that one as well, and loped his horse across the swale of land toward the next high ground, expecting to see more of the same. What he did see was angry-looking, black-streaked, gray-white clouds of smoke boiling upward as if a thunderstorm had formed on the ground instead of in the sky. As he gaped at the sight, the first wave of yellow and red flames crested the hill and started down toward him, dancing red sparks reaching out ahead of the fire line like angry bees. As he watched, a herd of deer ran across the slope of the hill, headed toward the river, twelve or fifteen miles away.

"Great God Almighty," Marty moaned, "a wildfire." He jerked the reins on his horse and put his spurs to use. "Come on, Horse. We gotta get back to the wagon train, pronto."

Marty slapped the flanks of his animal with the ends of his reins, and the gallant bay responded by fairly flying across the prairie. "Dear God, don't let this horse step in a prairie dog hole. The wagon train is doomed if he does and I don't reach them in time." Marty slapped the reins even harder and, shouting encouragement, galloped at full speed back the way he had come.

As Marty reached the top of the hill where the wagon train was just beginning to labor up the gentle slopes, he took off his hat and shouted at the top of his lungs, "Prairie fire, headed right for us. Circle the wagons—hurry!"

Marty continued shouting as he rode up to Gabe Laderman. "Gabe, quickly, man. Get the wagons in a circle. Drive the stock inside. Hurry, hurry. We don't have much time."

"What's happening, Marty? A fire you say, headed our way? Let's run for the river."

Marty grabbed Gabe by the arm. "We don't have time, man. You'll kill everyone if you try. Our only chance is to start a backfire around us so the flames from the main fire won't reach us." Marty ran toward the second wagon in line, waving his arm in a circle over his head. "Circle the wagons! Circle the wagons!"

In response to his shouts and thanks to their doing just that every night, the wagons formed up a circle in rather quick order. Marty glanced to the west. The dark smoke was high in the sky and appeared to be not more than a mile or two away. Marty stopped Walt and Driggs as they started to drive into the circle. "Wait, just a minute." He shouted at the drovers with the herds, "Drive the animals into the circle. Quickly! Hurry!"

As the cattle followed the horses toward the wagons, Marty shouted at the drovers, "Circle them around the wagons one time. Knock down all the grass near the wagons." He shouted at Gabe, who was running toward him. "Gabe, have every wagon soak a couple of blankets in water, then throw water on the canvas of the wagons. We gotta keep them from catching fire from blowing embers."

Gabe nodded and hurried off. As the cattle completed their circle of the wagons, Marty directed them inside to join the nervous horses milling about the confined space. He turned to Walt and Driggs. "Circle the wagons a couple of times, as fast as you can. I want the wheels of your heavy wagons to cut into the earth and throw it up, just like a plow would. Whip your animals, make 'em run. I want deep ruts cut into the ground. Then get inside the circle. Hurry now, hurry!"

Marty looked up. The writhing smoke and flames were at the top of the hill. "Gabe!" he shouted. "Start setting fire to the grass outside the beat-down area. Put out any flames that head for the wagons. Get all the men you can to start setting backfires. Quickly, we don't have much time." Marty ran outside the circle of wagons and lit a clump of bunchgrass. He ran down the line for fifty feet, setting fire to the dry grass. Then he grabbed a wet blanket and beat down the flames attempting to eat their way toward the wagons.

Gabe had a dozen men doing the same thing. Marty lit another clump of grass. He looked up through the flames and smoke of the backfires. The wildfire was already halfway down the rise to the circle of wagons. Tom and Walt beat back several streamers of fire headed for their wagons. Ever so slowly—it seemed to the desperate members of the wagon train—the backfire moved toward the boiling cauldron that was the advancing edge of the wildfire bearing down on them.

Marty looked around. A solid carpet of darkened, smoking ground surrounded the wagon train. The burned-out barrier was over thirty feet wide and growing with every precious moment. Marty prayed it would be enough.

The wind blew the hot, throat-searing smoke and heated air past him, and he convulsed in a spasm of choking coughs. Shaking himself, he moved back to the front of the wagons, his wet blanket in his dirt-encrusted hand. Walt and Tom joined him, their grins starkly white against their soot-blackened faces. It was more like a game than a matter of life and death to the two youngsters. "Watch the canvas," Marty croaked, his parched throat dry and filled with soot. "The sparks'll set it on fire if you're not quick with the water and your wet blankets. Tom, take Julia's wagon. Walt, you look after the big wagon. When the two fires hit, there'll be an explosion of burning embers shot into the air. I'm gonna check on the other wagons."

"Don't worry, Marty," Walt shouted over the increasing crackle and rumble of the advancing burning grasslands. "We'll handle things here. Right, Tom?"

Tom shouted his agreement as he scrambled up the side of the wagon to beat out a half-burned stalk of grass that had just blown onto the canvas of Julia's wagon. Marty saw her come around the end of the wagon, carrying a bucket of water to resoak the wet blankets. Marty ran down the line of wagons, shouting instructions and encouragement to the harried immigrants as they prepared to meet the roaring inferno. Coughing and gasping in the dense smoke, he hoped to make a complete circle and get back to his wagons.

Marty did not see the confluence of the twin walls of flame. He was too busy running from wagon to wagon, shouting quick instructions, helping beat out hot sparks that were showering down from the smoke-filled sky like raindrops, as well as calming excited horses, mules, and oxen, who were feeling the sting of hot embers on their exposed hides.

Marty paused from beating out a small circle of fire that had started on the canvas side of one of the wagons when Gabe stumbled up to him, coughing and hacking dirty globs of sooty phlegm. "Did you see it?"

"See what?" Marty coughed.

"The fire. It hit the backfire like an explosion. Fire musta shot a hunnerd foot into the sky. Sparks and fire danced up like there was no tomorry, then—*boom!*—there was nothing. Just some smoke and a few small clumps of grass still burning. Just like that it was past us and we're still here. You done it, Son. We're saved. Way to go, my boy."

Marty waved his hand to clear a space of air so he could breathe. "It's past? Thank God. That was a close one." He grinned at the soot-covered face of the grizzled Gabe, wondering if he appeared as black and singed as the man he smiled at.

"What do we do now?"

"Make certain there's no fire still smoldering in any of the canvas, then we've gotta get out of here. Find water and good grass. The animals will plug up if we drive them on the ash for too long."

"Whatever you say, Marty. I jus' want you to know, I thought we was goners when I saw them flames racing down the hill toward us. You sure saved our bacon fer us, and you can be certain we won't fergit it."

Marty returned to his wagons. Gabe started around the wagon train, checking on the welfare of everyone else. Walt and Tom met Marty at the wagons. Both were busy rubbing the backs of the mules with wet blankets to ensure that no embers were tormenting the animals. Julia was doing the same to the horses and the bull. Both boys had faces as black as coal miners', as Marty expected his was. Both were grinning like kids let out of school early.

"Holy cow, Marty," Walt exclaimed. "Wasn't that somethin'?"

"It was like hell was rollin' right down on us from above," Tom interjected. "I thought we was goners when the two fires hit. I could feel the heat clear over here."

Marty slapped each on the shoulder. "You boys did fine work. I'm proud of you both. You faced up head-on to what the Texas vaqueros call a *faieren,* or wildfire, and beat it. Julia, you and Johnny all right?"

"We're fine. There's a six-inch hole burned in the top of the canvas over the big wagon, but I can fix it with a patch soon as there's time."

"Good. When you get done, wipe out the nostrils of the animals with a wet rag, give each one a short drink, then perhaps you can heat up some water, if there's any left, so we can get some of this soot washed off. We'll be moving pretty soon, so you'll have to hurry."

"Very well. Tom, bring me a bucket of water, will you?"

Marty found Gabe busy wrapping the burned hand of one of the men from his group. "He'll be all right, Gabe?"

"Sure will. Tried to put out a fire in his canvas with a hand rather than a wet blanket."

"How'd we do?"

"We're good. Every canvas has a hundred pinholes in it from sparks, and most have a hole or two burned in 'em, but they're still serviceable. What's the plan?"

"Make the rolling stock ready to go. Wipe out their nostrils and give them a small amount of water. Then we've got to get going. We need to get out of the ash as soon as we can." Marty looked around. "You seen any sign of Black Jack or Junior?"

"Nope. They rode on ahead afore noon. Black Jack said

he wanted to find water. Said that he thought we could make it afore sundown."

"Well, get the wagons rolling as soon as you can. I'm going to try to wash off some of this soot on my face. I must look like a mule skinner who's quit bathing for Lent."

"You look like a savior from heaven to me, Son. I'm forever in yur debt."

"Thanks, Gabe. Let's get outa here—what do you say?"

Chapter 15

Black Jack's True Colors

The wagon train made its way out of the burned-out area in a shallow *V*, with Gabe's four-oxen-harnessed wagon in the lead. This formation reduced the amount of black ash churned into the air. Even so, every member of the wagon train was soon coated with the powdery residue from the fire. The animals had to breathe the suffocating soot, while most of the immigrants tied kerchiefs over their noses to block the worst of the irritant.

As usual, Marty and his wagons were on the extreme right and rear of the north leg of the V. Tom and Marty were on horseback, acting as a sort of flank security for the northern leg of the wagon train. Marty left Pacer to make his own way through the burned-out landscape while he kept his eyes on Julia Bennett, who was driving the small wagon, and the horse and cow herds, which were following in the lee of the wagons. The herders had it the worst. Trying to hold the unhappy animals close behind the wagons forced them to ride the flanks and drag of the milling animals, where they suffered from the full effect of the stirred-up ash and dust.

Tom suddenly called softly to Marty. "Marty, lookie up on the ridge yonder." He pointed with a move of his chin. "Ain't them Injuns?"

Marty swiveled his head around. About a quarter mile away, two Indians sat on their ponies, watching the progress of the wagons across the burned prairie.

"You want to shoot 'em, Marty?"

"Nope. They don't seem to be interested in doing us any harm. Leave 'em alone for the time being."

"But they might have been the ones who started the fire."

"We don't have any proof of that, Tom. Don't forget, killing an Indian usually begets a response from his friends, and we don't need that right now. Watch 'em, but don't do anything else for the time being."

Crooked Teeth and Little Dog looked down on the wagon train in amazement. They had waited for the fire to burn out and expected to ride into the soot-covered area and find scattered and burned wagons littering the landscape and horses running free, ready for the taking. Instead, they witnessed the white eyes rolling along as if nothing had happened.

Crooked Teeth had no explanation except bad medicine. His heart sank and he turned to tell Little Dog that they might as well go back to their camp; there would be no easy pickings that day. The young Indian must have read his thoughts. He made the Cheyenne sign for *quit*, like he was pushing something away from his path, and said, "I go. Bad medicine." Little Dog spun his pony around and trotted away, his animal kicking up puffs of ash and dust with every step.

Crooked Teeth glared at the wagon train with regret, then, cussing his bad luck and the white eyes' good fortune, turned his pony and galloped after the boy, anxious to get out of the fire's cloying ash.

Marty saw the Indians spin their ponies and gallop over

the top of the rise one at a time. He watched until they rode out of sight, then returned his attention to the front, where the lead wagon in the train was slowly gaining in altitude. Spread out before him, the plain of black ash suddenly turned into the softer brown of high desert. They had finally reached the end of the burn zone. Within half an hour they crossed the dividing line between the two extremes—one the sooty, burned ground; the other soft, sandy soil, free of the ravages of the fire.

Marty stopped his wagon and rode ahead to where Gabe had halted his, awaiting Marty's input on what should be done next. "We need to water the draft animals agin, Marty?" the old farm leader asked.

"Do we have enough water? We should, if we can, and wipe out the insides of their nostrils again."

"Black Jack and Junior said they was certain there's good water up ahead. They said the Arkansas River's within a day's march. I suspect we'll be runnin' in to 'em anytime now. I'd say we should go ahead and use up the last of our reserves."

Gabe and Dan trotted their horses around all the halted wagons, explaining what had to be done to relieve the suffering livestock. Tom and Walt carefully cleared the dust and ash from the mules' nostrils while Marty did the same for the extra horses and the old bull, Victor. The stoic breeding bull snorted and fussed but seemed to understand what Marty was doing and allowed it.

By the time Marty was done, the front of the train had lurched forward again. Marty waited until the Driggses' wagon started, and then fell his wagons into the wagon line as the train plodded its way across the sandy, rock-strewn landscape, toward ever higher ground to the west.

The sun was closing in on the western horizon when the wagon train crested a low rise and saw a welcome sight in front of them. A solid green line of trees marking fresh water stood only a mile or so to their front. Everybody's spirits picked up at the thought of fresh water to drink and cleanse in. A thin column of white smoke indicated a campfire already burning. The exhausted families headed for the Arkansas River, desperate to get to the fresh water to cut the soot and dust from their parched throats.

The thirsty animals needed no encouragement to push on; in fact, it was all the herders could do to keep the cattle and extra horses from stampeding straight toward the smell of cool water. Soon all were at the water's edge, drinking their fill. Marty drove his mules and horses to the river's edge and quickly filled a wooden bucket for Victor to drink from, then walked over to where Gabe and Dan were confronting Black Jack and Junior.

Gabe offered a ladle of water to Marty. "Some cool water, Marty?"

"Thanks, Gabe. I could use it." He took a long swallow, then, wiping his mouth with the back of his hand, returned the empty ladle to Gabe. "Mighty good. Thanks."

Dan was berating Junior and Black Jack for missing the fire. "You boys laid around here, cooking your prairie hen, while Marty there was savin' the whole train from a wildfire. How come you didn't come back once you reached the water here?"

"We didn't know we was needed," Black Jack lamely replied. He glared at Marty, angry to be judged wanting before the interloper. "You know we didn't say nuttin' about comin' right back, Gabe, afore we started."

"Well, no harm done, I reckon," Gabe answered. He turned to Marty. "We need to park here for a spell, Marty?"

Black Jack sneered as the wagon captain bypassed his advice to ask the new "hero" what to do.

"I think we ought to give the animals a day to rest up, Gabe. The pull through the burned-out area was hard on 'em."

"Good enough fer me. We'll rest a day. Dan, tell everyone to take their time and get recovered. We'll spend tomorrow here on the river. Black Jack says it's the last good water for maybe three days. Right, Black Jack?"

Never taking his jealous eyes off Marty, Black Jack nodded. "We'll hit a stream or two, if they ain't dried up all the way. But it's three days to another water spot as good as this one."

Marty wandered back to his wagons, wondering why Black Jack was so openly hostile to him. His curiosity was lost in the chores Julia set up for the men. Julia had all three toting water for her washtub and then for hot baths for everyone. Walt and Tom built her an enclosure, and the three of them patrolled the perimeter of their campsite while she bathed as well. Walt took Johnny swimming in the shallow water. Marty and the others from the wagon train watched from the bank and laughed at their happy abandon. Once again Marty vowed to himself that he would make an effort to get closer to Johnny. At the same time, the cold pain in his heart over the loss of his son, Matt, and his wife to the vicious outlaws who killed both of them would not allow it. The pain chilled any affection he felt for another man's son. This was a problem he needed to fix and he knew it.

Sighing, Marty headed for the picket line to brush down Pacer and the other horses. He would worry over his personal shortcomings while doing something worthwhile.

Black Jack and Junior sat by their campfire, both men angry at the cold shoulder they had received from everyone in the wagon train for missing the fire. Black Jack grumbled as he tossed small sticks into the flames. "Damned smartass. Who asked him along, anyways?"

"You talkin' about Marty Turner?"

"Damned right. I've half a notion to put a bullet twixt his eyes."

Junior nodded. "There's somethin' about him. I tell ya, I know I know him from somewhere. I jus' can't put my finger on it right now. He's trouble, Black Jack. I think we need to move up the timetable for our little plan."

Black Jack looked around, his eyes wary. "Talk soft, Junior. These damned plow-chasers'll hang us from the nearest tree they find out what we're up to."

Junior agreed. "I sure don't want to fight my way outa here. There's jus' too many guns agin us."

"Fer the pleasure of killing that smart-ass Marty, I might chance it."

"Kill . . . kill . . . Man-killer! That's it. Marty Keller, the man-killer. That's who he is. Not Turner, but Keller. I seen him in Fort Smith last year. He'd just brought in two brothers wanted fer bank robbery, shot dead. He's a famous bounty hunter, always brings his men in dead, I heerd. S'pose he's after us?"

"I don't know. You got papers out on you in Missouri, right? I don't think them papers from Californee about me would git all the way back here. Maybe, I dunno. We can't take no chances. We either gotta kill 'em right now, or do the thing right now and light out while he's hung up takin' care of the folks in his wagons. Lemme think a minute."

Black Jack swirled the coffee in his tin cup, watching the brown liquid reflect the firelight.

"No, he can't be after us. We run upon him by chance. He sure didn't know we was a'commin'. It's jus' bad luck on our part. We'll take him out iffen we git the chance, but if not, we grab the train's strongbox tonight and light out fer the Colorado goldfields. Keller don't owe these sodbusters nuttin'. He'll not come after us, most likely. Iffen he does, I'll kill him fer the pleasure of it. Even if he does find us, don't fergit, we won't be out where he can shoot us in the back. We'll be in a town, with lots of folks around to make sure he don't sneak up on us. I don't suspect he's so tough when he has to face a man head-on holding a gun of his own. I reckon he's mostly a coward anyhow. You seen how he wouldn't kill them mangy redskins that was a'doggin' us."

Junior drew a sharp knife from a hidden scabbard under his dirty shirt. "I could sneak over tonight and slip this twixt his ribs afore we go after the strongbox."

Black Jack shook his head. "Nope, I don't think so. The Turner wagons are quite a ways from Gabe's wagon, where the strongbox is. If somebody was to happen in upon this fella, Keller, after you got him or someone sees ya, it'd cause such a racket we'd be cut off from the money. Best we git the money and skedaddle as quiet as possible. Put together some supplies and fill the canteens afore you go to sleep."

"Yur the boss, Black Jack."

"I'm gonna ease over to the horse herd and git us three extra mounts apiece. If we keep changin' mounts every two hours, we can cover eighty, ninety miles a day. We'll be in Colorado afore these hay shakers even miss us."

Marty was stretching the kinks out of his back as the sunrise topped the eastern plains. He had just placed a coffeepot of fresh water over the campfire grates when a young boy ran up to him.

"Mr. Turner?"

"That's me, boy. What can I do for you?"

"Mr. Laderman sent me for ya. He says fer ya to come quick to his wagon. Somethin' bad's happened."

Marty trailed the boy, who darted across the open ground of the circled wagons to Laderman's wagon, the one closest to the ford they would take across the Arkansas River when they left the refreshing waters for the open plains ahead of them. Laderman was talking with his son, Dan, when Marty hurried up.

"Something wrong, Gabe?"

Gabe looked up at Marty, wringing his hands in anxiety. "Oh, my God, is there. Someone knifed Sam Driggs last night and stole our strongbox from my wagon. It's got all our settlin' down money in it. I had everyone put their savin's in the strongbox so it'd be safe for the journey. Now someone has stole it and maybe killed poor ole Sam in the process." Gabe was close to tears. "Sam was takin' his regular turn at guard; just his bad luck to be there, I reckon."

Dan smacked his closed fist against his thigh. "We gotta git that money back, Pa. It'll be the ruin of everyone if we don't."

Gabe's voice was flat with suppressed grief. "I know, Son. I know." Gabe turned to Marty, who was standing silently beside the disconsolate train captain. "Marty, I'm hopin' you'll help us. I want you and Dan here to go after who done this terrible thing and git our money back. Will you?"

"First things first, Gabe. Who did this?"

"I ain't rightly sure. I got Rafe Gibson circulatin' the camp right now, to see if anybody is gone."

"Is Mr. Driggs gonna be all right?"

"I hope so. The knife scraped twixt his ribs, but I don't think it punctured his lungs. I got him over to Doc Bishop's wagon, bein' worked on. He nearly bled hisself out afore I found him. His missus is there with him."

"Can the doc help him?"

"He's really more an animal doctor, but he can sew up cuts and dig out bullets with the best of 'em." Gabe grabbed Marty's arm and pleaded again. "You gotta help me git this money back, Marty."

"I've got my wagons to worry about, Gabe."

"I know, but you got two good boys workin' fer ya. I seen how good they are. I'll move yur wagons right up here next to mine, so's I can keep an eye on them whilst you're gone. I promise ya, they'll be looked after like they was my own till you git back."

"Show me the place where you had the strongbox." Marty found nothing there that would reveal who the cowardly thieves were. He climbed out of the wagon just as a stout farmer hurried up and reported to Gabe.

"Black Jack Reed and Junior is the only folks not in camp, Gabe. Their campfire's cold and there ain't nothing of theirs layin' around. I'd say they was long gone."

Marty spoke up. "Did they know about the strongbox, Gabe?"

"I don't know, but I guess they must have. Damn their rotten souls."

"I suspect you're right, Gabe. They must have found out about the money and were biding their time to make off with it. I'm surprised they struck so soon. Maybe my joining the wagon train upset their plans."

"Why's that, Marty?"

"I'm a bounty hunter, Gabe. Anyone on the wrong side of the law may have heard about me. They might have thought I was after them. Anyways, I suspect some of this may be my fault, so I'll go after them. Dan, you don't have to come with me. I'll be riding hard and resting little."

"That's fine by me, Marty. I can still ride and shoot a pistol. It were our stuff Black Jack stole. I reckon I'll come along."

Marty nodded. "Pleased to have you, Dan. Gabe, how much did Black Jack steal?"

"Nearly fifty-three hunnerd dollars, Marty. It was all our combined savin's. We was gonna use it to git us started in the new land. We jus' gotta git it back. I'm a'prayin' you boys'll be able to do that."

"Save your praying for Black Jack Reed and Junior. They're the ones who are going to need it." Instinctively, Marty eased his six-gun up and down in his holster, as if getting ready to face the outlaws head-on.

Chapter 16

On the Outlaws' Trail

"They sure ain't worried about coverin' their tracks, are they?" Dan's voice broke into Marty's musings as they trailed the two men who had betrayed their trust by stealing the wagon train's strongbox. Marty and Dan found the box, its hasp busted off by a heavy crowbar they found lying beside it on the trail. The two outlaws had carried the box until it was daylight and they could see what they were doing. Then they had busted into the heavy strongbox and taken the cash inside. Fortunately, they had left the valuable papers that contained the deeds to the new land Gabe and the other farmers had purchased. Marty and Dan left the important box in the middle of the trail for Gabe to find when he brought the wagons through.

Marty looked at Dan. "They probably think they've got a good jump on us. I doubt they expected us to notice they had taken extra horses from the herd so as to put a lot of miles behind them in a hurry." Marty glanced down at the worn earth that delineated the Santa Fe Trail. The tracks continued due west and were spaced out enough that Marty knew that the men he was after were still pushing their horses hard.

"We got the Jacobs boy to thank for that. Makin' a count of the horses was his idea."

Marty looked ahead, wondering if the whole thing would turn out to be just a horse race. The tracks seemed to lead on relentlessly toward the west. He decided they would stop at the next grove of trees indicating a stream cutting their trail, and switch saddles. "No need to ride you to death, old fella," Marty whispered to Pacer as he stroked the faithful horse's muscular gray-haired neck with his right hand.

Marty spurred Pacer to a slightly faster pace, glancing at a small cluster of sandstone stacked against the higher ground to the north, about two hundred yards up a gentle slope from the trail. He hoped there was nobody hidden there waiting to ambush him and Dan. It looked like an excellent place to spring a surprise on any pursuers. Since his gut had given him warning about the rocks, he looked around. To his left was a washout, a jagged cut in the earth easily six feet deep. If anyone shot at them, they could duck into the gully and have cover and concealment from the ambushers above.

"Keep your eyes peeled on those rocks up yonder to the north of the trail, Dan. A good ambush site."

"Gotcha, Marty."

Black Jack Reed and Junior had been lying in wait at the rocks for nearly two hours. Junior was stiff and bored, as well as a bit reluctant to waste daylight lying among some rocks rather than riding hard for Colorado and safety.

"Dammit, Black Jack. We've been here nearly two hours now and ain't seen nothin'. Why don't we light outta here and put some miles twixt the wagon train and us? We gonna wait fer it to catch up to us?" He uselessly swatted his hand at a pesky fly that was bedeviling him.

"My gut tells me to wait here fer a while longer, Junior. Iffen that smarty-ass Turner or Keller or whatever his name is rides hard, he could be right close to us. If we can git him here or, at the very least, kill his hoss, he'll be six hours walkin' back to the wagon train fer a replacement hoss and that many more comin' back. We'll put a lot of miles between us by then."

"Hold on. I think I see some dust," Junior announced. "Maybe you was right—someone is after us."

The two desperados watched as the dust cloud morphed into two men followed by two horses each.

"See, what'd I tell ya?" Black Jack jacked a round into his Henry rifle. "It's Keller. I know that big gray he rides. Who's the other?"

Junior shaded his eyes. "I think it's Dan Laderman. I'm pretty sure the fella only has one arm."

Reed snorted. "Keller thinks he can take us with just a one-armed cripple along to help? Wait till I give ya the word, Junior. Take yur first shot at Laderman and then aim fer his hoss. We want 'em either dead or afoot. Got it?"

"I got it, Black Jack. What iffen we don't git 'em both?"

"What d'ya think? Keep shootin' until all the horses is down. Then we light out over the hill and ride hard all night." Black Jack peered around the rock he used as cover. "They're gittin' close. Wait fer my signal and then cut loose with everything ya got."

Junior got to one knee and lay his Spencer rifle on the top of the rock he was behind. He sighted down through the *V* sight, laying the front post smack in the middle of Dan Laderman's chest.

Dan shifted his gaze back toward the rocks, just as Marty had instructed. He caught the movement of Junior's change in position and saw the reflection of sunlight off the barrel of Junior's rifle.

"Marty," he shouted, "someone's in the rocks!"

Faster than seemed possible, Marty yanked Pacer's bridle

and gigged him hard in the flanks with his spurs. The big horse was already galloping into the gully as the first shot echoed across the dry plains, the bullet zipping past Marty's head like an angry hornet. Marty jerked the line to his re-mounts and they followed, all under cover before Black Jack could lever a second shot into the chamber of his Henry rifle. Marty grabbed his big Sharps and pulled himself up to where he could peer over the edge. Dan was lying under his horse while his two remounts were thundering back the way they had just come, probably not to stop until they reached the familiar confines of the wagon train.

The one-armed veteran was trying to pull his leg out from under his horse, which appeared dead. "Dan," Marty shouted as another bullet zinged over his head, "stay down and lay quiet; you're protected by your horse. You all right?"

Dan pushed with his free leg until he was able to slip his pinned one out from under the body of his horse. He scooted around until he was safely hidden behind the carcass. "Sorry, Marty. I was just turnin' ole Sam to follow you when he caught one in the head. He's deader 'n a doornail, poor fella. He was a good hoss." Dan peeked over his saddle and got a shot in the dust near him for his effort. "Them bastards'll pay fer killin' Sam."

Marty ducked back into the ravine at the flurry of shots and got his Winchester rifle out of his saddle scabbard. He moved a little way down the gully and eased the barrel of the rifle over the edge. "Dan, I'm gonna open up on those jay-birds. When I do, you scurry into the gully. Understand?"

"Gotcha, Marty. Let her rip."

Marty banged out ten shots in half as many seconds while Dan scooted to the edge of the ravine and dropped in. Marty did not expect to hit anyone above him, but he sent dust and chips in all directions. The two ambushers had to keep their heads down and were unable to get a single shot at Dan while he was exposed.

Dan hurried over to Marty, wiping the dust from his face with his sleeve. "Thanks, Marty. What do you want me to do?"

"You have your rifle?" Marty asked without taking his eyes off the rocks where Black Jack and Junior were hiding.

"Nope, sorry. It's under Sam. I got my pistol, but it ain't worth much at this distance."

"You ever shoot a Winchester?"

"Nope. I got a Burnside single-shot carbine. Used one all during the war and got pretty good with it."

Marty took a fistful of fresh cartridges and reloaded the rifle. "This here is how you reload it. I want you to take a couple of shots and then move to another spot and take a couple more. I want those jaspers trying to spot you. Meanwhile, I'm going to move down there." He pointed. "I will either fire at them from there or I'll move on until I get a good spot. When I give you the signal, I want you to pour it on 'em. I'll try to maneuver around them and get behind them. Understand?"

"I gotcha, Marty."

"You'll have to keep their heads down until I reach the top of the rise. That's at least thirty seconds from here, so if you run out of bullets for the rifle, open up with your pistol."

"Don't worry. I'll keep 'em busy for you."

Marty handed Dan a handful of extra cartridges and then slipped away, crouching low to avoid being spotted by the shooters firing from the rocks above. He moved down the gully about one hundred yards and then edged up the sheer wall until he could peek over the top.

Dan was firing a couple of shots and then moving right or left a few yards and repeating the diversion. Marty strained to see anything of his quarry, but he could not, even when they fired at Dan. Suddenly, he saw the round outline of a man's hat slowly edging up over the top of a large rock. Quickly setting his vernier sight for three hundred yards, he aimed at the boundary between the rock and the crown of the hat. Ever so gently, Marty squeezed the double triggers of his mighty rifle.

The loud *boom!* of the mighty buffalo gun shattered the quiet interlude between shots from Dan and the ambushers. Marty jerked his head to the side, squinting to see through the haze of gun smoke. As carefully as Marty had aimed his shot, he had misjudged the drop of the lead bullet. It hit the large sandstone boulder an inch below his aim. Gouging a large groove in the soft stone, the heavy lead bullet bounced upward and tore through Junior's hat a half inch from the top of his head. The dirty, sweat-stained hat was knocked twenty feet away, but all Junior lost were a few strands of dirty hair instead of the top of his skull.

"Gawd Almighty," Junior screamed. "What was that?"

"What's wrong?"

"Somebody just shot at me with a cannon, from over there, to the left, by that big rock. Damn near took my head clean off."

Black Jack raised his head and looked toward where Marty had fired at Junior. Marty's next shot pinged off the rock next to his head and zinged into the air. Black Jack ducked back down, his face white. "The sumbitch is shootin' at us with a buffalo gun. We gotta git outa here, Junior."

"I'm with ya, Black Jack. Let's git while the gittin's good."

The two outlaws skulked away from the ambush site, crossed over the small rise, and leaped onto their horses. Leading their remounts, they galloped away, to ride for the next twenty hours without stopping.

Marty waved at Dan. As the one-armed veteran fired his covering fuselage, Marty ran hard for the top of the hill. He knew that at the distance he was from the rocks, it was doubtful the thieves could hit him. Once he reached the rise, he would flank them and should have a shot at their exposed backs.

With every step, his apprehension increased. He waited for the shots from Black Jack and Junior to whiz by. When he finally threw himself down at the top of the ridge, his breath was coming in short, jerking gasps. Dropping to the ground, he struggled to regain control of his heaving chest and looked for a target among the rocks. He saw no one. Unsure, he moved farther up the rise toward the rocks.

"Damn, have they skedaddled?" he asked the wind.

Marty stood and waved toward the gully until Dan stood and waved back. "They're gone, Dan. You see anything?"

"Nope," Dan shouted back. "You want me to come up?"

"No, you stay there. Get your saddle on one of my remounts. We gotta get after them right away. I'm coming down."

Marty hurried back to the gully where he had left Dan, growing madder at Black Jack and Junior with every step. They had killed Dan's horse and had obviously aimed to kill Pacer as well. "Mess with my horse, will you," he vowed angrily.

Dan was struggling to get the saddle off his dead animal when Marty arrived. Together, they pulled the saddle from under the carcass and carried it to the gully where Marty's three horses awaited.

"I'm sorry I dropped the leader to my remounts, Marty. I was slow to react, I guess. No wonder you Rebs shot off my arm."

"That's all right, Dan. If you hadn't shouted, I would be lying there next to poor Sam. Let's get you mounted on one of my horses and get after those two."

"The buckskin has a bullet in her left flank. She'll bleed to death if we ride her now."

"Damn those skunks. Well, we'll leave her tied up close to the trail. If she's still alive when your pa comes up, maybe they can save her. Now, let's get after those two. I'm gonna enjoy sending them to hell."

Chapter 17

Bad Men's Tricks

Dan shifted in his saddle and looked over at Marty, who was silently riding beside him. "I've said it before, but it bears repeatin'. These fellas don't seem interested in tryin' to hide their tracks, do they? When we came to where the trail cuts southwest to Santa Fe, they sure didn't try to make us think they went that way. If they'da left us a sign-post, it wouldn't a been more plain that they was headed fer Colorado."

"I've been worrying on that very subject, Dan." Marty scanned the flat, nappy plains. They were somewhere in eastern Colorado, still following a well-defined set of hoof-prints toward a little stagecoach stop called Limon Town. The terrain was high desert, with pungent sage and cactus as its predominate vegetation. Ever since the ambush three days earlier, Marty had been alert to a repeat, but they had seen nothing of their quarry, only the obvious, clear prints of their horses. Not once had the outlaws tried to hide their direction of travel.

"I've got to think these two jaybirds are the dumbest outlaws going, or they've got themselves a plan. I've just about decided that nobody can be this dumb, so they're up to something. I think they're trying to get us set up for a real double-cross."

"What'll we do about it?"

"Nothing we can do but follow along, and see what happens. But I'll bet they lure us into something real obvious, then do just the opposite."

"Looks like that must be the Limon stage stop up ahead there. The road splits there for either Denver or the Colorado Springs goldfields. I wonder what we'll see there?"

The two hunters soon found out the answer to Dan's question in the tiny hamlet of Limon. The first man they talked with, a burly blacksmith named Rogers, remembered Black Jack and Junior.

"Shore do remember them two. They had a string of horses and asked how the trail was to Colorado Springs from here. They asked where they could pick up some supplies. I sent 'em over to Colinson's tradin' post. He carries dry goods and such fer the travelers headed fer the goldfields."

"When were they here?" Marty inquired.

"Two days ago. I reckoned as to how they should wait out the big rain that was a'commin' toward us, but they jus' loaded up and headed out. I'm a'bettin' they got plenty wet afore the morning come."

Marty looked at Dan. "Sounds like we'd best get on after 'em, Dan. Let's see what we can find out at the trading post and get back into the saddle."

The skinny, balding clerk at the trading post certainly remembered Junior. "He bought hisself a new hat. Said his old one blowed off. I wondered why he didn't just ride it down, but I figgered it were none of my business. He was mighty particular about which one he took, too. I think he tried on every one in the store afore he made his choice. It were the finest I had in stock."

They had ridden only a few miles from Limon on the cut-off to Colorado Springs when the tracks disappeared. Dan rode up and down the trail a ways, then shrugged in defeat. "Here's where they must have been when the rains hit, Marty. I can't find nary a sign of 'em anywhere."

Marty sat on Pacer, gazing toward the west. He scratched at the corner of his mouth, his fingernails rasping across the four-day stubble of beard on his face. He was ready for a hot bath and a shave, that was certain.

"Here's the place, Dan."

"How's that, Marty?"

"Here's where they make their move to slicker us. No crook in his right mind would go to the very place where his victim was also headed. Reed and Junior know your pa is taking the wagon train to Colorado Springs. They'd be crazy to go there. Now, if I had a pocketful of money and wanted to get lost in a crowd, I'd head for Denver. I'll bet you a week's wages that they rode in the rain for a spell and then cut back north and picked up the road to Denver. We can follow a false trail to the south or we can cut north right now, save some time, and take a chance they went to Denver. What do you say?"

"I think I'll go along with whatever you say, Marty. You've been doggin' owlhoots long enough—I reckon you got a feel for how they think. If we miss 'em in Denver, we can always cut back to Colorado Springs. It ain't but a hundred miles or so."

"All right, let's ride on a couple of miles more. If we don't cut any sign that points us firmly toward Colorado Springs, we'll head north. Fair enough?"

"Lead the way, pard. I'm right behind."

They rode into the raw, bustling boomtown of Denver/Auroria three days later. Both were tired and trail dirty. They stopped at the first livery they came upon and stabled their mounts. "Give each a double ration of oats," Marty instructed. "They've earned it."

"Happy to," the crippled stable worker answered. He limped to them and gave each horse an experienced once-over. "You fellas have been riding these hosses hard."

"We've covered better than three hundred miles in seven days," Marty answered. "We're just about as broke down ourselves." He stretched a kink out of his back. "Where can we get a bath and a shave, Mr. . . . ?"

"Silas Kemp, mister. Try the Brown Hotel. Got the best barber in town. And plenty of hot water fer yur bath."

"Sounds like the place for us." Marty paused, then added, "I'm Marty Keller." He quickly flashed his Texas Ranger's badge. The livery worker's eyes widened as he looked at the symbol of the famous lawmen. "We're looking for a pair of backstabbing robbers. They were each leading a string of three extra horses. One of them was a paint with three black feet and one white. You happen to see 'em?"

"Sure did, Ranger Keller. Came in early day before yesterday, late-like." He paused and rubbed his nose with a dirty finger. "They wanted to sell their extra mounts, so I got 'em in touch with Mr. Shriver—he owns this here livery. That was yesterday mornin'."

"This Shriver, did he buy the horses?"

"Yep. Paid the tall, dark-haired gent four hunnerd dollars for six of 'em."

"Including the paint?"

"Yep. They're in the corral in the rear."

"Mind if we take a look at 'em?"

"Not a'tall. Right this way."

As they walked out the back door of the livery barn, Marty spotted his paint straightaway. "Yep, that's my paint. Silas, do you know if Mr. Shriver got a bill of sale for these animals?"

Silas shook his head. "I don't think so, Ranger Keller. I

think he's waitin' fer Mr. Reed to bring one by later. I think that's what was promised."

"Good enough. Silas, I want to get cleaned up and have a bath. If Reed or Junior shows up with a bill of sale or they show up and want their horses, I want you to stall 'em until after supper. I'll have my friend here, Mr. Laderman, check in with you about every hour so you'll know where we are. Pull a shoe off Reed's horse. That should slow him up if he tries to leave. You understand all this?"

"I shore do, Ranger. If he asks, I'll tell him I gotta find the smithy, and that'll give me a chance to come find you."

Marty slapped the man's bony back. "That's thinking, Silas. If Mr. Shriver comes in, tell him I will be talking with him later about those horses he bought without a legitimate bill of sale from the seller. Otherwise, let's surprise him to-morrow."

"I think I kind of like that, Ranger. Shriver is too quick to blame me when things go bad and take credit when they don't. You boys go on and git cleaned up. I'll come runnin' if Reed or his little buddy shows up."

Marty led Dan out of the livery. "I learned a long time ago from a good ranger buddy of mine that if we're gonna have to face up to some owlhoot, we might as well be clean and well fed. Makes facing the unpleasant side of our work a little more tolerable."

"Works for me, Marty. My stomach is rubbin' itself raw on my backbone anyways."

The Brown was brand-new and quite an impressive hotel. Marty and Dan bathed and got shaves. They changed into the clean clothes they had rolled in their bedrolls and made their way to the restaurant to enjoy an excellent meal of steak and fried potatoes. After coffee and peach pie, Marty led the way to the front veranda.

They smoked their after-dinner cigars and relaxed in the coolness of the approaching night. Marty spoke first. "Dan, we better check in with the local law. No need to court trouble with him later if we run into problems with Reed and Junior."

Dan nodded and flicked his smoking cigar butt into the street. "Lead the way."

Marty stopped a passerby and got directions for the town marshal's office. He and Dan casually walked over, scanning the pedestrians for sign of Black Jack or Junior.

The marshal had just walked into his office when Dan and Marty entered. He was taking his gun belt off to hang it on a nail in the wall behind his desk. He placed it in such a way that he could quickly grab it and put it on, then turned and looked intently at his two visitors. "Howdy, gents. What can I do for ya?"

"Hello, marshal. I'm Marty Keller. This is Dan Laderman, from Indiana. We are part of a wagon train led by Dan's pa headed to new land near Colorado Springs. A fella named Black Jack Reed and his buddy, Junior Raye, robbed us of a strongbox, carrying the train's start-up money and six horses. They ran a knife in the back of one of the settlers, who was guarding the strongbox, and lit out for here. We found the horses down at the Shriver livery, so we know they're here in Denver somewhere."

The sheriff was a bit past his prime but still radiated a sense of strength and purpose. As he stood straight, he was nearly six feet tall, with broad shoulders and mighty arms, more indicative of a blacksmith than a lawman. His brown hair was flecked with gray, and his curled mustache was almost completely gray, making him perhaps appear older than his years. His nose was Romanesque and he had a nasty scar that split his right eyebrow.

"You don't say," he rumbled. "Name's Zack Scott. Keller, umm, Keller. How is it that I've heard of you, Keller?"

"I was involved in the fight that wiped out the Carter gang in Bixley, Kansas, a while back. Maybe that's it."

"Sure, Keller. The bounty hunter. You after a bounty here, Keller?"

"No, Marshal Scott. I swear, what I've said is true. Reed and Junior Raye assaulted one of the men in our wagon train and stole money and horses. We trailed them to here and aim to catch them."

"Whatever they did out there is outside my jurisdiction, you know."

"I understand. We plan to find them and then bring 'em in to you. You can handle the legal end of it. If nothing else, you can try them for selling stolen horses."

"Shriver bought horses with no papers?"

"Well, to be honest and in his favor, he thinks Reed is going to bring him the papers in the next day or so."

"Well, if what you've told me is true, I'll be happy to look for these two hombres. One thing, Keller. I don't want you bracin' 'em and killin' 'em in my town. If you want 'em brought to justice in Denver, you'll have to let me handle it my way." Scott smiled faintly at Marty. "Of course, if you happen to catch 'em over in the gambling halls or saloons in Auroria, and something happens there, it's outa my control."

"What about the law over there?"

"They ain't quite so much a stickler as I am about following the letter of the law. If they give you a hard time, I'll step in—I promise. Just know that I won't brook no shoot-outs in Denver, no matter who's the one startin' it. Understand?"

"I do, Marshal. Dan and I will do our looking across Cherry Creek. I promise."

"All right, give me a detailed description of your men and I'll put my deputies to looking in Denver. Me, if my pockets were full of stolen cash, I'd be over at the Palace or the Golden Slipper in Auroria, trying to lose it on cards or loose women."

"Thanks, Marshal. We'll mosey over that way and have a look. I'll keep in touch."

"You do that, bounty hunter."

Marty and Dan followed the wooden sidewalk along Front Street. As soon as they crossed over the bridge into the raw village of Auroria, they found themselves in a world apart from the more refined Denver. The buildings were more crudely constructed, with green wood facades trying to make them seem more imposing than they really were. Saloons lined both sides of the street. Noise emanating from a dozen pianos crashed against their ears. The people who milled along the muddy street were all male, save for a couple of working girls standing in the doorways of their tiny cribs next to a building that housed a saloon and gambling house called the Golden Slipper.

Marty and Dan stepped through the double door at the corner of the building. The inside was dim with cigarette smoke, and it smelled of stale beer, spilled whiskey, and unwashed men.

A consumptive piano player banged away in a far corner and numerous tables were filled with men drinking and carousing with the floozies. One painted lady, sitting on a man's lap right next to Marty, shrieked in drunken exuberance and flounced away from the drinker with whom she had been sharing a bottle.

As she sauntered past Marty and Dan, she appraised them with an experienced eye. She sensed that they were not interested in her company and so continued on to the bar, where she put an arm over the shoulders of a drinker and whispered in his ear. The pudgy bartender quickly put a glass of amber fluid in front of her. Marty's eyes slipped past the little tableau and he blinked in surprise.

"Dan," he whispered. "Look over there, by the stairs.

There's Black Jack Reed, at the table with the five men play-ing cards. That's him, isn't it?"

"Sure is. And there's Junior, standing by the stairs, where he can watch Jack's back. Whata you wanta do now?"

"I say let's go get your money back."

Chapter 18

The Wages of Sin

They slowly, casually made their way toward the rear of the saloon. Marty's eye continually shifted between Black Jack and Junior, but neither man was very vigilant at the moment. Black Jack was deep in a card game and seemed to be winning big. His face was flushed with greed and his eyes never left the pot or the other players. Junior stared at himself in the mirror behind the bar, carefully positioning his new hat on his head from side to side or low in front or pushed back. From the silly grin on his face, it seemed he found himself irresistible.

"Some outlaws," Marty whispered to Dan. "So busy thinkin' on themselves they've forgotten to watch out for trouble." He stopped where he had a good view of both robbers but remained somewhat obscured by the drinkers and the floozies between him and them. "Dan, ease over there behind Junior. You keep your eye on him close. If he makes any sign that he's seen me or is about to raise a ruckus, draw down on him and keep him quiet." Marty eased his pistol up and down in his holster. "I'm going to move in on Black Jack. Once I start the hoedown, you take Junior out of it."

Junior Raye was so taken with his new hat that nothing else intruded upon his thoughts. He had never owned a fifty-dollar hat before. He could not take his eyes off his reflection in the mirror behind the long bar. He smoothed the brim and canted it on his head, tilting it up and down. His pride was so strong he was about to bust. He took no notice of the one-armed man who slid up to the bar just one man to his right and kept his eyes glued to his every move. Junior gave his reflection another big grin and adjusted his hat one more time.

Marty slowly edged through the milling crowd until he stood just behind and to the gun side of Black Jack. The dark-haired thief crowed loudly and pulled in another pot. "Yowee, boys, I'm hot tonight. You fellas may as well head fer the hills—I'm filled up with mama luck. I can't lose."

Another hand was dealt while Marty watched and waited for just the right moment to make his play. Black Jack bluffed the final man out of the pot and raked in another hundred dollars. Too much whiskey slurred Reed's words and clouded his judgment. He was playing recklessly. Marty surmised that the cardsharps at the table were setting the loudmouth crook up for a big fall.

As Black Jack wrapped both hands around the pot and started to drag it toward his pile of coins and greenbacks, Marty pulled his pistol and whispered just loudly enough for Reed to hear him.

"Looks like your luck's about to run out, Reed."

He stepped to where he could pull Reed's pistol from its holster and throw it on the floor. Reed froze in his seat, his eyes wide with surprise, his slack jaw about to hit the table, and his hands still wrapped around the pile of chips.

Junior caught the movement of Marty in the mirror as he pulled Black Jack's gun out and tossed it away. Gulping in shock, he spun around to draw down on Marty's blind side when, without warning, the lights went out.

Dan lay a solid whack across Junior's head with his pistol barrel, putting him down and out cold. He turned to the action at the gaming table.

Marty motioned with his gun and ordered the shocked Black Jack, "Stand up, horse-killer."

Black Jack slowly got out of his chair, raising his hands to shoulder height. "Don't gun me down, Keller. I ain't armed."

"You just stand still. I'd rather see you in the hoosegow, waiting on whatever the law wants to do to you. Anyone as ornery as you are is bound to have papers out on him from somewhere. Dan," Marty called out, "Junior all quiet?"

"He's out like a runned-over polecat."

"Get over here and see if Reed's carrying your pa's money." Marty scooped up the pile of bills stacked in front of Reed's chair.

"See here," one of the other gamblers at the table complained. "That's our money you're grabbin' there."

"It peers to me that you'd already lost it to Reed here, but if you want in this dance, I'll make room for you." The other gamblers shut up and eased their chairs back, putting distance between themselves and the two men.

Dan moved up behind Black Jack and patted him down. He reached under Black Jack's shirt and jerked out a money belt completely filled with cash. "Here it is, Marty."

Involuntarily, Marty's eyes drifted down to the money belt. The desperate outlaw had been waiting for just such an opportunity. He spun and grabbed Dan's shirt, then threw him against Marty. Without pausing, he headed for the front door, knocking startled customers left and right.

Marty regained his balance and fired a shot into the ceiling. Accustomed to ducking at the first indication of a gunfight, men dropped like falling rain. Marty snapped a quick shot at Black Jack, stopping him from moving any farther toward the front door. He would have to walk over men lying on the floor to get there, anyway. Black Jack veered to the bar, leaped over the top, and landed behind its welcome cover. He looked up and down until he saw a sawed-off shotgun stuck in its hiding place next to a pile of washed whiskey glasses. He pulled the deadly shotgun out and checked it to make certain it was loaded. He found two more brass shells sitting beside the gun and put them in his pocket. Reed hastily scooted back toward the rear of the room, hoping to catch Keller watching the front of the bar.

Marty whispered to Dan, "Get up the stairs. See if you can spot him or get a shot at him." Marty rolled an over-turned table in front of him for cover. Men were still scrambling out of the bar, but he had eyes only for Black Jack Reed.

Dan ran up the stairs two at a time. The overhung balcony did not extend to where he could see behind the bar, but he realized that if he moved down just a bit, he could see behind the bar in the long mirror hung on the back wall. He spotted Reed crouched at the rear of the bar, the shotgun in his hands.

He whistled to alert Marty, still poised to take on Reed coming out the front end. Marty glanced up at Dan.

"Shotgun," Dan mouthed, holding up two fingers and making the motion of breaking open a shotgun. Marty nodded his understanding. "Down here." Dan pointed at the rear end of the bar. Marty slowly moved in that direction, darting from overturned table to table. He did not want to take on a scattergun without some solid cover between him and Black Jack.

Reed could hear the two men whispering but could not make out exactly what they were saying. He glanced up and saw Dan's reflection in the mirror. He quickly rose and aimed the scattergun. Fortunately for Dan, Reed had misjudged where Dan was crouching, because of the reversal effect of the mirror. He swung his gun back toward Dan, who flung himself flat on the floor. The pellets from the shotgun whizzed over him and tore huge chunks out of the plaster on the wall. Reed quickly dropped the barrels toward Marty, who was firing and ducking behind a table at the same time. His shot missed Black Jack and smashed into a filled bottle of rotgut sitting on a shelf under the long mirror. Reed's shot slammed into the hardwood that was the top of the table Marty had ducked behind. The heavy lead pellets chewed out chunks of wood, but none passed completely through the table to hit Marty. Black Jack dropped back behind the bar, flipped the shotgun open, and replaced the two empties with fresh cartridges. He scooted on down behind the cover of the bar until he was too far under the balcony for Dan to see him or get a shot at him.

Marty shouted, "Reed, give it up. We've got you cut off from the door, and the law is undoubtedly headed this way. I don't want to kill you, Reed. Throw out the shotgun and show me empty hands."

"Here's empty hands, you son of a bitch." Black Jack stood and fired at the center of the table as he spoke, busting the fractured wood to splinters.

Marty saw him coming and knew he could not depend on the tabletop to withstand another assault from the buckshot. He threw himself to the left, firing his pistol as he rolled away from the ugly menace of the shotgun.

Marty's aim was deadly accurate. His first bullet hit Reed in the throat, and the second went into his open mouth, cutting off the scream of agony Black Jack was about to utter. The few brains Black Jack possessed went out the back of his torn-open skull and splattered on the mirror, then slid down the stained glass like foam down a beer mug.

Marty scrambled to his feet, hurried to the bar, and leaned over the top. Reed was crumpled in a clutter where he had fallen, the smoking shotgun lying beside him. Marty scanned the room. It was completely empty except for the four combatants. Dan scrambled down the stairs.

"You okay, Marty?"

"Yeah, I'm fine. Reed's done for. You know his and Junior's horses?"

"I think so, why?"

"I think we oughta get over to Denver before any law shows up."

Dan grabbed the still form of Junior by the shirt collar. He looked at Reed's lifeless body. "You need any help with him?"

"No, I can handle him." Marty grabbed Black Jack's coat and dragged his body toward the open door of the saloon. People were just beginning to stream back into the place, eager to see what was going on.

Dan pointed out Black Jack's horse and threw Junior over the saddle of the horse standing next to it. Marty and Dan led the horses carrying their grisly cargo back over the bridge across Cherry Creek and to the marshal's office in Denver.

They had scarcely recounted their story to the tall lawman when a beefy man wearing a sheriff's badge stomped into the office. "Hello there, Bill. You lookin' fer these fellows?"

"Damn right, Zack, if they the ones what shot that jasper outside on the hoss."

"Have a seat, Bill. Let me tell you what I know and then they can fill in the blanks. These two fellas are from a wagon train on its way to Denver."

By the time Marshal Scott, Marty, and Dan finished their stories, the Auroria lawman had settled down a good deal. "Sounds like the two had it coming, all right. Everyone I spoke to at the Golden Slipper said Keller here tried to get the deceased to surrender, but he pushed the fight." The sheriff looked at Marty and Dan. "You two has got to stay around until we have an inquest, but I reckon I can put it to-gether by tomorrow afternoon." He put on his sweat-stained hat. "They want your hospitality so much, Zack, you can put 'em up fer the night. Save Auroria a few dollars. I want them at my office tomorrow at two o'clock, sharp. Unnerstand?"

"They'll be there, Bill. Else I'll run them down myself." He gave a stern look to Marty and Dan.

"You can depend on it, Sheriff. We just want to set the record straight and get back to our wagon train." Dan held out his hand to the sheriff, who reluctantly shook it, then stomped off, back to his town across the river.

Marty grinned at Marshal Scott. "I wanted to have you hold Junior for me, Marshal. He's guilty of selling stolen horses in Denver, so you have cause."

"I'll put him up before the grand jury as soon as it con-venes."

"I wouldn't be surprised if those boys don't have a poster out on 'em. They're too crooked not to. If you put the heat on Junior, he'll probably crack and fess up for you."

"We'll see. In the meantime, can I count on you two showin' up tomorrow for the inquest over in Auroria?"

"Do we need to be worried about it, Marshal?"

"I don't think so, Marty. Bill's 'bout half the lawman he once was, but these jaspers hadn't been in town long enough to make many friends. I reckon it'll go pretty smooth."

"Sheriff, we need to get those horses back from Shriver. Does Junior have any of the stolen money on him?"

Scott went into the cell where Junior was still uncon-scious. He rummaged through the sleeping man's pockets and came up with a roll of bills. "Peers to have, umm, three fifty, four hundred, four hundred eighty-five dollars."

"We need four hundred to give back to Shriver."

Scott counted off the money and passed it over to Marty. "I'll keep the rest. It'll help the city pay fer his keep until he's tried or shipped off on an outstanding warrant."

Scott gave Dan a quick look. "You get your pa's money from the recently departed?"

"Yep," Dan answered. "Reed had fifty-eight hundred on him, more than enough to cover what he stole."

"Well, you'll owe the city twenty dollars to plant him."

Dan passed over the money, then replaced the money belt under his shirt. "Marty, I guess we'd better get down to the stable and buy back our horses."

Marshal Scott held up his hand. "Tell you what. I'll drop by Shriver's place right now and warn him not to sell those horses until he gets papers on them. You two pick them up the day you leave here. We'll let Shriver pay fer their keep outa his pocket. That'll teach him for taking horses without papers. As tight as he is, it'll hurt him like the blazes to have to put those animals up on his nickel." Scott chuckled at the thought.

Marty shook the marshal's hand as he prepared to leave. "You've been right square with me, Marshal Scott. I have to admit, I don't usually get treated as well from most local lawmen when I come around."

"I admire what you did over in Bixley. Wiping out a bunch of cutthroats like Long Tom Carter and his gang was a good thing, in my book."

"I had some good men helping, believe me."

"I'm sure you did. Still, it speaks well fer you in my book, so I'm gonna give you the benefit of the doubt. You boys stay close to the Brown Hotel tonight. I'll be in touch if anything comes up."

"Come on, Dan. Let's get some shut-eye."

Dan followed Marty out of the office and down the street toward the hotel. "Before I can get some sleep, I'm gonna need a drink, Marty. Buy you one?"

"A beer is all, Dan. Anything stronger and I might get reckless and I don't want that. You put that money belt under your pillow tonight, and sleep with your six-gun right beside your bed. Understand?"

"You bet I will."

The next day, after a leisurely lunch of ham and beans with cornbread, they walked back to Marshal Scott's office. The big lawman greeted them and gave them the news. "Junior spilled the goods. Reed has a warrant out for him in Sacramento, California—a big one. Junior thinks it's a thousand dollars. Junior is wanted in Sedalia, Missouri. Says he's got three hundred on him."

"That'll be yours, Dan. You got Junior. As for mine, if it comes here, Marshal, send my part to the Stockman's Bank in Dallas. I reckon you oughta keep two hundred to cover the expense of collecting for me." Marty smiled at Dan. "Where do you want your money, Dan?"

"I reckon you could send it to the postmaster in Colorado Springs. I don't really know where I'll be for certain."

"That's it, then. I'll git 'em out to you two as soon as the checks arrive. Now, mosey on over to Sheriff Dotson's and git the inquest over with. I had a talk with him earlier today and he assured me it was just a formality. Said he had several witnesses who verified that you tried to bring Reed in without gunplay. I also saw Shriver and made it clear he's not to sell them horses until I say so. When you're ready to leave, let me know and I'll accompany ya over to his place to git 'em."

Marshal Scott was right. In an hour, Marty and Dan had been completely absolved of any wrongdoing by the inquest jury. They walked back to the Denver side of Cherry Creek, bought some supplies, and picked up the Marshal before heading for the livery.

Shriver was a whip of a man, dour faced and mean of spirit. His jaw dropped when Marshal Scott ordered him to release the six horses to Marty. "Danggummit, Marshal. I bought them horses fair and square. What about the eight hundred I offered for them?"

"You paid half down, according to Junior Raye, and I have the money right here. Please have your man rope 'em up so we can get going immediately." Marty passed the roll of greenbacks to the grumpy livery owner, who immediately and carefully counted every bill.

"There's only four hundred here. I put these nags up for six nights. That's eighteen dollars more. Who's gonna pay that?"

Marshal Scott broke in. "I reckon you'll just have to write that up to the cost of doing business with crooks, Shriver. Might help you to remember to check papers afore you buy horses from strangers in the future."

Marty and Dan bid their farewells to the marshal and headed down the road toward the Limon stagecoach station. "Where do you reckon the train is by now, Marty?" Dan questioned.

"I'd figger it's coming up on the Limon cutoff in a day or two. We'll probably meet up with them there."

"I'm lookin' forward to seein' Pa's face when we give him back the money. He'll be mighty pleased and grateful. You'll be able to name your reward from him."

"I don't want anything except to get my wagons to Wyoming Territory and shed myself of Julia and her boy. I've got men I have to find."

"You mean the ones who killed your wife and son."

Marty's face was grim. "The very ones. They've got some dying to do."

Chapter 19

Wyoming-Bound

"There they are," Dan announced.

From where he had been dozing in the shade of a lone cedar tree growing next to the stage stop, Marty squinted through the heat waves. The wagon train had just crested a low rise to the east, about a mile away from where the two tired men were waiting. They had arrived only three hours earlier, dog-tired after their ride from Denver. A stagecoach driver they passed about a mile out of Limon had told them that he had seen the wagon train and that it would arrive at Limon within a few hours. Dan and Marty decided to wait at the small outpost of civilization rather than ride out and meet the train on the trail.

It was here that Marty and his party would swing to the north, leaving the company of the Laderman wagon train, which would cut southwest to Colorado Springs and their new lands.

The train moved slowly toward them in the *V* formation that the wagons had adopted to avoid eating dust kicked up by those in front. Marty was pleased to see Julia's wagon next to Gabe's, just as he had promised and just as Marty had expected.

Before the train grew close enough to overwhelm them with eager immigrants, Dan turned to Marty. "I jus' want to thank you again for lettin' me come on this little adventure, Marty. And thanks for Reed's horse. It's a fine replacement for ole Sam."

"You deserved it, Dan. After all, they killed your animal. And you sure as heck held up your end of the deal, so I oughta thank you."

As the train grew closer, the members recognized Dan and Marty, so by the time Gabe's wagon rolled to a stop, numerous people had gathered to hear the news of the chase after the robbers.

Marty and Dan waited until the listeners surrounded them, and then presented Gabe with the money belt and returned the horses to their rightful owners. "And if that ain't all"—Dan continued his story, one that left Marty feeling a little uncomfortable as his actions were described and amplified by Dan—"we also got back forty more dollars than was stole from us. How 'bout that?"

The crowd cheered mightily and Gabe pumped Marty's hand again and again. "Glad I could help, Gabe," was Marty's humble response to the adulation. "How'd my people get along while I was gone?"

"They're fine, just fine. We had no trouble a'tall since you've been gone. Everyone watched over 'em real good."

"Thanks. By the way, Dan was a big help to me. Couldn't have done it without him."

"Proud to hear that, Marty. The boy's been at sort of loose ends since he came back from the war, losing his arm and all."

"He's a whole lot of man in my book."

"Thanks, Marty. I'll tell him that."

"How's Mr. Driggs getting along?"

"He'll live, thank the good Lord. With rest and tendin', he'll be up and about in a week or so."

"That's certainly good news."

"He'll be mighty relieved to hear that you got our money back. He was feelin' real guilty that he allowed Junior to sneak up on him the way he did."

Gabe decreed the next day to be one of rest and celebration in thanksgiving for the return of the wagon train's money. Marty and his party stayed as well, although he knew that Julia was anxious to be on her way.

"We'll push hard up to Denver and on to Cheyenne. One day here won't hurt."

"Very well," she sniffed in derision, then abruptly turned away from Marty and engaged Mrs. Driggs in conversation. The next morning, Gabe slaughtered a cow that had injured a leg and was having trouble staying up with the herd. They spent the day feasting, relaxing, cleaning, and repairing clothes and tack. That evening, after the sun went down, they got out their musical instruments and had a real hoedown, dancing until nearly midnight under the stars.

A stage full of passengers bound for Denver even stayed over a couple of hours just to enjoy the celebration. Marty watched as Dan whirled Julia around during a lively Virginia reel, remembering with nostalgia the dances he and Meg had attended while living together on their ranch in Texas.

Dan brought Julia back to where Marty was sitting on the tongue of the big Studebaker wagon.

"Thank you kindly, Mrs. Bennett. I certainly enjoyed the dance. It's the first I've had since I went off to the war."

"Please, Dan, call me Julia. I enjoyed it as well." Julia sat down on a blanket next to the campfire, across from Marty.

Marty glanced at Julia, a bit taken aback by her willingness in allowing Dan to call her by her first name, and even more surprised that she had called Dan by his. She continued to address Marty only by his last name, Mr. Keller, when she had to talk to him, and preferred not to talk to him at all if she could avoid it.

Trying to start a friendly conversation, Marty remarked, "You and Dan cut a fine swath around the dance ring, Julia. Dan really seemed to be enjoying himself."

"And why not? Even though he's minus an arm, he's still a fine figure of a man. Any woman would be proud to be seen with him."

She wiped the perspiration from her face with a lacy hankie pulled from a hidden crevice somewhere in her dress. "We'll depart for Denver tomorrow, right?"

"Yes, that's my plan."

"And I can assume that you'll not be running off seeking someone to kill until we reach my land in Wyoming?"

"Damn, woman, it wasn't like that. Gabe asked me to go. He'd been good to us. I felt like I owed him."

"What you owe, Mr. Keller, is to get me and my son to our place in Wyoming and help us get our new life started."

"I thought all you wanted from me was to get you to Wyoming."

"No, Mr. Keller. You'll not get off that easy. I expect you to see that Johnny and I are well started in our new place. Then you can ride off and find more unfortunates to gun down."

"Dammit, Julia Bennett. You rile me more than a pesky horsefly, I swear."

"Just remember your promise, Mr. Keller."

Marty stomped away, knowing that if he sat there any longer, he would jump up and cuss her out so loudly the entire camp would hear him. Grumbling like a wounded bear, he headed for the main campfire and a cup of coffee from the big coffeepot hung next to it.

Dan Laderman came up as Marty carefully sipped the hot brew. "Marty, I've a favor to ask of you."

"Anything, Dan. You've earned it."

"I'd like to accompany you and Mrs. Bennett on to Wyoming."

Marty raised his brows. "Why, Dan, I don't see any reason why you shouldn't. But won't your pa need you when you get to the new land at Colorado Springs?"

"No, not really. My two brothers and their wives came out here last year. They're the ones that got the land and set up the purchases. Pa is sort of keepin' me around because he's afraid I won't be able to make it on my own, with just one arm and all. I think I'd like to try somethin' else for a while. I can always go home if it don't work out. I talked about it with Pa and he's fine with the idea."

"Dan, I'd be proud to have you. I think I oughta run it by Mrs. Bennett to get her okay first."

"I asked her while we was dancing. She's already said yes. I just thought I oughta get your okay as well."

"Thanks for the consideration, Dan. I told you why Julia Bennett is so down on me, so maybe you oughta stay a little distance from me, else she's liable to get her back up about you, too."

"Don't you worry none, Marty. I told her how much I think of you already. She just sort of sniffed and made a sour face." Dan grinned at Marty. "I happen to think she's all wrong, but I got to understand her reluctance to meet you halfway, considering what happened."

"I tell you, pard. She's got me by the short hairs and won't let go. I'll be the happiest man around the day she says my obligation to her is done and I can go about my business again."

"Well, for what it's worth, I'll do my best to make that happen as soon as possible. You planning to leave the wagon train tomorrow mornin'?"

"Just as soon as we can get put together and saddled up."

"I'll be ready. See you then. I'm going over and tell Julia that you're okay with me comin' along."

"It peers she doesn't give a houn dawg's scratch about what I think."

Dan smiled. "Aw, don't be too hard on her. She's got a lot of worries of her own, too."

"Not if she can put them on my back. Well, I'm headed for the sack. I want to get away early tomorrow. Night, Dan."

"Good night, Marty. See you in the mornin'."

Marty and the others took their leave of Gabe Laderman's wagon train and its band of Indiana travelers early the next morning. The old farmer shook Marty's hand. "You're always welcome at my place, Marty Keller. You come on by, you ever in the neighborhood."

"Good-bye, Mr. Laderman. Thanks for letting us travel with you. Dan, take your time saying good-bye to your folks. You can catch up with us."

"I'll be right with you, Marty. Well, Pa. Be seeing you. Say hello to Luke and John and their families. I'll write you once I get settled."

"Don't be a stranger, Son. Take care of yourself." The two men gave each other a warm hug, then stepped back in the awkward way men do when they become emotional with another man. Dan kissed his mother, then climbed onto his horse and cantered away from the camp beside Marty, followed by the two wagons and the three horses and one bull.

As they crested the rise on the far side of Limon Station and looked back, Gabe Laderman stood where they had left him, staring at them until they rode out of his sight.

"I think your pa is gonna miss you, Dan," Marty observed.

Dan patted the neck of the black gelding he had "inherited" from the late and unlamented Black Jack Reed. "Yeah,

'a has worried about me plenty since I got home from the
war without my arm. At first I sort of figgered my life wasn't
worth livin', but now I know I can go on from here and
make somethin' outa myself."

"I'm in your corner, Dan. All the way."

Their first night away from the company of the wagon
train was a lonely camp. It was a somber group that gathered
around the campfire.

"I reckon we best go back to standing guard duty," Marty
said, breaking the silence. "We'll be crossing Indian lands
from now on until we reach our final destination." He
looked over at Julia, who was mending one of Johnny's
shirts. "Julia, do you want to pull a guard watch with the rest
of us?"

She looked over at Dan, who was helping Tom repair one
of the trace lines from the four-up tack. "I think I shall, Mr.
Keller. I would be happy to always take the first watch, since
I simply cannot go to sleep before the middle of the night."

"Good enough. Dan, you're up to pulling a guard watch,
I suppose?"

"Certainly, Marty."

"Fair enough. Julia, you take the first, Dan the second.
Tom, you take the midnight to two. Walt, the two to four. I'll
finish up." He patted Johnny's dog, who was currently nuz-
zling his pants leg. "We'll use ole Pawpaw here too. Every
guard will keep him close, so he can alert us to any tres-
passers."

They pushed hard and reached Denver in four days. Dan
escorted Julia and Johnny into the town, where Julia purchased some needed supplies to sustain them on to
Wyoming. Marty and the boys sold their buffalo hides to a
tannery and then purchased warm buffalo-hide coats and
blankets for everyone. He dropped off the two boys at a
somewhat quiet saloon with the admonition "Remember,
fellas, only one beer apiece." Then Marty joined Dan and

Julia at the dry goods store. Dan had purchased a fistful of sugar candy for Johnny, a gift that endeared the likable farmer to the young boy. Marty mentally kicked himself for not thinking of doing exactly the same thing.

Dismissing the lost opportunity to gain favor with the quiet, reserved child, Marty waited until Julia had made her purchases, and helped Dan load them onto the wagon. He stopped off at the saloon where Walt and Tom were drinking beer and collected the two young men. They put four hours between themselves and Denver before the sun set.

The countryside slowly rose up before them as they traveled north toward Cheyenne. Julia and Dan were the first to remark that it was getting harder to get a good breath of air.

"It will get easier. After a week or so, you'll become adjusted to the higher altitude of Wyoming. I suspect the ranch we're headed for is even higher yet."

They were relieved to see the outline of Cheyenne ahead as they crossed the rugged sagebrush-covered terrain. It would mark the last phase of their journey. The town had grown even larger since Marty's last visit. Railroad workers crowded the muddy streets, along with those men and women dedicated to separating them from their money.

Julia and the others went to the dry goods store while Marty headed for the headquarters of the Union Pacific Railroad. He was admitted to the station agent, a Mr. Hartman. "I used to work for the railroad, Mr. Hartman," Marty explained. "One of my close friends was a big Irishman named Mick O'Rourke. Any chance he's still boss of the track layers?"

"Big Mick? Sure is. I reckon he's at end of track, somewhere near the Utah border. Why d'ya ask?"

"Can you get a message to him for me?"

"Sure can."

"Tell him that Marty Keller will be in Laramie in four days and would like to see him if it's at all possible."

"I can do that. Since you once worked fer us, consider it professional courtesy."

"Thanks, Mr. Hartman. I surely appreciate it."

Julia had replaced the items they required to finish their journey by the time Marty rejoined everyone. They headed west the next morning toward Laramie, a new town built as a switching station for the transcontinental railroad.

By following the road that had been built beside the track, they made good time. In four days they were at Laramie, only three days from their new home, forty miles to the south.

"We going on?" Julia inquired.

Marty shook his head. "Not just yet. There's someone I want to see first. Let's make camp there, by the stream. I'll ride on into town and see if I can find him."

Marty stopped at the rowdiest bar, judging by the loud music and louder voices inside. He swung down from Pacer, climbed the two wooden steps up from the street, and pushed his way past the twin glass doors into the smoke-filled interior. A lusty crowd of men cheered their throats out as two men strained at a game of arm wrestling. With a grunt, the larger of the two men finally slammed the arm of his opponent against the table. Grabbing a mug of beer, he took a mighty swallow and shouted loudly, "Who's next? Who wants their arm broke by Big Mick O'Rourke?"

Marty smiled. "Anybody got a sledge? That's the only way to beat this hardheaded Irishman. I'd be happy to pound a few knots on his thick skull. Who's got a spike hammer?"

The big Irishman laughed and pushed away from the table. "Only one man dumb enough to talk that way about me to my face. Marty Keller, you ole buffalo-shooter. How the hell are ye?"

Chapter 20

A Short Cattle Drive

"Hello, Mick, you big galoot. Good to see you again."

"Marty, me lad. You've been busy since I saw ye last. I read in the papers about your shoot-out with the outlaw gang in Kansas. Why didn't ye call fer me?"

"I should have, Mick. It all happened so fast, I just got overwhelmed and didn't have time to think about it."

"Well, just remember fer the next one. Otherwise I'll think ye don't like me no more." The large but amiable Irish track boss slapped Marty on the arm with a blow that would have knocked Marty off his feet had he not braced himself.

"Let me make it up to you, at least a little bit, by buying you a drink."

"Now yur talkin', me bucko. Bartender, whiskey. And leave the bottle. Me pal Marty Keller is buyin', and may the saints preserve him for his generosity."

Once Mick had slammed down a couple of stiff drinks, he began to quiz Marty on all that had transpired in the months since they had last seen each other. Mick listened intently, then asked the obvious. "Why are you back here, and what do you want from me, laddie?"

Marty laughed. "Am I that transparent?"

"Depends on what that word means."

"It means you saw right through me like a pane of window glass. But you're right, Mick. I do need help." Quickly, Marty explained why he was escorting Julia to her new place in Warm Springs.

Mick nodded his leonine head. "I know the place well. We've got a big operation cutting cross ties down there. I've even been there. They have a place where the water comes outa the ground as hot as steaming coffee brewing over the campfire. The Injuns used to come there and soak, but a few years ago they all quit, so only the white man uses it now."

"Why is that?"

"They had a bad pox epidemic a few years ago. The Injuns sent all their sick over to the hot springs to soak, but they died anyhow. Now the Injuns think the place is bad medicine. They're happy to let us whites have all the bad luck." Mick drained his whiskey and motioned for the bartender to pour another. "Now, about this here widder gal, Bennett. You want me to cover fer ya while you make tracks fer Texas?"

"No, I'm willing to finish what I started. I want her settled and secure, then I'll put a lot of dust between us in a hurry."

"Whatever ya say, bucko. Now, tell yur ole pal Mick what he can do fer ya."

"Mick, I need you to find me a couple of men who are cowboys. Then, I need to get some cattle. Julia Bennett has to get a herd on her land if she is going to make a success of her ranch. I thought among all those men you have laying track, a few should have worked as cowboys before."

"By the eyes of Saint Margaret, is that all you want?" Mick turned toward the bar and shouted over the din in the crowded saloon. "Paco, Paco. Come over here."

A young man turned and headed toward the table. He grinned shyly at Mick. "You wanted me, Senor Mick?"

"Paco, this is Marty Keller. He needs some good men to work on his ranch near Warm Springs. Didn't you say you worked for an Englishman there?"

"Sí, I worked for Senor Stonecipher for two years. I like him very much. I am very good sheepherder."

"Sheepherder! I need cowboys. I don't know anything about raising sheep," said Marty.

"Senor Stonecipher raise sheep. His land no good for cattle. Only sheep can do good on his land. I am Basque. We are the world's best sheep men."

"What happened to Stonecipher?"

Paco sighed and quickly made a sign of the cross. "He kill himself two years ago. Senor Wolf come to the ranch and say Senor Stonecipher dead and we must go. Then, I hear him tell his men to kill and run off all the sheep they could find."

"Who is this Wolf?"

"Senor Wolf owns most of the land around Warm Springs. He is not very nice, I think. He wanted Senor Stonecipher to sell ranch, but my patron say no. He want to raise sheep to sell to the railroad, which was being built soon, Senor Stonecipher say."

Paco sighed again. "Then Senor Stonecipher die and Senor Wolf run me off. After that I am hungry most of time, until Senor Mick hire me to build track for railroad."

Mick turned to Marty. "This here lad's a good fella. He's familiar with the area where you're goin' and says there's a lot of sheep still running around the hills that he can gather up and bring to you. I suggest you take him." Mick turned to Paco. "You worthless spike driver, you, do you know any cowboys that come from around there?"

"Oh, sí. Little Roberto Short used to work for Senor Wolf. He not like the senor and quit to lay track with Paco.

He's very good cowboy, I think, but he do not like laying track."

"Where is this cowboy?" Marty inquired.

"He's at end of track, I think," Paco answered.

"Don't worry, Marty, me son. I'll send fer him immediately. He'll be here tomorrow." Mick turned to Paco. "As fer you, Paco, from this moment on, you're a sheepherder agin, workin' for Marty Keller. Unnerstand?"

"*Sí,* Senor Mick. I understand."

Marty measured the round face of Paco. There was not a trace of guile or deceit in the man. Marty nodded. "It's a deal. Get me Little Bob and I'll be fit to go, I reckon."

Mick swallowed another shot of rotgut whiskey. "Consider it done."

"Mick, what ever happened to Bill Cody?"

"He quit the railroad not long after you did and joined the army. I heered that he's a scout fer the Fifth Cavalry now, out of Fort Leavenworth, in Kansas."

"Do tell. I never would have thought Bill would try that." Marty smiled. "Whatever Bill Cody is doing, you know he'll turn it into something bigger than life."

Marty was more than satisfied when he met Little Bob the next day. The forty-plus cowboy was not much more than five feet tall and a hundred twenty pounds soaking wet, but he had the look of a steady man who had faced his life head-on and never shirked the task at hand.

"What do you want me to do first, Boss?" Little Bob asked once he agreed to take up again the cowboy way of life.

"We need to find some cattle. You have any suggestions?"

Bob nodded emphatically. "Do I? We're in luck. Just last week there was a big train derailment not twenty miles from here. Among the cars derailed and broke open were ten carryin' over three hundred cows. We had just got most of them rounded up when one of the overturned engines exploded and the cattle stampeded all over hell and gone. The railroad washed their hands of the whole lot. They're up in the hills to the south of here. We should be able to gather up fifty to a hundred with no problems."

Marty shook his head, excited and amazed at his good luck. That they could obtain a few cattle without having to buy them on the open market in Cheyenne was very welcome news. He turned to Mick O'Rourke and shook his burly hand. "Thanks, Mick. You've been a lifesaver. I'll be in touch, once I get settled down in Warm Springs. Maybe you can come down and enjoy the hot baths. Soak some of the weariness out of those old bones of yours."

"Maybe so, me bucko. Meanwhile, I've got you fixed up and I'm needed at end of track. Good luck, pard. Holler if you need me."

"I surely will, Mick. Paco, Bob, if you two will follow me, I'll introduce you to the rest of my group of pilgrims."

Julia's tight lips and furrowed brow sent a clear signal: she was smoldering about something again. As the two new hires were putting their gear into the wagon, Marty followed her to where the mules were picketed.

"What is it, Julia?"

"Why do we need to hire more hands right now? We don't even know what we'll find when we reach the ranch."

"According to Paco, we won't find much. These two can herd cattle or sheep, and you're gonna need them. Walt and Tom can't, even if they were going to stay with us, which, the last time I checked, they aren't. As soon as we get a little settled, both will head back to their families in Missouri."

"You're right," she admitted. "I had forgotten they weren't planning to stay on with me."

"Bob thinks he knows where some stray cattle are. We're gonna try to pick some up on our way to the ranch. When we get to where he thinks the cattle are scattered, I'll take everyone but Dan and see if we can round up a few."

"Should Dan and I go on to the ranch?"

"I don't think so, Julia. There've been some strange things happening concerning the ranch, perhaps including murder and suicide. I think we'd better go in as a group. There's safety in numbers. I don't plan on being gone more than a couple of days. We'll find a good place to camp and you can wait for us there."

They made camp that night near a mountain stream of clear, cold water. It was a convenient spot to wait for Marty's return. He and the men built a small rope corral for the mules and prepared to spend the next couple of days chasing stray cattle among the many small valleys and glades of the low mountains.

Bob pointed out the obvious. "The cattle won't go too far into the high country—there's too much grass down low. We oughta be able to find some of 'em purty easy-like."

Marty and Bob smiled at the buoyant spirits of Walt and Tom as they departed the campsite. Both of the seasoned cowboys knew just how much work finding and gathering the cattle could be. The five men rode into the foothills and fanned out, looking for any sign of cattle. Marty had gotten Johnny's permission to use Pawpaw during their search. The faithful dog had the makings of a real herd dog, according to Paco. Marty put Tom next to him and Walt next to Bob, with Paco in the middle. They rode deeper into the foothills, vainly looking for their first cow. Pawpaw picked up several scent signs, but they were disappointed when they trailed the dog higher into the mountains to no avail.

Around ten in the morning the next day, they saw their first solid indication of cattle and about an hour later hit pay dirt. Walt and Bob stumbled onto twenty-three head calmly grazing in a small pasture surrounded by high pine trees. They left them there with Paco watching the cattle and pushed on. By dusk, after some hard riding, including Walt's being swept off his horse as it ran under a tree branch while chasing a runaway cow—they had twenty-four cows and thirty steers rounded up and shoved together in the small holding area.

Marty wiped the sweat from his hat brim. "I reckon we've got enough to get started with. Let's have some supper and bed down. We'll start them down the mountain toward our camp tomorrow morning."

They had the cattle on the move early, expecting some resistance from the animals, but the cows had recently trailed all the way from Texas to Wyoming and still had the herd mentality. It was relatively easy to move them on down the mountain, and in the process they were lucky to find six more females and a yearling bull, which they added to their herd.

Their arrival at the campsite caused quite a stir. Pawpaw was running around, barking furiously at the cattle, which ambled along as if being herded were the most natural thing in the world. Tom and Walt were in the drag, darting back and forth, keeping the stragglers closed up. Dan and Julia, looking pleased at the number of cattle delivered, walked over to where Marty stopped the herd.

Julia shaded her eyes and counted the cattle. "Looks like you did real good, Marty. I never thought you'd find so many."

"Sure did. Got thirty steers and thirty cows, plus a yearling bull. It'll make a nice start for the herd. If we need any more, we can buy some from local ranchers."

Julia broadly smiled at Marty for the first time. "And you say Paco might be able to find some sheep for the ranch as well?"

"That's what he says. If he does, you'll be able to utilize your land to the maximum. The sheep can graze the higher elevations, and the cattle the low land."

Julia's expressive face was serene and peaceful. Her normally pursed lips spread into a gentle smile. Marty basked in the satisfaction of a job well done. After a minute, he mentally shook himself and ordered the camp struck. "We need to get on down to the ranch. Bob, you and Paco will have to herd the animals. Tom and Walt, get the wagons hitched up. Let's get going."

It was early afternoon when Marty heard Bob whistle at him from his place with the ambling cattle herd. The wagons had just crested a small rise offering a great view of the vista below. Marty held up his hand as he saw Bob trotting his pony toward him. Tom and Walt halted their wagons and waited.

"Mrs. Bennett." Bob pointed toward the east. "There she is, Mrs. Bennett. That land to the east yonder, it's all yours."

The surrounding land was typical high desert. Baked, dusty soil, clumps of bunchgrass, and sagebrush covered the terrain. The minty smell of sage filled the air whenever they stopped. The land to the east dropped slightly into a shallow valley, with high ground on three sides. The first layer of moderate hills that formed the valley was covered in brown grass and low shrubs. Taller mountains loomed up farther to the east and north, their blue-green appearance indicative of thick forest. Only to the southwest was there any opening in the circle of mountains. At the northeast end of the valley was a bright cluster of green trees, stark against the monotonous brown. Spreading outward from the trees was a circle of green grass.

Marty pointed toward the trees. "There water there?"

Paco answered, "Only in the spring. There must be some just under the surface, but the creek runs dry about the first of August and stays that way until the snowmelt."

Marty estimated. "There must be two hundred acres showing green around those trees."

Bob nodded. "A good place for the horses year-round,

and some left over for winter graze for the cattle. The rest of the property is bone-dry year-round. The land hereabouts takes ten acres to support one cow."

"Looks like a road over there."

"That's the logging road. The railroad has a crew cutting timber back in the hills to the east, beyond that first low range. The hills are much higher and covered in pine forest. The road is the southern boundary of the ranch. The road we're on is the main road to Walcott, where the railroad is putting in a central maintenance facility. It's the western boundary of the ranch. There's a stagecoach line runnin' twixt Grand Encampment and Walcott, which stops over in Warm Springs fer the night. Wolf has a real nice hotel in town fer the stage passengers to stay in. He owns most of everything hereabouts."

Bob shaded his eyes as he looked to the west. "Wolf Larkin's land starts here and runs for ten miles or more west, to the North Platt River." Bob pointed toward the southwest. Marty could just make out the faint outline of buildings in the thin but clear air. "That's Warm Springs, 'bout seven more miles down this road."

"Where's my ranch house?" Julia interrupted the two men.

"It's over in those trees, ma'am. It was a right nice little place when Mr. Stonecipher had it. I don't know now."

"What do you say we go find out?" Marty gigged his horse. "Come on, folks. We're almost home."

Chapter 21

A First Step

Two hours of continuous riding brought them to the grove of trees that marked the center of Julia Bennett's new ranch. Stonecipher's original cabin was still there, sheltered by the grove of mighty cottonwood trees. It was a solid two-room structure of stout timber logs chinked with dried mud to keep out the weather. A heavy front door and two windows covered with glass faced the open vista of the valley to the southwest. Cedar shingles covered the roof, and the over-hung front porch gave the inhabitants a place to relax at the end of the day.

Inside, the smaller room served as the kitchen and dining area, while the larger was arranged as a combined living room and bedroom for the previous owners. The large rock fireplace on one wall was blackened from heavy use during the cold Wyoming winters. The cast-iron stove in the kitchen would serve as an additional source of heat as well as a cooking tool. Julia slowly walked around the house, taking its measure.

"Another bedroom for me and one for Johnny off the back and this place will be nearly perfect."

*   *   *

Marty and Dan inspected the log building that had once been used as a bunkhouse. A half dozen bunks were scattered about. Though it was in need of a good cleaning, it would be satisfactory as a place for the men to sleep. The barn had burned down sometime in the past two years, leaving a stone foundation and blackened timbers as the only evidence of its location. Next to the burned barn, a sturdy corral still stood.

After the mules were unhitched, Walt and Tom got busy unloading Julia's belongings. Marty stood on the porch with Bob and pointed at a small herd of cattle that were grazing at the far end of the green area, south of the buildings.

"Bob, you and Paco ease those cattle off Mrs. Bennett's land. Push 'em slow but don't let them stop until they're off the property. Dan, let's herd our cattle toward where those cows were grazing. There must be some good grass there."

Everyone worked until dark, Bob and Paco being the last back. They rode in just as the others were sitting down to a hot meal from Julia.

"You get those cows all moved off?" Marty inquired.

"Yep. Me and Paco got her done. They didn't want to go. They probably got better grass here than where we pushed 'em."

"See anyone?"

"Nope. Nary a soul. Wolf Larkin's place is easy ten miles away. He probably leaves his cows up here all summer and winter, then gathers 'em in the spring for branding and sale."

"That reminds me. Julia, what brand do you want to use on your ranch? We gotta brand those cows we found; otherwise anyone that comes across them can take 'em along."

"A circle B. That's what Jim wanted. He even made the branding iron. I'll get it for you after supper."

"Good," Marty answered. "We'll do it tomorrow."

"I don't relish that job," Dan remarked. "Lassoing grown cattle for a branding is tough work."

"We won't do it that way. We'll use a stringer."

"How's that?" Bob asked.

Marty smiled. "Saw one in use in Texas once. You build a runway from one corral to another. Only big enough for one cow at a time. As we push a cow through from one side to the other, you stop him with a barrier, brand him, then send him on his way and stop the next one in turn. It works out real fast and easy."

Marty sopped up the last of his gravy with a piece of corn bread. "We'll build the stringer first thing tomorrow and get the branding done right away. Then we need to get some lumber and nails, so we can rebuild the barn and Julia's bedrooms."

Marty slept well that night, perhaps the soundest since he had agreed to undertake the mission of delivering Julia and her son to Wyoming Territory. In the morning they quickly built a narrow runway for the branding, wide enough for only one cow at a time, and, after some effort, finally got the sixty-one cows into the corral. The two boys herded the cows into the runway one at a time. Marty pushed one log in front and one in back to bar the cow's passage; Bob slapped a hot branding iron on one flank, marking it as a Circle B cow; then it was shooed back to the pasture. Every cow was branded before daylight ran out, leaving the men some time to clear the burned-out rubble from where the barn had once stood.

The next morning, Marty had instructions for everyone. "Dan, you and Walt take the wagons up to the logging camp. We need house-building logs and lumber. I'm hoping we can get both there. They ought to have plenty of cut logs that were too small to make good cross ties. And they'll have a sawmill to cut lumber for bridges. Anyway, fill up the wagons. Tell the head man up there that we're ready to sell him beef and mutton whenever he wants any. Tom, you need to replace some shingles on the roof. I saw a pile behind the chicken coop. I expect you to keep an eye on the place until we return. Paco, head for the hills and round up all the sheep you can. Use Pawpaw as your herd dog. Stay out as long as it takes to find some. Clear?"

"*Sí,* Senor Marty. I will find many sheep, I am certain."

Julia turned her attention from her mixing bowl to Marty. "What are you going to do today, Mr. Keller?"

"I'm going down to Warm Springs and then over to Larkin's ranch. He needs to know that we're here and this range is no longer available for his private use. I'm also going to try to find us some skilled carpenters. We need to get the barn and house additions done before the bad weather sets in."

"Is that wise?" Dan asked. "Going alone, I mean."

"I don't think Larkin will do anything. I suspect he'll be too surprised to even think of any mischief," Marty said. "Julia, I'd like you to come with me to town. Do you think Johnny would be all right here with Tom?"

"I suppose. Why do you want me?"

"I want to get your claim to the land properly filed. We could use some supplies as well. Also, I want you to buy some laying hens and a rooster, if you can. We've got a good coop here and I think we all would welcome fresh eggs from time to time."

They left within the hour on their assigned tasks. Marty and Julia watched the others depart and then headed for the little hamlet that was Warm Springs. Julia kept looking back as they rode down the road. Tom and Johnny were already busy hauling shingles from the pile to the ranch house and were too absorbed in their work to acknowledge Marty and Julia's departure.

*   *   *

They arrived in Warm Springs two hours later. It consisted of a few buildings, including a dry goods store, a livery, a stage stop, and a tack shop. Wolf Larkin's hotel, a two-story brick building, was proudly proclaimed the WOLF HOTEL in red letters a foot high on a white sign above the double doors in the lobby. Across the street was a two-story clapboard building painted a bright, bilious shade of green, with white trim on the windows and the front door. The high facade in the front was intended to increase the grandness of the building but really only emphasized the opposite. It bore a sign above its double doors identifying it as the MEDICINE BOW COUNTY GOVERNMENT OFFICE. A CLOSED sign hung from the doorknob.

Marty and Julia rode across a ford in the sparkling North Platt River, over fifty feet wide and flowing toward the south and the east. The stage stop was just across the ford, and next to it was another livery with a large corral holding numerous horses. The sign said that Mr. Charlie Ruut was the proprietor. Marty stopped there first. A burly man, his blond hair receding from his forehead, watched from the office door.

"Hello," Marty greeted the man. "You Mr. Rut?"

"That's pronounced *Root,* mister. Charlie Ruut. That's me. You?"

"I'm working for Mrs. Bennett here. She's the new owner of the Circle B ranch, the old Stonecipher place. Call me Marty. We'd like to rent a wagon for today, to take supplies out to the ranch. I'll return it tomorrow."

"Do tell. I heard Sam Bennett had some family comin' out here. Pleased to meet ya, Mrs. Bennett. Your husband comin' along later?"

"I am a widow, Mr. Ruut."

"My apologies, ma'am. I've got just the wagon fer ya. Cost five dollars, if you return it before dark tomorrow."

"That'll do. Hitch it up for us and park it in front of the

dry goods store." Marty thought for a second. "Mrs. Bennett needs to file her ownership with the county commission. I saw the county office was closed. How do we go about doing it?"

"Oh, Jimmy Joe Campbell will be there shortly. He's the town registrar, the county commissioner for Warm Springs, the local land speculator, the county magistrate, and the part-time bartender over at the Lazy River Saloon, which opens at noon, if yur thirsty."

"Thanks, maybe later. By the way, is that river we just crossed always that cold?"

"That's the North Platt. Fed by the snowcap in the mountains year-round. She's got some of the best fishin' in her you'll ever see."

Marty nodded, noncommittal. "I can take it or leave it, for the most part. Pan-fried fish is good now and then, I reckon."

"Well, you ever want me to show you the best spots, you just come on by. I'd as soon fish as about anything."

Marty looked down the street. Someone was just unlocking the door to the county building. "That'd be Mr. Campbell?"

"That'd be him. Nice meetin' you folks. I'll be seein' you agin, I reckon."

"By the way, Mr. Ruut, we've got four good mules that hauled us out here. You have any interest in them for stagecoach teams?"

"Fer a fact. I'll give you top dollar fer 'em."

"I'll bring them by later. Thanks again, Mr. Ruut."

"So long. I'll be along directly with yur wagon."

Marty and Julia walked their horses to the hitching post in front of the unusually bright green building that housed the county government offices. They stepped inside and approached the only ajar office door. A tall, ruddy-cheeked man with rust-colored hair looked up at them, a lively twin-

kle in his green eyes. He had just about the reddest hair
Marty had ever seen, and his mustache and beard were red-
der still. He nodded pleasantly and smiled brightly at Julia.
"Howdy, folks. I'm Jimmy Joe Campbell. You folks interested in some good land?"

"We have some, thanks. This is Mrs. Julia Bennett. I'm
her brother, Marty. She has the deed to the old Stonecipher
place."

Julia passed over the deed she had carried with her from
Missouri.

Jimmy Joe solemnly intoned, "Sam Bennett's family. I
sent you the letter about his death. My condolences."

"How did Sam die?" Marty asked.

"He was found dead, out in the hills behind his place.
Shot in the back. Nobody was ever brought up on charges
for the murder."

"What did the local law say about it?"

"It so happens that I'm the duly appointed law officer for
Medicine Bow County. I looked into it, but couldn't discover anything that would shed light on the murder. Sam
was on his horse and was shot with a rifle from some distance away, it seemed, as there was no cover around where
his body was found."

"Well, who would profit by his murder?" Marty persisted.

Campbell's round, boyish face grew clouded. "I can't
really say, Mr. Bennett. Some say that he and Wolf Larkin
had a set-to a few days earlier, but there was no indication
Wolf had anything to do with Sam's murder."

"Didn't Stonecipher kill himself where Larkin could find
him?"

"Yes, but there was no evidence that anything other than
what Larkin said happened did happen. Wolf Larkin is the
largest rancher in these parts. He has twenty thousand acres
of land and a couple of thousand cows on it. Why would he

kill for four thousand acres more that's as dry and barren as
the Stonecipher place is?"

"What about the creek that runs across the north end?"

"Deer Creek. The problem is that it runs dry about this
time every year. In a couple of weeks, your pasture will be
as brown as the rest of the grass around these parts. That's
why the best land fronts along the river." He looked at
Marty. "That's why Stonecipher wanted to sell his land to
Larkin the day he kilt hisself."

"What was it that Larkin said happened?"

"Larkin said that Stonecipher came to his place and tried
to sell his ranch, but when Wolf declined the price, Stonecipher rode off and then Wolf heard a shot. When he got to
where Stonecipher was, the man had put a gun to his temple
and blowed his brains out. It was really tragic."

Marty nodded. Time enough later to worry about that.
"Mrs. Bennett and I would like to pay our respects to Larkin.
Any idea where he's at right now?"

Campbell's face smoothed out. To Marty's experienced
eyes, the man knew a lot more than what he had just dis-
closed. "We can find out over to the hotel. Wolf has a man
there named Fredrick Wolf, who runs the place for him. A
German fellow, educated and dependable. He should know
where Wolf is."

"Wolf's got a Wolf working for him, huh?"

"Yeah, Larkin laughs about that all the time. I think that's
mostly why he hired Fred. He just got lucky to get a good
man in the bargain. Mrs. Bennett, I'll get your deed registered right away. If you'll follow me, I'll introduce you to
Fred."

As they stepped outside, they saw a stage splashing
across the ford toward them. "There's the Grand Encampment stage headed out. The Walcott stage just left as well,
headed north."

"We'll be wanting a couple of good carpenters, Mr. Campbell. You have any suggestions?"

"Luther, hold up there," Campbell shouted at the driver as the stage passed them. "I got a favor to ask you."

The driver pulled hard on his reins, and the stage stopped in the middle of the street. "Whatcha want, Jimmy?"

"Luther, this here is the Bennetts. They need a couple of good carpenters. Your brothers still doin' that over to Grand Encampment?"

"Sure are. The best in the county, I reckon."

"When can they get up this way?" Marty asked.

"I'll put 'em on the stage day after tomorrow. They'll want ten dollars a day. How long will you need 'em?"

"At least ten days. We'll give them room and board while they work out at the ranch."

Luther nodded. "I'll drop 'em off to you, Jimmy. You can get them out to this fellow's place."

"My pleasure, Luther. Be seein' ya."

"Eeeyah, git up, you hosses. Get a'goin' now." The stage rumbled off in a cloud of fine dust.

"Luther's a good man. Been driving the Encampment-to-Walcott stage for the last three years now. Don't matter if there's a mountain of snow on the ground. He pushes right ahead."

Marty and Julia followed Campbell across the street to the Wolf Hotel. They walked inside the lobby. Save for a solitary customer at the front desk paying his bill to a man dressed in a severe dark suit, the place was empty.

Off to the side was the hotel bar, a large room covered with bright red flocked wallpaper above varnished bead-and-board wainscoting. The bar itself was constructed out of cedar lumber and was also brightly varnished. The walls were hung with stuffed animal heads; deer, elk, moose, bear, mountain goat, and lion stared blankly into eternity. It appeared more like a museum than a watering hole for thirsty drinkers.

The paying customer finished his transaction and, hoisting his carpetbag, walked away from the front desk and out the door. The desk clerk smiled at Campbell. *"Guten Morgan,* Jimmy. Vat you vant? Ready to open de bar already?"

Chapter 22

Meet Wolf Larkin

Campbell made the introductions and then asked the hotel manager, "Where's Wolf Larkin, Fredrick?"

"I tink he is at his ranch. He say to me yesterday dat he must do some paperverk and dat he vill not be in town today."

Marty turned to Julia. "You want to ride over right now and pay our respects today, or not?"

"I really don't care to meet him ever, if you want the truth."

"I understand. Well, let's get our supplies and head on back to the ranch. I'll drop by his place this afternoon and give him the bad news."

Campbell broke in. "What news is that?"

"Larkin can't run his cattle on Circle B land anymore. We pushed several hundred head off the place when we arrived."

Campbell nodded, but his face was worried. "I suppose that's only fair. Wolf has been using that grass for free ever since Sam Bennett was shot. I'll mention it to him the next time I see him, as well. Let him know the law favors you in the matter."

"I'll make it clear enough when I see him; don't you fret. By the way, the men who Larkin sent to Missouri to buy the ranch last spring . . . One was killed in a fight with Jim Bennett. Who were the other two?"

"Harry Slocum was the one kilt. I'm not certain who the other two were. You'll have to ask Wolf." Campbell held out his hand to Marty and Julia. "Well, I need to get back to work. Welcome to Warm Springs, Mrs. Bennett, Marty. Stop by anytime you're in town. Next time, maybe you two can partake of the warm baths with me. It's quite a treat."

"Men and women together?" Marty's voice reflected his shock at the notion.

"Oh, no. The women have a little bathhouse built just for them. The men use one of the Indian bathtubs just a ways further down the river."

"What's an Indian bathtub?"

"The Indians have used the hot springs for hundreds of years, until just a few years ago."

"Yeah, we heard the story about the sickness."

Campbell nodded. "Well, they built a really nice pool, with rocks to sit on and a place to swim out into the cold water of the river. It makes for a nice place to relax and soak away your pains and troubles."

"Maybe next time. Good day, Mr. Wolf, Mr. Campbell."

"Please, Marty, Mrs. Bennett. Call me Jimmy Joe. Fredrick, I'll see you later. Good-bye for now." Marty and Julia watched him hurry across the street to the curious green building.

"Is it my imagination," Marty asked, "or is that the oddest shade of green paint ever put on a building?"

Julia chuckled. "It's dreadful, isn't it?"

"Almost criminal, if you ask me. I wonder where they got it."

They walked toward the Bear Creek Trading Goods Store. "I think Jimmy Joe Campbell is a little bit under the thumb of Wolf Larkin." Julia's insight drew Marty's agreement.

"You're dad-gummed right he is. He was practically doing a waltz around the subject. I imagine we'll find Mr. Wolf Larkin is a man who is accustomed to having his own way in just about everything."

"Will you be able to handle him, Mr. Keller?"

"If not, ma'am, then you and Johnny will be homeless before the snows come, I have a hunch."

"Will you be able to handle him?" Julia persisted.

"I reckon so. He's used to pushing folks around. Let's see how he does when someone pushes back." Marty held the door to the dry goods store open for her. "Make no mistake about it, Julia. If I fail, you've got to get your boy and get out, fast."

Julia said no more. They filled the wagon with food and hard goods, including two cases of iron nails and a small barrel of coal oil. Marty also bought some additional ammunition and some of the new petroleum cleaning solvent.

A young woman walked in as they were concluding their purchases. She was in her early twenties, with corn silk hair tucked under a blue bonnet. She was taller than many men and somewhat gangly, but she had a wholesome, friendly face with wide, rosy cheeks and shiny blue eyes. She marched right over to where Marty and Julia were standing.

"Hello there. Jimmy Joe told me that we had a new woman in town. I'm Pam Olsen. My folks own the ranch to the north of the river, just across the logging road where your land ends. I sure hope we'll become friends."

"Hello, Pam. I'm Julia Bennett. This is my brother, Marty. You must come out and pay me a visit as soon as possible."

"I'd like that, Julia. May I bring you a housewarming present? What do you need?"

"Why, thank you, Pam. If you could spare a chicken or two, it would be wonderful. I want to get a flock started."

"Consider it done. Day after tomorrow, I'll come callin'."

Julia's smile brightened the room like the sun had just come up. "I'll look forward to seeing you, Pam."

Marty drove Julia back to the ranch house and helped her and Tom unload the supplies. Tom had already completed the repairs to the roof and asked to accompany Marty to visit Larkin. "I just want to get out fer a while. I'll stay close to you, honest."

Julia agreed with the young man. "Larkin is less likely to try anything funny if you have him with you. Even a cad might shy away from hurting one so young."

Unable to counter their arguments, Marty finally agreed. "You do exactly what I say, Tom, and when I say it, without argument, agreed?"

"You bet, Marty."

They rode together toward the ranch of Wolf Larkin, Marty pensive and Tom so thrilled to be off on an adventure with Marty that he simply savored the moment and kept his mouth shut.

Larkin's place was a rugged-looking utilitarian ranch that had never seen a woman's touch. The main building was ample enough, but it had been made from green logs and mud plaster. There was nothing of style or color about the place. The ranch did not make a visitor feel welcome. The barn and the corral were all business, however. The roof of the barn had recently had numerous new cedar shakes emplaced, and the corral had sturdy new poles all around. Several quality purebred horses watched the strangers ride up, then returned to their munching of hay from a feeder along the inside of the corral.

Marty and Tom rode easily to the front porch. Marty

shouted out, "Hello, the house," then waited for a response and invitation before dismounting. Tom sat beside him, looking around.

A man stepped outside, his facial expression flat and non-committal. "Howdy, stranger. What do you want?" The tone of his voice held not one iota of welcome.

Marty carefully measured the man whom he was destined to confront in the current fix he had allowed himself to be lassoed into. The man was nearing fifty, fit, well dressed and groomed, including a carefully shaped mustache with curled ends. He looked as if he was the owner of the ranch but hired others to do the work. The man's eyes were dark, cold, even cruel. They focused on Marty without blinking.

"Hello. You Mr. Wolf Larkin?"

"I am. Who are you?"

"I'm the brother of Julia Bennett, the widow of Jim Bennett and the sister-in-law of Sam Bennett. She has brought her family here to Warm Springs and taken over ownership of the old Stonecipher ranch, the one to your north. We're going to put cattle and sheep on it and your cows will not be able to graze on it any longer. We drifted two hundred or so off the place yesterday. I came by to let you know so you can make other plans for 'em."

Wolf Larkin's face grew red with anger. "Mister, nobody touches my cows. Nobody."

"Fair enough. Keep 'em west of the Walcott Road and that's how it'll be. Let 'em drift east, across the road, into Circle B range and they get run off or, if they're unbranded, get a Circle B slapped on their rump."

Larkin struggled to appear unruffled, but the steam was almost about to blow out his ears, he was so riled up. "See here, fella. I give you fair warning. Brand any of my cattle and I'll hang you for a common cow thief."

"Maybe. Maybe not. You'll have to learn the hard way, I reckon. Anyway, I've given you the message. What you do about it is up to you. Come on, Tom. Let's go home. Good day, Mr. Larkin. Remember what I told you."

Larkin had to get the last word in. "Remember what I told you, hay-raker. I need that land and I mean to have it. And you stay away from my cows." He glared at the receding figures of the two riders until they crossed over a low slope to the north of his house. Then, slapping a fist into the palm of his other hand, he stomped back into the house.

A second man of medium height and build, with hair turning gray and typical cowman's garb, stepped away from the window where he had observed the exchange of words and covered his boss's back. "Who was that, Boss?"

"Some damned hay-shaker from the widow of the man who owned the Stonecipher place. Told me to keep my cattle off his land. Damned cheek of the fella. I oughta shot him where he stood."

"I don't know, Boss. He looked sort of familiar with them two six-guns he was a'carryin'."

"Hell, Beecher, how many times I told ya that a real gun-slinger only needs one gun? If ya can't git someone with six shots, then ya ain't worth yur salt."

"Still, Boss. That fella looked like he's more than any ole hayseed from the farm. Don't ya think you'd better sort of feel out the competition afore you jump in with both feet?"

"Otis, I pay you to ramrod my cattle. There's three hundred of 'em wanderin' around up by the Stonecipher ranch. Get on up there and drive 'em over to the west pasture. I was plannin' on saving that graze until the winter snows, but we'll have to put 'em in there early, thanks to the widder Bennett and her hayseed kin."

As Otis Beecher hurried off, Larkin thought about what his faithful ramrod had advised. "Reckon I'll just have to head over that way real soon and pay my new neighbors a visit. Get an ideer about just what they're a'plannin'." He headed for the cupboard and poured himself a stiff drink of whiskey. It was too early in the day, but his dander was up and he needed to cool off so he could think.

Marty and Julia were sitting on the front porch when Dan and Walt drove up in their wagons. Both were loaded to capacity with six-inch logs that were about ten feet long and sawed lumber of various lengths. Dan hopped down, a big grin on his face. "I'll bring down another load tomorrow. They practically gave away the logs; they're too small to make good cross ties. The lumber only cost one cent a board foot. You find any nails?" He looked at Marty.

"Yep. Also ordered out two carpenters from down in Grand Encampment. They'll be here tomorrow."

"Great. I'll have enough wood by then to build the additions to the house and the barn. Come on, give me and Walt a hand unloading. You too, Tom."

After they finished supper, Dan sat on the front porch with Julia and Marty. "The foreman up at the logging camp, calls himself Dutch Charlie, said they'd be happy to buy beef and mutton from you at a fair price. They said they feel like the person supplying them right now, a fellow named Larkin, is asking a pretty dear price for scrawny cattle."

"What are they paying right now?" Marty asked.

"Twenty-eight dollars a head, picked up at the road junction outside of town."

Marty looked at Julia. "You'd make money at twenty a head, plus they could pick them up right here, saving a ten-mile drive from Larkin's place. Looks like you'll have a ready market for any cows you decide to sell."

Julia nodded, her expression remote. Marty turned his attention to Dan. "Dan, did you see any sign of Paco while you were up in the tree line?"

"Nope. He said that he'd be gone for a few days, didn't he?"

"Yeah, it's just I'm a little uneasy about what Larkin is up

to. He got so mad when I told him about Julia here taking
control of the ranch, I thought his head was gonna explode.
I think he's a dangerous man. I want us to always ride in
pairs whenever we're away from the ranch house. You take
your rifle when you go up to the lumber camp tomorrow.
Walt too."

"Sure enough, Marty. Well, if you'll excuse me, I'm
gonna hit the hay. It's been a long day."

Marty tried to engage Julia in conversation, but she
seemed more content to sit in silence, so he did as well,
watching the stars brighten in the darkening sky. Finally,
Marty spoke out. "Julia, keep a close eye on Johnny. Don't
let him wander off where someone could get at him."

"Never fear, Mr. Keller. That's not going to happen."

"Damn, you just aren't gonna call me Marty no matter
how many times I ask you, are you? Well, good night. I've
got a busy day tomorrow."

The next morning, Marty sent Little Bob and Tom out to
check on the cattle. "Bob, try to give me some idea as to
how long the cows can graze down on the south pasture.
And see if you can come up with another site for us to use
when the good grass is gone. Keep your eyes open for trouble. Tom, you keep an eye on Bob and do what he says, understand?"

After Dan and Walt left for the lumber camp, Marty
hitched up the team to the rental wagon. "I'll run the wagon
back into town. You need anything you forgot yesterday?"

Julia shook her head. "I'm going to make some curtains
for the kitchen today. Be careful."

"I will. It's probably too soon to worry about Larkin, but
I've got a gut feeling he's gonna give us trouble."

"I'm not worried. That's why I brought you along, Mr.
Keller."

"That's what worries me."

Chapter 23

A Surprise Visit from Wolf

Marty drove the rented wagon into the little town of Warm Springs before nine o'clock. He dropped off the wagon at the Ruut Livery Stable and asked the owner to replace all the horseshoes on Pacer. "I'll need the wagon again tomorrow, Mr. Ruut. I've got a couple of carpenters coming in from Grand Encampment and they'll need a ride out to the ranch. What time does the stage usually arrive?"

"About two in the afternoon or so. I'll have the vagon ready fer ya, don't vorry."

Marty walked over to the county building. Jimmy Campbell was unlocking the door as Marty walked up behind him.

"Morning, Jimmy."

"Hello there, Marty. You're up early."

"Ranch work is never done. Want to get some coffee?"

"Sure. In fact, I was thinkin' about having some fried eggs and ham over to the Wolf Hotel restaurant. You want some?"

"No thanks. Julia made us some flapjacks this morning already. A cup of coffee will do me just fine. I'll drink it while you eat."

They walked over to the hotel restaurant and ordered from a young man with a clubfoot. Marty sipped his coffee and carefully worked to instill a sense of friendliness between him and the gregarious Jimmy Joe Campbell. He might need him if Wolf Larkin caused trouble in the future.

As Jimmy gobbled down his eggs, Marty described his service under General Forrest during the war. Jimmy immediately warmed up. "No fooling? I was on General Joe Johnson's staff. Hell, we might have even seen each other during the Atlanta campaign."

"Might have. You come out here right after the war?"

"I knocked around a couple of years, then when the railroad construction got going, I drifted this way. Met a fellow named Devin Charlie who worked for Tienack Logging Company. He described the area around here, and I sort of followed him to Warm Springs. Been here ever since."

"You must have known Stonecipher, then?"

Campbell's face grew nervous and wary. He absently rubbed his red mustache, as if ridding it of biscuit crumbs. "Yes. I did. He was a nice sort of fella. A bit odd, but not a mean bone in his body."

"You know where I'm headed with this, Jimmy. You think Stonecipher was the sort of man to shoot himself in the head because Larkin wouldn't buy his ranch?"

"To be honest, no I don't. I know that Larkin wanted Stonecipher's ranch, but I don't know why. His land ends at the North Platt and Stonecipher's place is mostly dry. It doesn't make much sense. Larkin's the big dog in these parts, Marty. He's been here since before the war and gets most all of what he wants. I looked into Mr. Stonecipher's death, but there was nothing I could find that said it weren't a suicide."

"You certain he was shot with his own gun?"

"It was in his hand with one bullet gone. The bullet had passed all the way through his head, so I couldn't take a look at it. It was mostly Larkin's word, with nothing to prove it weren't the truth."

"And that brings up another question, Jimmy. How much you figger the Circle B land is worth an acre?"

"Oh, about two dollars or so, maybe three if you sell when the land by the creek is green."

"Sam Bennett wrote his brother and Julia that he had found something that would make the land worth fifty dollars an acre. Any idea what he was talkin' about?"

Campbell's eyes widened and he shook his head at the incredible price. "No way that could be. There's copper and silver in some of the mountains around here, but I've looked over your place. There's absolutely no sign of any valuable ore on it. I can't imagine what he was talking about."

"I can't either, but Julia said Sam was plenty smart and was positive there was something about the land that would make it very valuable someday. Something more valuable than gold."

"I wonder what he meant. Some around here might say water is more valuable than gold, but your place is dust dry except the little bit you get when Deer Creek is running in the spring."

"If there were water there, the land would jump in value, right?"

"Like cold water on a hot griddle."

"Interesting."

"If you ever figure it out, let me know. Maybe there's some more of whatever it is on other land around here."

"I plan to look, I assure you. Just as soon as we get a bit more settled. Any chance that Wolf Larkin would know what it is?"

"I have no idea. If he does, it would explain why he's trying so hard to get it. I know he was furious when Sam Bennett bought the land for back taxes. He fired his lawyer up in Laramie because he didn't notify Larkin in time for him to get up there for the auction."

"Well, I suppose I'd best get on back to the ranch. I'll be in town tomorrow, to pick up the carpenters from Grand Encampment. Maybe I'll see you then."

The two men exited the restaurant. Jimmy waved good-bye and walked to his office. When he got there, he stopped in surprise as he saw Wolf Larkin sitting behind his desk. "Why, hello there, Wolf. I didn't see you come in."

"I reckon not—you were so busy swapping yarns with that damned hay-raker from Missouri."

"What you got against those folks, Wolf?"

"Just that they're keepin' me from growin'. I want that land. I need it. I aim to have it. If you know what's good fer you and fer Warm Springs, you'll help me git it."

"Why on earth do you want that dry dirt ranch, Wolf? You got a lot better land on your spread."

"Never you mind. You just remember who was here first and who'll be here last. Don't be gittin' too close to them newcomers. They ain't gonna be around here too long."

"You seen the widow Bennett?"

"Nope."

"Well, she's a real handsome lady. You might try a little honey instead of vinegar to convince her to give up her place."

"Hummp. I was plannin' on ridin' out that way and meetin' her anways. I guess I'll see for myself."

"Might be a good idea, Wolf. I aim to take my Hattie out to visit her in a day or two myself."

"Just don't get too chummy with that brother of hers."

"Whatever you say, Wolf. Now, if you'll excuse me, I gotta get some work done."

Wolf walked out of the office and crossed the street to the dry goods store, where his foreman, Otis Beecher, was buying some supplies for the ranch. Wolf waited impatiently until Otis had completed the purchases; then Wolf briskly barked out his orders. "Otis, we're ridin' over to the Bennett place. Have the cook take the wagon on back to the ranch."

"Sure enough, Boss. You hear, Cookie?"

"Sure. I'll be on my way as soon as I've had a beer. You promised, Otis."

"I did, Cookie. Have yur beer and then git on home."

Larkin and Beecher rode out to the Bennett ranch without much conversation. Larkin was struggling to get his mind around a way to get the ranch without putting what he had already accumulated at risk. He had been lucky so far. How much more could he push Lady Luck, he wondered. "How much?" he whispered to himself.

Marty rode into the front yard of the ranch and saw Julia and Pam Olsen standing by the chicken coop, animatedly talking to each other. "Hello, Ms. Olsen," he tipped his hat to the visitor. "I see you found us."

"Oh, certainly. I came over here now and again to visit Percy Stonecipher. It's a real pleasure to have a woman to visit."

"And she brought four lovely sitting hens and a rooster. Isn't that sweet?" Julia was positively beaming with appreciation. "We'll have fresh eggs in no time."

"Mighty nice of ya, Ms. Olsen. I hope the coop will keep them close to the house."

Pam smiled at Marty. "They seem to be settling right in. After a day or two you won't be able to drive them off." She turned to Julia. "Julia, there's a church social this Saturday night. Won't you come as my guest and let me introduce you to the locals? Everyone will be anxious to meet you." She gave Marty a quick glance. "Bring your brother and the others too. Give everyone a chance to meet all of you."

Julia smiled brightly at her new friend. "That sounds just wonderful. We'll be there. We can use some relaxation." She grabbed Pam's hand. "Come on inside. I want you to have a look at what we're going to do with the house. And I want to get any ideas that you might have as to brightenin' up the place." She pulled Pam away from Marty, and the visitor obediently followed, casting a somewhat reluctant glance back at him.

"Damn," Marty murmured to himself. "I don't think Julia wants me to get anywhere close to that little Olsen gal." He shook his head, somewhat amused. "Maybe she's got some idea I'd run off with Pam afore this thing is settled."

He walked Pacer to the corral, where he unsaddled the gray horse and turned him free to rest up from the ride back from town. He then ambled over to where Tom was working on the well cover.

"What's happening, Tom?"

"I'm trying to get this danged pulley fixed so's we can draw water easier. It's in need of a good greasing, but I'm havin' trouble getting it off the crossbar. The knot in the rope is so old and dried out, I can't get it undone."

"Heck, we have plenty of rope. Cut it and we'll replace it after you grease the pulley."

"Okay, Marty. Whatever you say."

"Tom, how far down to the water table?"

"Less than ten feet."

"No kidding. That's close to the surface. And as cold as it is, it must be running fast from the mountains up there. Doesn't even have time to warm up any." Marty looked at the almost dry Deer Creek. It was only a couple of inches deep and barely a foot wide now, as the late summer progressed. Yet not ten feet down was a veritable river of running water. Marty looked across the sloping valley toward the meadow where their cows were grazing. Even from where he stood, he could see the dried brown grass slowly replacing the lush green blades as the land dried out in the late-summer sunshine.

He supported Tom as the young man stood on the well

wall and cut the pulley away from the crossbar over the opening. "Tom, we need to take us a ride around this place. Sort of get a feel for the lay of things."

"Today?"

"No, not today. We've got too much to do. But soon. Real soon."

Marty helped Tom take apart the pulley on the farmer's anvil, which they had set on the ground next to the rock foundation of the burned-out barn. As soon as they liberally slapped a heavy coating of wagon grease around the pulley's axle, the device worked easily. Soon it was back on the well's crossbar and ready for service. As they finished, Tom spotted the riders headed toward the ranch on the town road.

"Company comin', Marty."

They watched as the two riders came nearer. "It's Wolf Larkin and his foreman, Otis something." Marty stepped around the well and nodded politely. "Howdy, Mr. Larkin, Otis. Welcome to the Circle B."

"Mrs. Bennett around?" Larkin's voice was haughty and aloof. He was making it clear that he wanted nothing to do with Marty. He addressed Marty as if Marty were a hired hand. "I want to speak to her."

"Certainly, she's here. Tom, run up to the house and tell Julia that Wolf Larkin is here. Step down, Larkin. Help yourself to some cool water, if you've a mind."

"No thanks. Otis, let the horses get a drink from the creek, then wait for me by the corral."

"Okay, Boss." He did as he was bade, leading the horses down toward the stream.

Tom hurried back from the house. "Julia says for you to come right up, Mr. Larkin."

"Excellent." Larkin sneered at Marty and marched off.

"I wonder what that was all about," Marty whispered to Tom.

"Looks like he's got his dander up. We musta made him pretty mad, when we were there."

"I hope Julia can handle him. I reckon she'll call for me if she needs me. I'm gonna try to talk to Otis. Take care of his horses, why don't you?"

Marty's efforts were in vain. Otis would answer only the most general of questions, avoiding any that were outside his expertise, cattle and horses.

Julia held out her hand. "Mr. Larkin. Welcome to my place. You know Pam Olsen, don't you?"

"Luther Olsen's girl?"

"That's me, Wolf. Well, Julia, I'll see you at the social on Saturday. Around six or so. Good-bye, Wolf."

"Oh, Pam, you have to leave so soon?" Julia asked.

"Yes, I need to get on home. I'm looking forward to seeing you Saturday. All of you, at the social."

After Pam left, Julia turned to Wolf Larkin. "And you, Mr. Larkin. What can I do for you today?"

Larkin smiled broadly at Julia, but she was not taken in. His smile did not reach his eyes, which failed to register the slightest degree of warmth or friendliness. "I just wanted to say welcome, Mrs. Bennett. You've come a long way and I know it's not been easy for you. As I sent word to you earlier, I am anxious to increase my land holdings in this part of the country. I would like to make you a very generous offer, if you will listen to my proposal."

"First, forgive my manners, Mr. Larkin. May I offer you a cup of coffee?"

"Coffee would be fine."

Julia put several cups and saucers, along with the coffeepot, on a large tray and headed for the front door. Larkin followed, perplexed. She motioned to one of the chairs on the porch. "Please sit, Mr. Larkin. Here, let me pour you some coffee." She motioned toward Marty. "Come join us. Mr. Larkin has a business proposition he wants to make us."

Marty strode over from the corral, Otis right behind him. Julia smiled sweetly at Larkin. "I think I need to have my brother listen to this as well, Mr. Larkin. He has such a good head for numbers and dollars." She gave the flustered Wolf a simplistic smile. "Please go on."

"Well, Mrs. Bennett. I didn't figure to discuss this out in the open like this. I wanted to sort of keep it between ourselves."

"Nonsense, Mr. Larkin. I would not make any decision concerning the sale of my place without discussing it with my brother anyway, so just say your piece here and now so we can give it the consideration it deserves."

"Well, if you insist. I was gonna offer you four dollars an acre, and an additional five dollars an acre for the five hundred acres at the end of Deer Creek. That's eighteen thousand five hundred for your place. You have to admit that's an impressive offer."

"Yes, some might say that. However, Mr. Larkin, my brother-in-law said he had found something that would make this land increase in value by ten times. You have any idea what he was talking about?"

Marty caught the quick change in Larkin's expression. It was immediately replaced with a bland expression, but it had revealed that Larkin knew something. Marty said nothing, keeping his mouth shut and watching the discussion between Julia and Wolf Larkin.

"Why . . . why, I assure you Sam was mistaken. This whole country has been gone over with a fine-tooth comb. There ain't no mineral deposits on any of it. It's cattle country, and not very good cattle country at that. There's no way you're going to git any more fer your land than I just offered you. No way. Ask anybody."

"We'll see, Mr. Larkin. We'll see. In the meantime, I

would like very much to talk to the two men you sent to Missouri to try to buy this property. You know, the two who said my husband shot their friend in the back from ambush."

"Unfortunately, I hired those men for the express purpose of buying this property. When they failed, I let them go. I have no idea where they are at the moment."

"You did put up the reward on my husband, didn't you, Mr. Larkin?"

"Yes, ma'am. But I assure you, it was only because my agents swore to me that Harry was shot in the back from ambush. That's the only reason I guaranteed the reward money."

"My husband did not shoot your man in the back, Mr. Larkin. If I ever get my hands on those two others, I'll prove it. I don't suppose you would mind giving me their names?"

"I have them among my papers at the ranch. The next time we see each other, I'll have them for you." Larkin set down his cup and saucer. "Come on, Otis. It's time we got back to the ranch. A pleasure, Mrs. Bennett. You think real hard about my offer. It's the best you're gonna git from anybody."

"Good-bye, Mr. Larkin."

As Larkin and Otis rode out of the yard, Larkin barked orders at his foreman. "Otis, head to town. Send a note to Willis and Louie to get out of Laramie for a while. Tell them to go on down to Denver and enjoy the scenery. They're not to come back this way until they check with me." He rode silently for a few moments, thinking, then spoke up again. "Then put a note on the stage for Big Nose George, down in Encampment. Tell him to get on up here. I got another job for him."

Chapter 24

Trouble's Coming

"Damn, Boss. I sure wish you wouldn't bother with him. He's meaner than a rattlesnake at moltin' time. And don't you never call him Big Nose where he can hear ya. I heerd that he beat a man to death in Cheyenne for doin' jus' that."

"Let me worry about that, Otis. You just git 'im up here."

"Boss, I'm worried about this. The last time he was here, Sam Bennett was shot dead from ambush. I got a pretty good ideer it was George Parrott what done it. We don't need no more killin' around these parts."

"Dammit, Otis. I pay you to ramrod my cattle operation, nothing more. If you ain't comfortable with how I do business, you're free to leave. Know anyone else that wants to pay you eighty a month and found?"

"No, I don't. I like being your foreman. It's just that I don't think—"

"That's right; don't think," Larkin interrupted. "Now, head for town. I'll meet you back at the ranch."

Marty had waited silently until Wolf and his foreman were out of earshot; then he turned to Julia. "Did you see that look on Larkin's face when you mentioned Sam's statement about something of value on this land?"

"I certainly did. And I'm also certain he does know where the two men are who framed Jim." Julia's face was grim. "If I ever get my hands on them . . ."

"We're going to have to be doubly careful. Larkin is too used to having his way. He'll try something, and soon."

"You think we ought to send the boys back to Missouri?"

"I think I'll suggest they take off. However, I'll bet you they both insist on staying until our problem shakes out."

"Well, give them the option, anyway. I'm worried about Paco. You think he's all right?"

"I imagine we'll be seeing him soon. He only took a couple of days' rations. If he doesn't show up tomorrow by the time I get the carpenters back from Warm Springs, I'll go look for him."

As they were washing up for supper, Walt and Dan arrived with two more wagonloads of lumber and logs. Paco rode in on his little pinto mare.

"Hey, Paco. You have any luck?" Marty shook the Basque sheepherder's hand just moments later.

"Oh, sí. I bring in maybe one hundred head. There are more to be found, up in the hills. Maybe some will even come on their own to join the herd. I need supplies for a week. I will get the sheep settled in the high country and used to me and Pawpaw. He is gonna be a very good sheepdog, that Pawpaw. They will stay close to home once they have been here for a while. But to start, I should stay with them all the time."

Marty glanced at Julia. "Will it be all right to leave Pawpaw up with Paco for a spell?"

"Certainly. Everyone has to pull their load on the ranch. That includes Pawpaw and Johnny." She looked at Paco. "Could Johnny be of help to you with the sheep?"

"Oh, sí. I will teach him to be a good sheep man."

Julia asked Marty, "Do you think Johnny would be safer up there with Paco than down here at the ranch?"

"Well, perhaps. Paco, you'll have to keep an eye open for trouble. If Larkin sends his men up to roust the herd, you get Johnny out of there."

Paco's face grew very serious. "Oh, *sí,* I will. I will be very careful of little Juan. They will have to kill me to hurt him."

Julia nodded emphatically. "It's settled then. I think I'll rest easier knowing he's out of the way, up in the hills with Paco rather than down here, where we may be forced to fight anytime."

In an hour, Paco and Johnny rode out of the ranch on Paco's pinto, leading a mule packed with supplies. As they disappeared into the tree line, the look on Julia's face did not waver. She stood straight and remained steely-eyed and determined.

Marty said, "Julia, I gotta admit, you're one tough lady. You definitely got a pound of grit in your craw."

She glanced imperiously at Marty, then marched inside without saying a word. Shaking his head and muttering to himself, Marty headed for the bunkhouse. Tomorrow was going to be busy and his bunk currently held a lot of appeal.

The next morning Marty hurried into Warm Springs. He was talking with Jimmy Campbell while awaiting the stagecoach from Grand Encampment. "You going to the church social on Saturday night?"

Jimmy nodded. "Sure am. My misses is in charge of the refreshments. We've got a fiddle player hereabouts that's as good as any anywhere. You enjoy dancin'?"

Marty smiled. "I used to shake a leg or two, way back when. I suppose it's something you never quite forget."

"Glad to hear yur comin', Marty. Give folks a chance to meet and welcome you and Julia."

"Here's the stage, right on time." Marty and Jimmy watched as the stage came to a stop in a shower of dust, its mules snorting and swishing their tails.

The stage discharged six passengers, one of whom was a woman. Two of the men hoisted carpenter toolboxes and headed their way. The two looked to be about forty, and were definitely brothers. One spoke up. "Howdy. Either of you two fellas Jimmy Joe Campbell?"

"That's me. You kin to Luther Stagg?"

"Our oldest brother. I'm James and he's John. You the man we'll be workin' for?" He gave Marty an open, honest look of appraisal.

"That's right. You'll be building a barn that burned down and adding a couple of rooms to the main house. I have lumber and nails at the ranch. What else do you want?"

"Windows?" James asked.

"Good point. We'll pick up four at the dry goods store. Anything else?"

"Dry cement. We'll use that to set the foundation."

"Well, there's my wagon. Throw your stuff in the back and let's get over to the store. See you Saturday night, Jimmy."

Marty bought the items the Stagg brothers needed to complete the barn and room additions, then drove them out to the ranch. He put Tom and Walt to work helping them. "If you fellas aren't gonna take my advice and get out of here like you had a lick of sense, then you may as well learn something about good carpentering."

While Dan helped Julia put in a garden, hoping to get a few of the faster-growing vegetables cultivated before the snows came, Marty took Little Bob and rode out to look over the cattle and their graze.

"What do you think, Bob? How much longer can we leave the cattle on this grass?"

"We oughta take 'em off now, Marty. This area needs to grow some so's the cows can graze on it when the snows come."

"Where can we put the cattle instead of here? The slopes are already burned out from lack of water."

"We'll have to take 'em up into the high country. There's places up there where there's plenty of grass. We just have to find it. I scouted the area a couple of years ago fer Wolf Larkin. I think I can find some spots that'll work for us. We only have sixty cows to feed."

"Okay, Bob. You want to take 'em up tomorrow?"

"Sure. That'll be fine. I'll get 'em settled in somewhere and let you know where. Can I take one of the boys with me?"

"Take both of them. That'll get them out of the way for a spell, in case there's trouble."

"If there is trouble, Marty, I want to be dealt in."

"You don't have to, Bob."

"It ain't a subject fer discussion, Marty. I've throwed in with the Circle B and I aim to stand up fer it when the time comes."

"I appreciate that, Bob. I'll not forget you when or if the time comes."

"That's all I ask, Marty." Bob pointed to the ground. "If there was more water outa Deer Creek, we could support several thousand cows on this place, not just several hundred."

"After you get settled in with the cows, let's you and I take a ride around the property together. You can show me the lay of the land and we can decide on how we're gonna handle the coming snow season."

"I'll start the cows out tomorrow at first light. We oughta be back by Saturday at the latest."

Marty grinned at Bob. "You've heard about the church social, I gather?"

"Yep. Wouldn't want to miss it."

Marty assigned himself and Dan to help the two Stagg brothers the rest of the week. By Saturday, they had a forty-by-forty barn framed and covered, with six stalls and a work area on the ground floor and a hayloft overhead.

The carpenters had Marty and Dan bring in a load of creek rock between four and eight inches in diameter. Using it and the cement, they expertly laid the foundation down for the room additions. "We'll be done by next Friday," they promised Marty at the end of the day. "We'll be going to the social with you folks tonight, if that's all right."

Everybody was eager to go to the church social except Paco. He immediately volunteered to stay and guard the place for the time they were away.

"You certain, Paco? I'll stay if you want to go into town," Marty offered, trying to be fair.

"No, Senor Marty. I have been to these socials before. Someone is always wanting to fight with me because I herd sheep, not cows. I will stay here with Juan. We get along jus' fine, him and me. We will watch the ranch while you are in town."

Wolf Larkin watched the lone rider slowly make his way toward the porch of his home. As the rider grew closer, it was easy to discern the odd discrepancy between the sizes of the man and the horse. The rider was huge. He dwarfed the horse he rode even though it was an extremely large Morgan itself. The man's head was just shy of being monstrous. His nose was huge; even on the man's oversized noggin, it was grossly large. Broken and badly set, it leaned hard to the right. Tiny red veins crisscrossed the beak, betraying numerous bouts of drunkenness. Dark hair spilled out of the nostrils like animal fur. Wolf cautioned himself not to slip and call the man Big Nose George to his face. As the rider drew up to Wolf, he spoke. His voice sounded as if it rumbled out of a cavern.

"Good afternoon, Wolf. Well, here I am."

"Mr. Parrott, welcome to Wolf's Lair Ranch." He motioned with a hand. "Climb on down and come in. Ready for a drink to cut some of that trail dust?"

"Yeah, that'd be jus' fine."

It did not take Wolf long to explain the reason for his summons. "The only thing is, George," he intoned very carefully and forcefully, "I don't want no shootin' unless I say so. There's a big shindig tonight and the Bennett wider and her brother'll be there. I want you to get in a fight with him and knock his smart-alecky block clean off. If he ends up broke up so bad he even dies, that's okay. But no gunplay. You with me on this?"

"I understand," the big man rumbled. "I'll kill him with my fists."

"Whatever," Wolf said casually. "Just git the job done." He poured another round of whiskey into the glass of the hulking brute. "You can sleep in the extra room in the tack house, George. Why don't you get settled and grab some sleep. Come 'round to the social about nine or so. You know what to do after that."

Marty helped Julia out of the wagon at the Grange Hall, the biggest building in Warm Springs. She was wearing a pastel dress with lace trim. It was the first time Marty had seen her in anything but household gray or black. "You look very nice, Julia," he whispered. She did not answer.

Walt, Bob, Dan, and Tom were tying their horses to the wheel of the wagon, and the Stagg brothers were clambering out the back. "Come on, boys," James hollered. "Let's get something to eat and drink right now, so's we're ready when the dancing starts."

Dan held back, accompanying Marty and Julia into the

hall. One side had tables set up with food of all description: sandwiches, cakes, cooked vegetables, several plates of fried chicken. There were punch and tea, each in a large bowl with a chunk of ice floating on top. "Lookee there. They've got ice in the tea," Dan announced. "How 'bout that?"

The other side of the room had meeting chairs set up for folks to sit in and talk or eat. Eventually, the chairs would be removed and dancing would commence.

Marty and Julia were introduced to several ranchers and townsmen and their wives. Jimmy Campbell's wife, Hattie, was especially friendly and soon had a commitment from both Julia and Pam Olsen to visit for coffee and a "hen session."

The chairs were eventually pushed back against the wall, and the fiddler Jimmy had praised so highly, along with a guitar-picker and a bull fiddle–sawer, climbed onto a small stage set up at one end of the building. In a few minutes the place was hopping with lively music and dancing couples.

Dan got the jump on Marty and had the first dance with Julia. When they returned, Julia's face was aglow with enjoyment. Marty smiled at her and gallantly bowed, as he had been instructed in the social-skills class at Virginia Military Institute. "Care to share this dance with me, Julia?"

"Sorry, I promised Jimmy Campbell this one." She moved away with the likeable redheaded man while Marty looked on, his face carefully kept neutral. Once again she had rebuffed his overtures of friendship. She was not going to let him ever get on her good side.

Pam Olsen swirled into his view. "Care to try your dancing legs, Marty?"

"Thanks, Pam. That'd be fine by me. I have to warn you, however—it's been a while since I danced a jig. You might be in for a hard trip around the floor."

Pam laughed. "I'll take my chances. Come on, let's try it."

Marty spotted Wolf Larkin talking with some other ranchers near the small bar. Next to him, Otis Beecher was amiably conversing with several cowboys, who must have been from Wolf's or one of the other ranches in the valley. Marty's eyes met Wolf's for an instant, but Wolf quickly turned his back. Marty shrugged. He had better things to do than worry about Wolf Larkin and his big ambitions.

It was around nine when a huge man lumbered into the room. Conversations stilled as people recognized the new-comer. Marty found he was staring at the biggest fellow he had ever seen. Six and a half feet tall, weighing well over three hundred pounds, the man dominated the space around him. His head was about as large as the rest of him, with the biggest, sharpest hooked nose Marty had ever seen on any-one. His eyebrows met in a single dark line, and numerous scars around his eyes and lips attested to countless fights. Cauliflower ears stuck out like flappers from a head covered with dark, greasy hair. His beard and mustache were stained with food and tobacco juice. Marty wondered how anyone could ever stand up to the imposing giant. He was wearing dirty clothing and boots that looked like they had been old ten years earlier.

"Man, oh, man," Dan remarked. "That is one big, ugly fellow, ain't he?"

A cowboy with Wolf Larkin walked over and whispered something to the brute. The big guy's eyes swept the dance floor and settled on Julia, who was swinging around in a waltz with one of the smaller ranch owners she had just met. The big fellow pushed away from the wall of the building and lumbered out onto the dance floor, shoving aside any couples who got in his path. He stopped behind the man dancing with Julia and tapped him on the shoulder.

The dancer's face blanched. He was surprised to see the

massive outlaw so close. He quickly surrendered his place
with Julia and slunk toward the table holding the punch
bowl and the beer keg.

With a worried frown, Marty watched as the lumbering
man took Julia in his massive arms. "Who is that fellow?
You know, Bob?" Marty asked Little Bob, who was standing next to Dan, sipping a glass of beer.

"Damn, Marty, that's Big Nose George Parrott. He's
about the meanest no-good SOB to ever live 'round here. I
think he's one of Larkin's cronies, especially when it comes
to dirty work."

Marty watched uneasily as the man gathered Julia into
his embrace. The man dropped his head and whispered
something in her ear. Julia's face immediately registered
shock, then anger. She tried to disengage herself from the
big man's grasp, but he held her effortlessly.

"Uh-oh," Marty groaned. "Trouble. Watch my back,
Dan."

Chapter 25

A Deadly Challenge

Julia was hopelessly trapped in Big Nose George's massive arms. Her struggles were unnoticed by the others on the dance floor, but not by Marty. He maneuvered his way past several twirling couples to the side of George and Julia.

Julia quit struggling when she saw Marty. She turned her face away from Parrott's foul breath, which was sickening her. Her gaze avoided his malicious sneer, which she found both terrifying and disgusting. Her eyes pleaded with Marty for help.

Marty reached up to tap the man's muscled shoulder. "Pardon me, I'd like to cut in."

Parrott ignored Marty's request and drew Julia even more tightly into his embrace.

She gasped out desperately, "Let me go, you wretched beast, or I'll scream the roof off."

"Go ahead, pretty lady. Ain't nobody gonna do nothin' noways. I think I'll jus' keep on holdin' you close till you agree to my ideer."

Parrott's rotten breath, courtesy of bad teeth, and oppressive body odor from a lack of contact with bathwater nearly made Marty puke. He could only imagine what Julia was experiencing in his unwanted embrace.

Marty firmly tapped George's shoulder again and spoke in a voice loud enough for everyone in the room to hear. "Let her go, you parrot-beaked son of a bitch."

George spun around more quickly than Marty would have thought possible for a man his size, his eyes blazing hot with anger. "Damn you, fella. Nobody talks to me that way. I'm gonna tear yur head off fer ya and spit down yur throat."

Marty placed himself between George and Julia. "The lady doesn't want your attentions, so excuse us." He pushed her toward Dan and Bob, ignoring Parrott and hoping the enraged giant would not launch himself while his back was turned. As soon as he reached Dan, he whispered, "Watch her, Dan. That fella's up to no good."

Marty tensed as he saw the image of Big Nose George in Dan's widening eyes. He was grabbed by the arm and swung around. "Did you hear me, you loudmouth bastard? I said I'm gonna rearrange yur face. Put yur dukes up."

"I heard you, big man. And my answer is 'No thanks!'" Marty turned his back on the enraged George and tried to talk to Dan and Julia.

Parrott swung him around again. "I said put up yur dukes and fight."

"And I said no thanks." Marty looked at George, fixing him with a steady gaze of indifference. "You want to try me with a gun, be my guest. But I'm not gonna fight you with my fists, not now or ever."

"Why, you lily-livered coward. You stinkin' sheepherder. Yur afraid to fight me."

"On the contrary—I'm too smart to fight you. Why should I let you pummel me senseless just because you're half again as big as me. I'd be happy to put a forty-four slug through your thick skull, but I'm not gonna fight you. Get that through your head."

A crowd of people had silently drawn around Marty and George by then. They watched in morbid fascination while the two angry men jawed at each other. Parrott shook a meaty fist in Marty's face. "I said I'm gonna bust yur head, and by God, that's jus' what I'm gonna do. Get yur sorry butt outside."

Marty's face was calm, but cool and deadly. "No. I am not going outside for you, now or ever. I'll have my gun on when I decide to leave, if you want to try me. I'll put you in hell before your gun clears leather, but I'm not fighting you with my fists."

"You sorry, worthless coward. I'm givin' you fair warning. The next time I see you, I'm gonna break yur yellow back with my bare hands. I'm lookin' forward to it." He glared at Marty malevolently, then turned and stomped out of the room, muttering curses and shoving his way through the crowd of people.

"Way to go, fella," someone cheered from the onlookers. "Big Nose needs to learn he ain't the only man in Warm Springs. Fill his big belly with lead if he bothers you agin."

Jimmy Campbell pushed his way through to Marty. "Sorry I didn't get here sooner, Marty. I was out to the little house when this all started. I told Wolf to git his fightin' dog outa here."

"What did Wolf say?"

"He claimed he didn't have nothin' to do with it. He said he heard you threaten to shoot Big George. He reminded me that George don't carry a gun and if you shoot him, I'd have to do my duty."

"You mean that you'd arrest Marty for defending himself, but not stop the brute from beating Marty to death with his fists?" Dan sarcastically asked.

"All you gotta do, Marty, is not fight him, no matter how much he provokes you."

"You ask a lot, Campbell."

"Well, you can't shoot him unless he's packin' a gun, so maybe you'd best stay out of his way."

"I'll try, but I'm not gonna hide under my bunk with a blanket over my head either."

"Stay out of town for a few days. Maybe he'll get tired of hangin' around and move on. He's not one for stayin' anywhere too long. Certain law enforcement officials might find him."

Marty nodded. "I'll make no promises, Jimmy. I'll try to make myself scarce, but at the same time, I'm not hiding out from him either." Marty looked at the others. "You all ready to leave?"

The evening was spoiled for any further enjoyment. Julia led the men from her ranch out the door of the social hall, her head high. The men had their hands poised over their guns, ready for trouble, but Big Nose George was nowhere to be seen.

On the ride back to the ranch, the talk was all about the new threat from Wolf Larkin. "What you need," Dan announced suddenly, "is that Irish tracklayer from the railroad. If anyone can stand up to the fella, it's him."

Marty shook his head. "I don't know. Even Mick gives up two inches and fifty pounds to that monster. I'd hate for him to get hurt on my behalf."

"I sort of thought he asked to be dealt in if he was ever needed."

"Well, it hasn't come to that yet. Let's hope it doesn't."

Unfortunately, it was not to be that way. Dan and Bob accompanied Julia and Johnny into Warm Springs the next morning for church services. When they returned, Dan immediately sought out Marty. "That Big George is talkin' all over town as to how he's gonna wait for you to show up and then drag you off your horse and beat you senseless in front of everyone. They were talking about it after church. Jimmy Campbell says to stay away from town. He'll try to get Big George to leave the area. Personally, I don't think he's gonna be very persuasive about it." Dan looked at Marty, his brow furrowed with concern. "You want to send for the Irishman?"

"No, dang it. I don't want Mick to risk himself for me. I'll just have to shoot that monster the moment I see him and take my chances that it'll work out all right." He rubbed his hand through his hair. "Maybe I'd better go brush Pacer. I got some hard thinking to do."

Dan and Bob sought out Julia. "We think we oughta send Bob here up to Laramie to get O'Rourke. He's probably Marty's only chance at avoiding a fight with that fella. Win or lose, Marty's liable to find himself in real trouble."

Julia nodded. "I agree. Bob, do you think he'll come?"

"He told me that he thought the world of Marty. I guess all we can do is ask."

"You can leave as soon as you're ready. I'll tell Marty that I'm sending you to pick up some medicine I ordered from St. Louis." Julia swallowed a smile. She had just done what Marty was always after her to do: call him by his first name. Sternly, she reminded herself that he was still the man who had killed her husband.

Marty continued to manage the construction of the barn and the house additions, unaware of their plan. By the end of the week, the two Stagg brothers had done all they had promised. Two large, airy bedrooms were added to the back of the main house. The barn was also ready for use, so Marty put Tom and Walt to gathering hay for winter feed for the horses. Dan went into town to sell the big Studebaker wagon and four of the mules, one of which was Walt's, to the livery

owner. Marty presented Walt with Junior Raye's roan gelding in trade, making Walt a mighty happy young man.

Marty ended up two hundred dollars to the good over
what he had paid for the wagon and the mules in Missouri,
leaving him nothing to complain about. When Little Bob
showed up with Mick O'Rourke in tow a few days later,
Marty was secretly relieved.

"Mick, I don't want you to get yourself hurt. This guy
we're going up against is damned big. A monster. He out-
weighs you by fifty pounds and is two or three inches taller.
He has to turn sideways to walk through a door."

"Tsk, tsk, me bucko. I haven't spent twenty years per-
fectin' me skill in fisticuffs to let some overgrown hooligan
get the best of me. He's that big, he'll have a weakness or
two. Something he never considered because of his size.
You'll see."

Marty shook his head. "If you're willing to chance it,
okay. We'll ride into town tomorrow and see what happens.
I don't want you to get into trouble missing work because of
me."

"I'm on official leave of absence for a couple of weeks. I
got plenty o'time off coming, me worryin' friend."

The next day was a Saturday, providing everyone with an
excuse to accompany Marty and Mick into town. Paco once
again agreed to stay behind with Johnny to guard the ranch
while the others were gone. Marty was quick to notice that
every one of his friends had his six-gun strapped to his waist
with the holsters tied down against his legs.

"We're not going into Warm Springs to start a war, fellas," he complained, to no avail. Everyone was grim and
silent as they rode toward the showdown, save for Mick,
who was his usual exuberant self. But then, he had not seen
Big Nose George.

They rode into the small town at midafternoon and tied

their horses in front of the dry goods store. Julia climbed down off the wagon before anyone could help her. She thanked the Stagg brothers, who were headed back to Grand Encampment now that their work was done. She went into the store with a final word of encouragement to Mick and Marty.

"Good luck. I'll have bandages and salve if you need it." She gave Mick a quick kiss on the cheek. "Take care."

"Oh, yes, ma'am," Mick mumbled, blushing a deep red.

Marty smiled and held out his hand to James and John. "You two did a fine job. I'll spread the word about just how fine the place looks, thanks to you two."

"Thanks, Marty. Me and John has sort of decided we'll go along with you boys while you git a drink."

"You fellows don't have to do that, James. There's liable to be a whole lot of trouble."

"We're more'n willin' to be part of it, if it comes to that. You folks are good people and we're throwin' in our lot with ya."

"I appreciate it, men. Well, come on. Let's face the lions in their den. Walt, Tom, no matter what, don't be the first to draw your guns. This is a fistfight, not a shoot-out. Only if you have to defend yourself. Understand?"

The two youths hitched up their pants and tried not to show their excitement. "Yep," they answered in unison. "Lead the way, Marty."

Marty led his little army up the steps of the Wolf Hotel and through the double doors into the saloon. He glanced over his shoulder at the numerous townsfolk flowing along in their wake. Everyone wanted to witness the coming fight.

The saloon was busy, crowded with rowdy cowboys from the surrounding ranches in town to enjoy the Saturday evening. Several lumberjacks sat talking among themselves at two tables pushed together. A couple of floozies were circulating among the patrons, listlessly seeking some man to buy them a drink of high-priced tea.

When the customers saw Marty and his men, their conversation died. Big Nose George was at the far end of the bar, drinking and talking with Otis Beecher and half a dozen other Larkin riders. Otis saw Marty first. His eyes widened, and the words he was speaking died out.

Mick O'Rourke took advantage of the silence to shout merrily, "Now, where's this despicable brute named Big Nose George?"

Parrott spun around, his eyes bulging in rage, his face growing purple with anger.

"May the saints preserve us," Mick said, laughing. "You are one ugly brute, aren't ya? My God, how did the good Lord make a nose that big? Use a horse's arse?"

Chapter 26

A Legendary Brawl

"Who the hell are you, you shanty-Irish pile of cow dung?" Big George slammed a meaty fist against the bar, causing the glasses stacked on it to rattle against each other. "Nobody talks to me that way. I'll bury you."

"Well, bucko, take yur best shot, 'cause that's all yur gonna git. Then I'm gonna wipe up the floor with yur dirty hide, just fer the sheer pleasure of it."

With a mighty roar of rage, Parrott lunged at Mick. The two human behemoths collided with the force of two bull elk in mating season, scattering the customers looking on like chaff in a wind. Sounding much like a club smacking a slab of beef, Mick and George traded blows. George staggered back, surprised by the intensity of Mick's initial assault. He charged at the still-grinning Irish foreman and drove him into a table of lumberjacks, scattering them and their drinks across the room.

The offended tree cutters came up swinging. Walt, Tom, and Marty were quickly engaged in defending the two battering rams, who continued to trade mighty blows without pause. Marty threw a feisty lumberjack into two others, then turned to see what the other riders from Wolf's ranch were going to do about the mayhem. To Marty's amazement, Otis Beecher had restrained his men to sit the fight out. Not one man came to Big George's aid.

Gratified at Otis' response, Marty turned back to the melee, just in time to catch the full brunt of a head-down charge into his midsection by a drunken cowboy who could not stay out of the fight any longer. The exuberant cowboy shouted at the top of his lungs and swung both fists like a windmill, without causing much damage to Marty. Blocking a wild roundhouse swing, Marty punched the drunk cowboy hard in the jaw and let him slide down the bar to repose on the floor with his arm tangled up in the foot rail.

Dan was struggling with the bartender over a sawed-off shotgun. As Marty moved to help him, Dan jerked the gun away from the bartender and swung it to cover the mob of fighting men.

"No guns or knives, Marty. I'll see to that," Dan shouted.

Nodding, Marty leaped over a downed man to pull a burly tree cutter off Bob's back. He spun him around and punched him senseless, then dropped him to the floor. Bob wiped the blood from his nose and then leaped onto the back of a man who had Tom's head in a viselike grip. With one hard bite to the man's ear, he forced him to release the dazed Tom and turn his attention to the man on his back. Shrugging Bob off, the man squared up for a mighty blow. Swinging from the heels, the husky lumberjack would have torn Bob's head off had he connected, but the quicker Bob easily ducked under the blow and then drove several quick lefts and rights into the man's exposed stomach. Gasping for breath, the man dropped to his knees, out of the fight.

John and James were slugging away with two drunken cowboys who had joined in the ruckus for the sheer joy of it. Seeing that they were holding their own and that Bob and Tom had pulled away the two men who had been plummeting Walt, and were now savagely pounding their heads with their fists, Marty turned his attention back to Mick and his opponent.

The two main antagonists had worked their way over to a corner of the room, still slugging and weaving, Big George trying to get Mick encased in his massive arms, and Mick pounding George's midsection with hammerlike blows. Marty shoved his way through the clusters of battling bodies to where he could watch Mick's back. Someone swiped a fist past his cheek and he retaliated so quickly and accurately that he was not bothered any further.

Marty struggled to stay in a position where he could protect Mick's back and still watch both the fighting Irishman and the rest of his men. James and John threw their opponents over the bar like two sacks of cornmeal and turned back, ready to take on anyone who wanted some of them.

Wiping the blood from his cheek, John shouted happily at Marty, "A hell of a fight, ain't it?" Then he and John waded into a pile of who that had gathered around where Bob and the two boys were struggling with three drunken lumberjacks.

Soon Marty could not tell who was fighting whom. He pushed a whooping drunk waving a bottle back toward the center of the room and moved to follow Mick and Big George as their epic battle took them down the wall toward the bar again. George grabbed Mick in his huge arms and dragged both of them to the floor. They rolled around awhile, slamming fists into each other every chance they got, but without much success. Finally, Mick flipped George over his back into the back wall with a crash that shook the building.

Otis caught Marty's eye, shrugging in resignation. Then he released his hold on the arm of one of his cowboys. With a shout, the man rushed toward Marty, eager to get in a few licks before the fighting stopped.

Instead, he ran into a rock-hard fist and collapsed on the floor, out of the battle before he even got in a first swing. Otis said something to another man, and that man stepped toward Marty. This one was more deliberate and Marty took a couple of hard blows to the head before he got in the clincher, dropping the cold-cocked cowboy for the count. Marty turned his attention back to Mick and George. Mick and George were back on their feet, both men repeatedly slamming hard blows into his opponent's midsection. Mick's strategy seemed to be working. Big George was dropping his hands ever lower as the hammer blows took their toll. Suddenly, Mick switched tactics and gave the gasping George a mighty uppercut, snapping his massive head back and spraying blood from a cut chin all over George's face.

Marty sensed that the end was near. He felt someone tap him on the arm. It was Otis. He flashed a wry grin at Marty and took a halfhearted swipe at him with a long arm. Marty easily ducked under the blow and snapped a quick strike at Otis's jaw. While the blow probably would not have hurt a frail grandmother, Otis folded as if he'd been hit with an ax handle, and slumped to the floor. He made himself comfortable before he closed his eyes and settled in to await the end of the brawl. He had done his duty to his master, Wolf Larkin, and could say he fought until knocked unconscious.

Mick pelted George Parrott with a series of lefts and then a hard right hand to the unfortunate man's bloody chin. George groaned and slumped to the floor, his eyes rolled back in his head.

With a roar of triumph, Mick O'Rourke declared his victory over his foe. He wiped a trickle of blood from the corner of his mouth and turned to see who was next.

No man in the bar wanted any part of Mick. His mighty roar was a signal to the other combatants to cease and desist. Bob and the two boys waded out from a cluster of lumberjacks, their faces bloody but their grins wide and their shoulders square and proud. James and John each dropped an unfortunate cowboy whom they had been plummeting senseless, and waded through downed bodies to the side of Marty and Mick, their eyes bright with victory.

Marty looked around at his battered little army. "Everyone all right?" At their nods, he laughed and slapped the bar with the palm of his hand. "Bartender, drinks for everyone. On me and the Circle B ranch."

As the crowd stampeded to the bar, Otis got up and gathered his men. They picked up the still form of Big Nose George and hauled him out the door, leaving the place to the victors. Amid the laughing customers who had witnessed the cross between a riot and a drunken brawl, one spoke for all of them when he slapped Marty on the shoulder and pushed another beer toward a beaming Mick. "Yesiree, Bob. That's one fight fer the ages. Why, there'll be folks talkin' about it fer years to come. Hell, fellas, ya'all became a legend tonight."

And he was right. For years afterward, people stopping off at Warm Springs would ask to see the bar where Big Nose George got whipped by Big Mick O'Rourke.

When the exuberant Circle B men left the saloon around midnight, they had hoisted so many drinks in congratulation and celebration that none could begin to walk a straight line. "How you feeling, Mick?" Marty asked. He had noticed that his friend was gingerly rubbing his left side from time to time.

"I think that palooka cracked a couple of me ribs. I'm mighty touchy on that side."

Marty pointed toward the river. "Follow me, fellas. We're headed for the Indian bathtubs for a spell of soaking in the healing waters of the hot springs."

"Take a bath?" Mick grumbled. "I dassent think so."

"No, a soak in the hot springs. It'll make us all feel a lot better. Come on, let Doc Marty be the judge of what's best for you."

In quick order, the drunken and sore men were soaking in the hot sulfur springs, moaning and groaning but in reality savoring the soothing warmth of the hot waters that flowed over their aching bodies.

When they arrived back at the ranch, only Dan and Marty were still awake. The others were sawing z's in the back of the wagon. One after the other, they had tied their horses' reins to the jouncing wagon and climbed in the back to fall into drink-induced sleep. It was a quiet bunch that arrived at the bunkhouse. Paco came out and helped the groggy men into their bunks.

Marty walked over to the main house and knocked on the door. He saw the light and figured that Julia had stayed awake worrying about them.

"We're back and everyone is fine," he announced. "Mick cleaned the clock of Larkin's hired bully."

"Thank God," Julia answered. "I was afraid to go to bed, fearing you'd all show up with your heads busted."

Marty then realized that he had left Julia and Johnny at the dry goods store. "How'd you get home?"

"Jimmy Campbell brought us in his buggy. I think he saw it as a good way to be out of town during the ruckus."

"Smart of Jimmy. Well, good night."

"Good night to you. See you in the morning."

The next morning Marty was relieved to find that all except Mick were none the worse for their barroom battering. Walt and Tom proudly displayed their shiners and cuts as badges of honor.

Mick was moving a little slowly. He limped back to the bunkhouse from breakfast and sat heavily on his bunk. When Marty inquired about his needs, he replied, "That jasper had a right hand like a mule kick. I feel like I was stomped on and left fer dead, bucko. If it's all right by you, I'm gonna stay close to me bed this day. Some rest is what I'm needin'."

"That's probably a good idea, Mick. You take it easy today. By tomorrow perhaps you'll be feeling more like your old self."

Marty went outside and bid another farewell to James and John Stagg. Dan was to drive them back to town to catch the afternoon stage to Grand Encampment. Julia and Johnny were also accompanying Dan to attend church.

"So long, Marty," John said, shaking his hand. "We had a grand time, didn't we, James?"

"It was somethin' fer the books. I'll be tellin' my grand-kids about the time I cleaned out Warm Springs with Mick O'Rourke and the Circle B cowboys. You ever need us agin, jus' send the word. We'll hurry on up. Right, John?"

"In a bedbug's fart we will. So long, fellas."

Marty watched as the wagon rode off; then he turned to Walt. "Walt, you and Tom are gonna guard the ranch today. Bob, you and Paco get saddled up. I want to take a look at the high country we own. And the lay of the land beyond that."

"Be glad to, Marty. Paco, you know much about the land beyond the ranch boundaries?"

"Oh, *sí,* Many times I herd Senor Stonecipher's sheep well back into the hills in search of good graze."

"Well, let's get our canteens and some chow. I want to take a good look at what we have up there," Marty said.

Paco led the way on his paint, chattering about his time working for Stonecipher and their plans for furnishing the railroads and the logging camps with mutton. As they reached the boundary between grassland and the forested slopes leading to the high mountains, Marty looked back toward the ranch. As high as he was, he had a good overview of the ranch land below. It was easy to see the grove of trees and the surrounding green of Deer Creek, the gentle rising away from the low point of the valley, where the creek bed wound its way southwest toward the flat land beyond. He could even make out the logging road that was the southern boundary line for the ranch. Across from the road was the Olsen ranch, which went all the way to the river on its southern boundary.

Even in the short time he had been at the ranch, the green area had shrunk noticeably. Marty looked to the west. The Walcott Road was not visible, but it could not be far outside his range of vision. Just beyond the road lay Wolf Larkin's ranch. Marty turned and looked to the east. The trees blocked his view, so he turned to Paco and Bob.

"How far does the forest go before we run into mountains high enough to still have snow on 'em?"

Bob scratched his chin. "I'd say we've got six or more miles afore you reach the upper tree line. Wouldn't you think so, Paco?"

Paco nodded in agreement, then pushed his horse on ahead. "Let me show you the sheep, Senor Marty. They are just over this small hill, in a valley with green grass."

Marty followed Paco as the young Basque wove his pony through the trees. Suddenly, they broke out of the forest into a small valley filled with lush grass and completely surrounded by heavy forest. Marty's interest immediately increased. The sheep were clustered at the far end, contentedly munching grass and ignoring the interlopers.

"Paco, are there other small valleys and meadows like this around here?"

"Oh, *sí*, Senor Marty. There are many of them. Some are clear to the high mountains and some are not far from here."

"Are we still on Circle B land?"

"I think so. I am not certain where the line is, to be honest."

"Bob, anybody ever run cows up here?"

"Not that I know of, Boss."

"Tomorrow, I think we ought to bring our herd up here. Let the grass recover down in the valley, so there's some winter feed when the snows come."

"I think we'll have to put a man with the herd all the time. There are wolves up here. They'd have a feast on beef if we just let the cattle run free."

"I agree. Other than that, it should work, don't you think?"

"I think so, Boss."

"Okay, tomorrow you and the boys run the herd up here. We'll switch herders every three days or so. You start, Bob. I think we've just made a big discovery. Paco, lead us up on higher. Let's go all the way to the tree line."

They ran across a couple more mountain meadows as they worked their way up, ever deeper into the forest and always climbing. About three miles farther on, they came across a bright, blue lake, tucked in a slot in the mountains, the sun sparkling off its clear, cold water.

"My gosh, this is one beautiful lake!" Marty exclaimed.

"It is Deer Lake, Senor Marty."

"It feeds Deer Creek?"

"I think so."

They rode around the lake, following the shoreline. They crossed over several fast-moving streams feeding icy water from the high snows into the lake. At the far side, Marty stopped and let Pacer have a drink. He looked back at the spot from which they had ridden.

"Where does it go? The water, I mean. If it feeds Deer Creek, why isn't the creek running hard? As big as this lake is and as fast as water is feeding into it, there oughta be a hell of a lot more water flowing down Deer Creek."

"I don't rightly know," Bob answered.

"I don't either. Bob, find me a place where I can see down into the valley. Somewhere high."

Chapter 27

Río Escondido

"Whatda ya thinkin' about, Boss?"

"Bob, you ever hear the Mex term *río escondido*?"

"No, can't say that I have. What's it mean?"

"It roughly means 'hidden river.' I see a lake that's got half a dozen streams feeding into it, each one bigger than our Deer Creek, yet I don't see any water flowing out. I think that there's an underground opening somewhere around the bottom of that lake and it's flowing down below the ground. Some or all of the water from here is going past our place right below the ranch house. That's why the well water is so cold and why the valley is so green in the spring. When the water is really running out of the mountains, it must push up to just below the ground."

Bob led the way out of the tree line and upward on the high slopes of the mountain. Short grasses and lichen were all that survived that high of an elevation and cold, thin air. Marty kept looking over his shoulder until he finally said, "Stop. We're high enough."

Marty turned in his saddle and pointed at the lake. "See?

The water can't flow north or south. Too much high ground. It has to be going west, until it comes out at the North Platt."

"Why, it does," Bob announced. "Right below Warm Springs is a big spring that feeds ice cold water into the river. Everyone is always sayin' how funny it is that there's the hot springs and just a half mile away the springwater is near to freezin'."

As they rode back down the mountain and through the woods toward the Circle B, they stopped at the same mountain meadow they had passed on the way up. Marty suggested they stop and eat their sandwiches there. Afterward, he walked the meadow, checking the grass quality and quantity. As he did, he worried over an idea that kept flittering around in his mind. As they came out of the trees above the ranch house, it became clear to him.

"Bob, you ever see a windmill? The ones like the Sears and Roebuck catalog have?"

"Yeah. Round, with paddles that are way up in the air. Pumps water outa the ground. I ain't quite sure how."

"That's the kind. What I think we should do is drill some wells, one up there at the northeast end of the property, another by the ranch house, a couple more over there, where the green grass runs out." Marty pointed.

Bob nodded. "Yeah. Then what?"

"Look." Marty got off Pacer, took a small twig, and drew in the dust. First he made a rough outline of the ranch property. Then he put small x's where he wanted the windmills placed. "If there's water under the ground, like I think, we put windmills pumping up water at these points. The one to the northeast will feed all the land above the ranch house. The one in the middle will feed Deer Creek. Keep it running all year. The ones to the south will irrigate the land that's dry now, increasing our grass coverage."

"How will you get water from the windmill to where you want it to water grass?"

"Like the farmers do in Arkansas when they plant rice. They dig little trenches with a plow, then run water down it. Everywhere they want water to flow over the land, they cut a little slot in the trench. When it's wet enough for them, they fill it in." Marty scratched a line in the dirt and drew radiating lines running away from it. "See, you could get a lot of coverage from just a few offshoots from a water trench running down that high ground to the east of Deer Creek."

Marty nodded. "This is what Sam Bennett meant when he said that the land had something that made it ten times the value he paid for it."

"The way you describe it, we oughta be able to grow grass on the entire valley floor. Man, that'd be something. I wonder if Wolf Larkin knows about this." Bob looked again at the drawing in the dust, visualizing what Marty had described.

"I'd bet my Sunday shirt he does. That's why he's so damned anxious to get his hands on it. Paco, you'd better go back and night over with the sheep. I'll send Tom up to relieve you in a couple of days."

"Sí, Patron. Send Tom with some supplies and little Juan maybe. I will stay until Friday. I enjoy being with my sheep."

"Good. Come on, Bob. We gotta get into town and see if Jimmy Campbell knows where any well-diggers are."

"Someone will dig the wells fer us?"

"Sure. I saw 'em doing it in Nebraska. If they can dig there, they can dig in Wyoming."

"Fellas with picks and shovels?"

"No, they have a really interesting system. They have a steam engine and a tall tower. The steam engine pulls a real heavy iron spike up and then drops it. You should see them cut through the earth. They can drill ten, twenty, or even more feet a day."

"Well, I'll swan. I can't imagine. What'll they think of next?"

Marty and Bob made the ride to Warm Springs. They found Jimmy Campbell working in his garden, next to his wood-clapboard-and-batten house built on the west bank of the North Platt River. The house was painted a gleaming white, with green shutters the same color as the paint job on the county building.

"Howdy, Marty. Step down and rest yur rump. Hot, ain't it? Care for a drink or maybe a glass of lemonade?"

"Lemonade sounds good. Thanks. How 'bout you, Bob?"

"Suits me too."

"You Bob Short? Used to work for Wolf Larkin?"

"Yep, that's me."

Campbell shook his head, his ruddy face a bit concerned. "Wolf ain't gonna like that, Bob. He's a big believer in stayin' loyal to the brand."

"Well, he shoulda thought of that afore he brought Big Nose George Parrott up here to deal with Sam Bennett."

"Did he?"

"You bet he did. I heard him give the order to Otis Beecher to send for him. The next thing anyone knows, Sam is back-shot. Then Parrott rides off, his pockets full of money."

Jimmy's wife, Hattie, appeared with three glasses of cool lemonade, and the three men chatted for a few minutes. As soon as she retreated into the house, Jimmy turned his attention back to Bob. "You willing to repeat that in front of a judge if I can find corroborating evidence?"

"Sure will."

"Good. I'm gonna start looking into the shooting again."

"First thing to do, Jimmy, is get ahold of Big Nose George's rifle. See if it shoots the same bullet that killed Sam," Marty said.

"I'll do that. You have any idea where Parrott is right now?"

Marty shook his head. "Nope, can't help you there. He may have slunk off after the butt-whippin' Mick gave him yesterday."

"He may be out at Wolf's ranch. One of the guys said they loaded him into a wagon and drove off that way yesterday." Bob grinned at the memory of the barroom battle.

"I'll look forward to hearing what you find out, Jimmy. Meanwhile, we came to town to ask you if you know of any well drillers around these parts?"

"Well-drillers? You gonna dig yourself a new well?"

"We might be, yes."

"Well, lemme think. Seems to me that a fella down in Grand Encampment has hisself a rig and digs wells. Want me to find out for ya?"

"Please. If you find someone, tell him I've got a couple of weeks' work for him at the ranch. Well, we'd best get on back. I'm still not sure whether Wolf will try anything shady against Julia or not. I don't want to get too far away from her for the time being."

"I understand. If I hear from the well digger, I'll give him your message."

Marty and Bob mounted up and rode away from the house. Bob waited until they were out of Jimmy Campbell's hearing range. "You ain't gonna tell him about the water under the ranch?"

"Not yet. It may not come to pass. If it does, the less anyone knows about it for the time being, the better."

"Whatever you say, Boss. While we're here, I need to git a few things if I'm gonna be up in the high pasture with them cows fer a spell."

"I'll go with you. I need some cartridges for my six-gun as well."

*   *   *

As they headed for the store, Julia and Dan were exiting the church with the rest of the Sunday worshippers. Julia spotted Pam Olsen and waved her over. "Hello, Pam. Lovely day, isn't it?"

"Sure is, Julia."

"Pam, this is one of my hands, Dan Laderman. Dan and I met on the wagon train trip out west through Kansas."

"Hello, Dan." Pam smiled at Dan, heartily shaking his hand. "Please call me Pam. Hello, here's Otis. Hey, Otis. Have you met Julia Bennett? Julia, this is Otis Beecher. He's the foreman at Larkin's ranch. I've been trying to get him to come over and work for my pa for several years now."

"Aw, Pam. You know your pa ain't gonna make me no foreman while Wil Horner's still able to climb into a saddle. Howdy, Mrs. Bennett. I was at your place with Wolf a few days ago. You're fixin' it up right nice."

"Hello, Mr. Beecher." Julia's voice was cool and formal.

"Oh, Julia, Otis is an alright fella. He's stuck working for a man he doesn't like or respect. Isn't that right, Otis?"

"Now, Miss Pam, don't talk like that. A man's gotta be loyal to the brand he rides for."

"If you ask me, Mr. Beecher, a man shouldn't work for a man he does not respect," Julia said.

"There ain't that many foreman jobs available around here right now, Mrs. Bennett. I'd rather work than starve."

"Well, I'd rather starve than work for Wolf Larkin."

Pam touched Julia's arm. "Now, Julia, let's don't argue on such a nice day. Why don't you and Johnny come over to my place for lunch tomorrow? I'll make my dried-apricot pie. It's good, isn't it, Otis?"

"Oh, my, yes. I always try to buy it at the fall cake and pie sale at the school fund-raiser. It's the best pie in the county, maybe the territory."

The four continued to talk for a few more minutes, then went their various ways. Julia turned to Dan as they drove the wagon toward the ranch. Johnny was happily playing with his toy soldiers in the back. "You think I was rude to Beecher?"

"No, not really. I think he's gonna have to make a decision real soon as to where he wants to stand. Marty has things moving along real fast. Larkin is gonna have to make his play soon or just give it up."

"I hope he'll just leave us alone. That's my hope."

"If he doesn't, I'm glad we've got Marty on our side."

"He's a killer, Dan. Don't ever think he can be your friend."

"If you mean do I know he's a bounty hunter, I do. Still, I think he's got more integrity and honor than most men I'll ever meet."

"He killed my husband. I'll never forgive him for that."

"What?"

Julia spent the rest of the trip home telling Dan her story. After he had put away the mules and returned to the bunkhouse, he sat quietly on the porch, smoking his pipe and thinking about what he had heard. He had to get his mind around the concept of Marty as the cold-blooded killer that Julia had described. His impression of Marty and her story seemed so far apart. He stayed up late, wrestling with the problem. When he went into the bunkhouse, everyone was fast asleep, Walt's soft snores reverberating around the room. Dan put his hand under his head and stared at the dark ceiling, trying to sort through all he had learned.

Marty had everyone working the next day, and when it was time for Julia and Johnny to leave for Pam's, he was the only other person at the ranch house.

"If you'll wait a minute, I'll ride over with you and Johnny," he told the impatient Julia.

"No thanks. We're not going anywhere near town or Larkin's spread. We'll be just fine. I'll enjoy being away from everything for a little while. I really don't need nor want you to accompany us."

"All right, Julia. But you keep your eyes open and don't get careless. Agree?"

She nodded and flicked the reins against the rumps of the mules. "Giddyap, mules."

Marty watched her go with a nagging feeling of trepidation. However, the herd of cattle was just about to enter the tree line and he really wanted to see them safely displaced to the mountain meadow. Spurring Pacer toward the herd, he cast one last glance at the receding figure of the wagon.

Pam warmly greeted Julia and Johnny and showed Julia around the place while Johnny played with the Olsens' two wolfhounds. The pie was as good as Otis had promised. The afternoon slipped quickly past and soon it was time to go. "Come agin, real soon," Pam shouted as they rode out of the yard and up the road toward the logging road.

"You have a good time, Johnny?"

"Yes, Mama. I like Pam's doggies. Me and the dogs jumped from the hayloft into a big stack of hay."

Julia did not answer. Something in the rocks to her left had caught her eye.

Chapter 28

Desperate Measures

While Julia was on her way to Pam's, Wolf was busy cursing his failed bullyboy.

"By the Lord Almighty, what do I have to do? Take matters in my own hands and do yur jobs fer ya?" Wolf Larkin was in a snit and his attitude was only getting worse. Big Nose George Parrott was hunched in a cowhide chair, holding a drink in one meaty paw and his throbbing head in the other.

"I'm shore sorry, Wolf. He caught me with a lucky punch and then kicked me whilst I was down. I'll beat him dead the next time we meet. I promise."

"I don't give a rat's ass in hell about who beat you up, you thickheaded idiot. I want the Bennett ranch in my hands, once and fer all. We gotta git that woman and her smart aleck brother to give us the deed. That's what's got to be done. We can whip his ass later."

Wolf poured himself another drink and walked over to the window to glare out at his world. He was fuming about the time and opportunities lost. He knew that had he offered a few dollars more, rather than trying to buy the property on the cheap, he might not have had any of this trouble. When Stonecipher rode over to tell him that he would not accept Wolf's offer, Wolf had lost his temper and shot him dead. He had been fortunate that no one was in the house when he killed the weird Englishman. He had taken the body out near the Walcott Road and dumped it. He had fired one round from Stonecipher's pistol into the air and then gone for help. Jimmy Campbell had bought his story about Stonecipher killing himself, but then, in the mother of all screwups, his lawyer had missed the sale of the land in Laramie and Sam Bennett had shown up. He had tried to get Bennett to sell, but his dogged persistence had aroused the man's curiosity about the land. When Wolf had tried the last time, and Bennett had laughed at him and blurted out his awareness of the underground water source, Wolf knew that Sam had to die as well.

"At least you did that one right," he snarled at the miserable Parrott. Parrott had slipped into town and ambushed the man deep in the woods in back of his house, with no witnesses. Wolf figured his luck had changed when the other Bennett brother had gotten into a fight with his emissaries back in Missouri. When James Bennett had killed one, even though the fight had been provoked by his men, and he had gotten a reward out against James, Larkin had thought it would be easy pickings to obtain the land from the wife. Who would have thought she would show up in Wyoming, planning on making the ranch her new home?

He saw Otis riding into the front yard. Why on earth did he allow his foreman to waste every Sunday morning listening to the town Bible-thumper? He walked out onto the front porch. "Otis, tomorrow I want to ride over to the Bennett place. I want to talk with the widow lady about selling the ranch."

"She's gonna be visitin' Pam Olsen fer lunch, Boss. I suspect she'll be back at her place around four or five in the afternoon. I heard 'em talkin' about it after church services this mornin'."

Larkin was quiet for a moment, thinking furiously. He stared at Otis, a determined look on his face. "Fergit what I said. First thing tomorrow, you take some men and run a couple of hundred head from the east range across the Bennett place and up into the hills beyond. I want our beef on their property. Understand?"

"I understand what you want, Boss. I just don't understand why."

"Don't you worry about it. You just do it." Larkin turned back into his house and went to the chair beside Big Nose George. "George, you listen to me. I've decided to take matters into my own hands. Here's what we're gonna do." Wolf Larkin and Big Nose George spent the rest of the day refining their plan.

As soon as Otis and six of his most dependable cowboys left the next morning, Wolf walked over to the bunkhouse. The three men who were left behind were the gun hands Wolf had hired when Sam Bennett had bought the Stonecipher ranch. Otis would not use them when it came to herding cattle. "You boys stay close to the bunkhouse. Me and George are gonna need you later today," Wolf told them.

"Otis told us to ride the south pasture and push the cows there toward Rock Springs," the oldest answered. Called Grubby by everyone else, he was a slender, balding man with a bad eye, the result of a knife fight that went against him years earlier.

"Just do what I told ya. I'll handle Otis," Wolf snarled.

Shortly after noon, Wolf ordered everyone mounted up and ready to ride. He led the way to a small hill covered in man-sized boulders, just a few hundred yards from the logging road that separated the Bennett place from the Olsen ranch. "Settle down, boys. We're a'waitin' on a lady and her brat coming from the Olsen ranch. She oughta be along in an hour or two. One of you git up there on that big rock where you can see her coming. The rest of you find some shade and take it easy. We're here until she shows up, no matter how long it takes."

It was three hours later when Grubby called down to Wolf and the others. "A wagon coming. Looks like a woman and a kid."

"No outriders?"

"Nope."

"Good. Give a signal when they reach the bottom of the hill. Everyone else, git mounted and ready to follow me."

Wolf spurred his horse around the outcropping of large rocks on Grubby's signal. The wagon had stopped right where Wolf wanted to intercept it. Confident as a wolf closing in on a lame deer, he swooped down with the others on the wagon. Big Nose George leaped off his horse and climbed onto the driver's seat, grabbing the reins from Julia's hands.

"What do you want, Mr. Larkin?" she asked with icy contempt.

"I think you need to come with me, Mrs. Bennett. We got some business to do. Tell that boy that if he don't shut up, I'll have George wring his neck."

Julia immediately gathered her crying son in her arms. "You'll pay for this, Wolf Larkin. Just you wait and see."

"I don't think so, Mrs. Bennett. Anyhow, you jus' keep yur mouth shut and do what yur told. If you do, you and the boy can go home soon. Otherwise, you and I are gonna git to know one another a lot better."

Julia rode the rest of the way to Wolf's ranch house in silence. With Johnny along, her options were limited. Her best bet was to cooperate until Marty and the others missed her and started to look for her.

When they reached the ranch house, Wolf hustled Julia

and Johnny inside. He left them in the back bedroom, guarded by George, and went out to confer with Grubby. "You boys hide the wagon over to the line shack at Rock Springs and hurry on back here."

"Gotcha, Boss."

Wolf, a look of victory on his face, watched them leave. He turned and walked back inside, heading directly to the bedroom. Julia was seated in one of the chairs, a sniffling Johnny on her lap. She was softly consoling him when Wolf stepped into the room.

"Well, Mr. Larkin. Now that you have us, what are you going to do with us?"

"It's like this, Mrs. Bennett. Tomorrow, you're gonna go into Warm Springs with me and sell me yur ranch. You'll be my guest tonight."

"What makes you think I'm going to sell to you?"

"If you give me any trouble, I will have George tear off your boy's arms and legs, one at a time. George, pick up the brat by one leg and hold him straight out."

Big Nose George grabbed Johnny and dangled him by one leg at head height, the boy wailing and thrashing in terror. George was grinning like the dumb brute he was. Julia's face blanched at the sight. She grabbed Johnny from George and squeezed him to her until he quit screaming.

"Wolf, Mr. Larkin. You can't be that cruel. He's just a child."

"And he'll never reach manhood if you give me any trouble. Tomorrow morning we go into town and you sign over the ranch or he gits tore apart. You understand?"

"Yes, yes, I understand. I'll do anything you say. Just don't hurt Johnny."

"Now, you two git comfortable. Here's a bed and a necessary pot. You ain't comin' out till tomorrow. The window's nailed shut and the door'll be locked. Don't ask, or cry, or try to git out. Just stay quiet and don't cause no trouble and everything'll be all right."

After the two were locked in the room and Wolf poured George a stiff drink, George asked the question of the day. "You ain't gonna let them two go once they sign the deed over to you, are ya?"

"Gawd, no. Once the deed is in my hands, you'll have to break their necks. Then we'll drive 'em in their wagon off a cliff on the Medicine Bow Peak Road. We'll say they sold out and left for Cheyenne using the peak shortcut and lost control. After that, you'll have a five-thousand-dollar bonus due you."

George grunted. "Sounds good to me, Wolf. Think anyone'll come looking fer them tonight?"

"I don't know. We'll keep Grubby and his boys in the house with us as insurance. They can keep watch until daylight tomorrow."

Wolf sipped his drink, a cruel smirk on his scarred face. His plan was working exactly as he had envisioned it. He wondered if the others at the Bennett ranch even knew that the woman was missing yet.

Marty believed that his plan for the cattle was going to work. As long as the cattle had good grass in the meadow, they were not inclined to stray off into the woods. He had run a few of the more adventuresome ones that did try back to the herd. He and Bob agreed that if someone stayed with the cows, they would not go far from the meadow. He waited until Bob was settled in and then left the meadow with Dan, Walt, and Tom, heading back to the ranch.

As they exited the tree line, Marty looked for the wagon on the road from Pam Olsen's. Then he squinted toward the ranch. He did not see the horses in the corral or the wagon. "Tom, you've got keen eyes. You see Julia and the wagon anywhere?" he said.

Everyone shaded their eyes and looked for any sign. "Nope," Tom announced. "Nary a sign of her."

"Damn," Marty grumbled. "She oughta be on the road or home by now. Something's not right. Tom, go get Bob. He knows this area better than anyone. Get Paco too. Meet us at the ranch. Go, boy.

"Dan, you make tracks to Pam Olsen's place. If Julia's there, escort her home. Me and Walt will head for the ranch house, just in case she's already there. Dan, if she's already left the Olsens', try to follow her tracks. We'll meet on the road no matter what. If the tracks leave the road, follow them, but leave us sign so we know it's you."

"Gotcha, Marty." Dan spurred his horse away, galloping hard toward the Olsen ranch.

"Come on, Walt. Let's get on down to the ranch house."

Their search was fruitless. Marty and Walt headed down the road toward the Olsen ranch, leaving Mick behind, in case Julia showed up there unexpectedly. The tracks of Julia's wagon were fairly easy to pick out in the dirt path, but now and then a layer of shale and rock sticking up through the dust showed no sign of the wagon's passage. Just as they reached the hill covered with rocks where Wolf had sprung his ambush, Marty spotted Dan and Pam Olsen and another man riding toward them.

Pam rode up to Marty, her face concerned. "Hello, Marty. This is my foreman, Wil Horner. Wil, Marty, and Walt, isn't it? Have you seen any sign of Julia yet?"

"Howdy." Marty's greeting was abrupt. He was becoming more worried by the minute. "Nope. When did Julia leave you, Pam?"

"Around three, I think. She's had plenty of time to get home by now."

"Dan, you see any sign of Julia's wagon headed toward the ranch?"

"It was clear as a bell just over the rise back there." Dan

pointed to the rear. "We lost it when she entered this rocky area."

"We never saw any sign of her coming out of this rocky stuff. She had to have turned off somewhere in here and the rocky ground hid her tracks." Dan rode his horse in a small circle around everyone. "Even on these rocks, there's bound to be a sign somewhere. We jus' gotta find it."

Marty nodded. "You're right. Dan, you and Horner ride to the east, making a wide loop. Keep your eyes peeled for any sign. Walt, you come with me; we'll swing to the west. Pam, would you be so kind as to go into Warm Springs and tell Jimmy Campbell about this? I have a strong hunch that Julia did not go off on her own. Have him hotfoot it out to the ranch. We'll meet him there."

"Certainly, Marty. You think Wolf Larkin has got her?"

"Damned right I do." Marty's eyes were as cold as the Grim Reaper's. "He'll pay for it with his life if he's hurt her or the boy."

Pam galloped away on her pony. Marty and Walt rode away from the dirt road, looking for anything that would give them a clue as to where Julia had gone. Walt made the first discovery. He was off to Marty's left when he gave a shout.

"Marty, over here."

Marty trotted Pacer toward Walt, who had climbed off his horse, the bay once owned by Junior Raye. He pointed to a scuffed place on the side of a small boulder. "Looks like a wagon wheel slid off this here rock and scratched it. Mighty fresh too."

"Good eye, Walt. Keep on looking. I'll move on down to the right some." Within a few minutes, Marty came upon a natural seep. Fresh wagon tracks and the hoofprints of several horses were still filling up with water. "They came this way, sure as shootin'," he mumbled to himself. "Walt,"

Marty shouted, "go get the others. Julia's wagon came this way." Walt waved his hand and galloped off.

Marty pointed out the sign when the others arrived. "Hasta be them," Wil Horner said. He looked back toward the road and then turned one hundred and eighty degrees on his heel. "Headed straight northwest."

"What will you run into if you keep going that way?" Marty asked.

"Wolf Larkin's place. Nothin' else out that way fer twenty miles."

Marty motioned with his hand. "Come on, let's get back to the ranch. It's almost dark and we'll need to make a plan before morning."

Marty rode with the others back to Julia's ranch house and waited there impatiently until Tom showed up with Paco and Bob. He introduced Wil Horner to everyone and put the boys to work feeding and watering the horses. "We'll be riding them hard before the night's over," he told them. "Make certain they're ready for it." He walked out of the corral and looked down the road. He could hear galloping hoofbeats on the hard dirt of the road. As he waited, Pam and Jimmy Campbell rode into the yard.

"Pam told me what happened," Jimmy said as he swung down from his horse. "You find any sign of her or the boy?"

"Yes, we did, plenty. It all heads for Wolf Larkin's place, straight as an arrow."

"Damn, I was afraid of that. Any chance that Julia went over there on her own?" Jimmy's face was as serious as Marty had ever seen it.

"Nope. The wagon was surrounded by half a dozen horses." He motioned toward the house. "Come on in. We gotta put together a plan to get her and the boy back unharmed."

Jimmy shook his head. "I don't think Wolf would harm a woman or a child, Marty."

"Wolf Larkin is desperate to get this land, Jimmy. He's likely to kill the two of them as fast as he killed Stonecipher or Sam Bennett."

"Now, Marty."

"Don't 'Now, Marty' me, Jimmy. You know Wolf Larkin had a hand in their deaths, so don't try to explain it any other way. The thing to worry about now is how we're gonna handle our problem." Marty got out a sheet of paper and a pencil and gathered everyone around the dinner table. He quickly drew a rough outline of the buildings around Wolf's ranch house. He passed the pencil over to Bob Short. "You have anything to add, Bob?"

Bob took the pencil and made a few adjustments, then handed the paper back to Marty. "That's about how it looks, I reckon."

Marty nodded. "Wil, you with us?"

"You bet I am."

"How about you, Mick?"

"Of course, bucko, although I must admit me fists is me best weapon. I ain't much fer shootin' a rifle or pistol."

"That's all right. We welcome your help." Marty pointed at a spot on the map. "Wil, you take Walt and set up a firing position on this little knob. If it comes to a firefight, you can cover the bunkhouse from there. I want to keep Larkin's men separated from the main house as much as possible. Jimmy, you, Paco, Dan, Mick, and Bob will come with me. We'll work our way down this streambed to just about the corner of the corral. We can cover the front and side of the house from there. Bob, where would you think Wolf would put Julia and Johnny?"

Bob drew the rooms of the main house on the paper. "Right here. This is an extra bedroom. There's a cot and dresser in it and only one window, too small to wiggle out through."

Marty studied the drawing. "If we're careful not to fire at

that window, Julia and the boy should be safe. The walls are adobe, and bullets shouldn't penetrate them."

"Whatda you want me to do, Marty?" Jimmy asked.

"You need to step up, Jimmy, in your job as county magistrate. You have to convince Wolf to let Julia and the boy go. That'll preclude any shooting at all. But, if he refuses, I'm gonna blast my way in there and get her out. Make him understand that. Give her up or die."

Chapter 29

Go Down Fighting

At midnight, Marty awakened everyone and gathered them in the kitchen of the main house for hot coffee, courtesy of Pam Olsen, who had stayed over even though Marty had urged her to return to her home.

"Nonsense," she had replied. "Julia may need me. We don't know what she has gone through. I'm not gonna be anywhere but close to you until Julia is safely back with us."

"Well, you surely don't think you're going with us when we confront Wolf Larkin, do you?"

"I most certainly am. I'll ride with you or after you, but I am going."

"Well, I know enough not to face off against a determined woman, but I have one requirement, and you'll follow it or I'll hog-tie you to a post until we get back."

"What is it?"

"You go where I tell you and you stay there until I tell you it's safe to leave. Will you agree to that?"

Pam grimaced but finally shrugged in defeat, afraid that Marty might indeed tie her down. "All right, I agree."

Marty gulped his coffee, then gathered his gear along

with the others. When everyone was ready, they rode out into the darkness, headed for Wolf Larkin's ranch. Bob took the lead, as he was most familiar with the way. Marty rode alongside Pam. She could not stay quiet; her adrenaline was so pumped up in anticipation of the coming confrontation.

"Remember your promise, Pam. If it comes to a fight, I want you where I put you. I don't want to worry any about your welfare. I've got the safety of the others to keep me busy."

"I gave you my promise, Marty. Don't fret so."

"I've been there before. I know how a gun battle can go bad."

"I know. Julia told me about you and her husband."

"And?"

"And I think she's lucky in some ways."

"How's that?"

"I imagine most bounty hunters would tell her to go pick daisies if she put her demands on them. I think, Mr. Marty Keller, that you're a man of rare character and principles."

The unsolicited praise left Marty unsure of how to respond, so he sort of grumped a snort of a reply and rode on ahead of the column, where he could watch for Bob Short. In fifteen minutes Bob rode out of the darkness and stopped the column at the foot of a small rise. Though it was probably unnecessary, he spoke in a hoarse whisper. "The ranch is just over the top of this rise. From there we can see the main house easily, in the full moonlight."

"Everyone off their horses," Marty commanded. "Pam, you take them over there, by that clump of trees." He pointed emphatically with a forefinger. "You stay there with the horses until I send for you. The rest of us'll go ahead on foot. Everyone bring his water and ammunition."

The group of men crept to the top of the rise. The ranch was bathed in the diffused blue-white glow of the moon. A light burned in the main house; otherwise the ranch was dark and quiet.

"It don't look like they're a'waitin' on us, do it?" Bob said.

"They have to be," Marty answered. "It's crazy to think any other way. Wil, you and Walt need to find a place over there, where you can cover the bunkhouse."

The Olsen foreman nodded. "Understand. We'll get us a good spot and wait fer you to call the tune." He and Walt scooted away, rifles at the ready.

Marty turned to Tom and Mick. He pointed to a stand of trees behind the main house, at a distance of about one hundred yards. "You two need to sneak down there and cover the back. Don't let anyone out. Be very careful. The room where Julia is will be just to the right of the back door. Don't fire any shots into it. Be sure and wait for my signal, unless they come out firing at you."

"Gotcha, Marty." Tom scurried off.

Marty turned to Jimmy Campbell. "Jimmy, there's a big water trough just to the front of the corral. Isn't that right, Bob?"

At Bob's grunt of affirmation, Marty continued. "Jimmy, take Dan and Paco with you and make your way to the trough. Paco needs to be close to use the shotgun effectively and Dan works best with a handgun. They can cover you when you talk to Larkin. Bob and I'll set up at those rocks to the left of the front gate. We'll be able to see the front and side of the house from there. We'll be about fifty yards from you, so you shout if you're forced away from the trough and we'll cover you as you go through the corral toward right where we are now. We'll fall back to here if we find out we're outgunned."

Marty looked up at the night sky. Some clouds were slowly drifting toward the moon. "Once the moon is obscured, we'll move in. Don't forget, we don't do anything until sunrise, unless it's forced upon us. If that happens, don't be kind. Cut them down in a heartbeat."

After a few anxious minutes, a thick cloud blew across the moon, and the men split up, headed for their fighting positions. Marty and Bob made themselves comfortable behind the cluster of rocks and prepared firing positions from which they had good views of the quiet ranch house. Marty followed the shadows of his men as they moved up, through the corral, to their place behind the long water trough. He carefully watched the house in case they were observed, but all stayed quiet. Everyone was in position. Now all they had to do was wait out the night until dawn. Twice men came out of the main house and walked around the yard, but they never came close enough to spot the hidden men.

Big Nose George carried a cup of steaming coffee into the living room and looked out a window at the new day. What he saw caused him to spill the hot liquid down the front of his shirt. "Boss! Boss!" he shouted at Larkin, who was asleep in a big chair by the fireplace. "Come here, quick. There's three men standin' outside by the corral."

Cursing like a drunken mule skinner, Larkin leaped from the chair where he had dozed off and headed for the window. Jimmy Campbell was standing by the main water trough along with two other men. One had only one arm, which meant he was probably Julia Bennett's hired hand.

"Dammit, George, how'd they git there? You're supposed to be guardin' the place. Git the men to a window, rifles ready. I'll find out what he wants." He shouted toward the kitchen, "Cookie, take the shotgun and guard the rear door. Don't let nobody inside, got it?"

"Gotcha, Boss," the grizzled old cook answered.

Wolf Larkin stepped just outside the front door, leaving it open for a quick retreat.

"Hello, Campbell. Whadda ya want?"

"Morning, Wolf. You got Julia Bennett and her boy in there with you?"

"What makes you think that?"

"We followed her wagon tracks here. She's in there, Wolf. I want to talk to her."

"You're in over yur head, Campbell. Best you git on back to town and mind yur own business."

Campbell took several steps toward the door. "Now, Wolf, you know I can't do that. Please, bring Julia out so I can talk to her."

"I'm tellin' ya for the last time, Campbell. Get outa here and mind yur own business."

"Please, Wolf. Before there's somethin' more serious to happen. Let me talk to Julia."

As Campbell took one more step, Big Nose George shot him from his position at the front window. Campbell went reeling back, his hands pressed against his forehead, then collapsed in front of the water trough.

Paco fired both barrels of his shotgun at the window, driving George to cover beneath the windowsill. Wolf Larkin ducked back inside, slamming the heavy wooden door, and raced to the window to peer outside. He was just in time to see Dan Laderman drag Campbell behind the trough and then start firing his pistol at the front door of Wolf's home.

"Dammit, George, why'd ya shoot Campbell?"

"I got tired of hearing 'im argue with ya. You're gonna have to kill 'im all anyhow, so let's git to it."

"There might be more than jus' them two; we don't know. Ya acted too quick and now we're stuck."

"You was stuck the minute ya grabbed the gal and her brat."

One of Wolf's men took aim with his rifle out the side window. "I see someone over there, by the rock pile." He slammed back, a spreading stain of red covering the front of his shirt.

Marty had seen Campbell mercilessly shot down. He had watched as Dan and Paco had recovered the friendly redhead to the safety of the big water trough. He had aimed at the side window as the outline of a man had become visible. "I hope that's Larkin," he had muttered to himself as he'd squeezed off a shot, driving the gunman back into the room.

Larkin gazed without emotion at the body lying on his living room floor. He fired at the water trough, then, swinging his rifle at an extreme angle, fired at the rock pile by the front gate. He received the return fire of at least two men, their shots sending him back a step from the window.

Bob hammered three quick shots at the front window, cussing softly. "Dammit, I had a shot at Big Nose George, but I think I missed 'im."

"That's all right. Take your time and make good shots. We've got them penned in there and they're not going anywhere." As if to punctuate Marty's statement, both Walt's and Wil's rifles started booming from the rise above the bunkhouse and Tom's rifle barked twice from the trees at the rear of the house. Someone inside fired a shotgun in Tom's direction, but at a hundred yards, its effect would be minimal.

A savage look crossed Marty's face. "We've got the rats trapped. Now to smoke 'em out."

Suddenly, one of the men in the bunkhouse burst out the door, running hard for the main house. Bullets from Wil and Walt kicked up dust at his heels but did not bring him down. Just as Marty took aim at the cow-puncher, Dan fired his pistol and hit him high in the thigh. The man fell in a heap beside the front porch and slowly crawled behind the side, seeking what small amount of protection it provided. He lay there, out of the fight with a busted leg, too busy trying to stanch the blood seeping out of his wound to be of further danger to Marty's men.

For twenty minutes the antagonists fired at each other, sporadic gunfire erupting and then dying out. During one of the lulls, Marty heard Wil shouting at someone in the bunkhouse, but could not make out the words. He realized that the fire from the bunkhouse had suddenly quit, but was it because his men had shot everyone inside or was it for some other reason?

Wolf Larkin wiped the sweat and gun smoke from his eyes with the sleeve of his shirt. He sniffed and realized that the dead man on the floor had voided himself as he'd died, and the stench was nauseating. "Sam, you and George drag Frank's body into the parlor. He's stinkin' up the room. Waco, you take Frank's place at the side window. Keep pepperin' those yahoos behind the rock pile."

As Sam moved to comply, Bob saw him pass by the window and thumbed off a snap shot. It caught the gunman high in the ribs, breaking one, and then bounced off to tear a goodly chunk of chest muscle away. Sam spun around and fell, cracking his head on the stone hearth of the fireplace, knocking himself out.

Big Nose George looked coldly at Larkin. "If you want Frank moved, you're gonna have to do it yourself." He fired a couple of shots with his rifle at the rock pile and then at the water trough. Grunting in disappointment, he crouched low and started reloading his rifle. He glanced up at Larkin, who was targeting the rock pile, hoping to get a good shot at the men hiding there. "They've got us penned up good. You got any ideers as to how we're gonna git outa here?"

As Wolf turned to answer Parrott, he heard Marty shouting at him. "Larkin, you're bottled up. We can stay here indefinitely. You want to give it up before anyone else gets hurt?"

"Like hell, you sodbusting SOB."

Chapter 30

End of the Line

Marty answered the defiant reply by slamming two shots against the window frame near Wolf's head. He crouched back down behind the safety of the rocks and said, "Bob, I think we're gonna have to flush that bastard out the hard way. You think you can cover me if I make a dash for the side of the house?"

"Sure, Marty. But maybe you oughta cover me. You're the better shot of the two of us."

Marty checked behind him. Someone was slowly approaching from the low ground to the rear of the rock pile, where he could not be seen from inside the house. As soon as he was covered by the rocks, he ran toward Marty and Bob. It was Walt.

"What's wrong?" Marty asked.

"Everything's fine. Otis Beecher asked why we was shootin' at him and when Wil told 'im, Otis convinced the rest of the cowboys in the bunkhouse that it weren't none of their business. They threw out their guns and are sitting the rest of the fight out. Wil is watchin' 'im while I come over here to tell you."

"Good. That's one less problem to deal with." Marty turned back toward the house, slamming a couple of shots through the nearest window. He crouched back down and looked at Bob and Walt. "The men inside must know that there are two men here. If you and Bob throw a bunch of lead at them, they'll duck back and perhaps not see me coming in from the left there."

He glanced over the pile toward the house, then toward the woods where Tom and Mick were hidden. "Bob, you heard any gunshots from the back of the house toward the woods in a while?"

"Nope, can't say that I have."

"Maybe Tom and Mick got the man inside who was shooting at them. Good. One less to handle there. Well, here goes. Bob, you and Walt keep firing from both ends of these rocks, to keep them thinking there're two men here. I'll slide off to the left. Walt, when I give you the signal, you and Bob open up with everything. I don't want anyone looking out the side window while I'm moving up." Marty eased away from the rock pile, keeping it between him and the house until he reached the small dry streambed. Staying low, he moved toward the rear of the house, cutting the angle of the side window.

In the cover of the trees behind the ranch house, Mick looked over at Tom, hidden behind a tree to his left. "That fella inside ain't shot at us in a while, has he, bucko?"

"I'm certain I saw him spin away after that last shot. You hit him, I'm positive." Tom inched his head up and looked toward the door.

"He may just be playin' possum, waitin' fer us to come out in the open. Let's find out. I'm goin' to that tree thar, halfway to the door. You comin', bucko?"

The young cottonwood offered limited protection. If they made it to the tree and then came under fire again, they would be cut off from moving back into the woods. Tom swallowed his apprehension and nodded. "Let's go, Mick. I'm with you."

They scampered to the small tree and lay down, only partially covered by its slender trunk. "There's Marty," Mick whispered. "Looks like he's gettin' ready to move in on the house. When he goes, I'm going in too, through the back door. You can cover me from here."

When Marty signaled, Walt and Bob opened up with everything they had at the side window. Paco and Dan also blasted away at the front of the house, forcing Wolf, Big Nose George, and Waco to cower behind overturned furniture from the fuselage of deadly bullets whizzing about like angry bees.

Marty dashed to the southwest corner of the house unscathed. Mick lumbered up to join him, breathing like a winded racehorse. "Whew, bucko," he whispered to Marty. "Gunfightin' is a mite tirin'."

"I'm going in through the window, Mick. You want to cover me from here?"

"Nope. That window, there?"

"Yes."

"When you do, I'm comin' through the back door. We'll hit 'em from two sides at once."

"It's mighty dangerous, Mick. Those men are desperate and will kill you without a second thought."

"Only if we don't kill 'em first. Right, bucko?" Mick's big grin was infectious.

"All right, you crazy Irishman." Marty pointed at the rain barrel sitting next to the downspout off the roof. It was nearly empty, thanks to the current spell of dry weather. "I'm gonna throw that barrel through the window. I did the same thing in Bixley, Kansas. It clears out all the glass. Then I'm diving through after it."

He pointed at the rear door. "When you hear the glass breaking, you bust through the rear door. That may draw

their attention away from me as I dive in after the barrel.
You ready?"

Mick chuckled, a deep rumble in his massive chest.
"Can't hardly wait, me bucko."

The two men split up, Marty lugging the barrel as he
carefully moved toward the side window. The splintered
window frame was a testament to the accurate rifle fire of
Bob and Marty.

Marty got to where he could just reach the window. He
hefted the wooden barrel, ready to toss it through the re-
maining glass shards left in the shattered frame. Bob and
Walt halted their firing in preparation for Marty's assault.

Inside the house, Wolf sensed that something was up. He
could see only one way out of the trap he was in. Slithering
across the wood floor on his belly like the snake he was, he
worked his way down the hall and opened the locked door
of Julia's confinement room. She and the boy were cower-
ing in the corner, with the mattress from the cot pulled over
them.

Wolf jerked her to her feet by the hair. "Come on, lady.
Yur gonna help me get outa here."

Screaming in pain and fear, Julia felt herself being jerked
around until Larkin was standing behind her, one hand holding a pistol to her throat and the other wrapped in her long,
brown hair. He reached the door and heard a mighty crash as
the barrel flew through the window and smashed on the
floor of the living room. Almost immediately, the back door
dissolved in a thunderous shower of splinters as Mick burst
through it and staggered to a stop in the kitchen.

The cook sat in the corner by the stove, clumsily trying
to wrap a bloody rag around the bullet hole in his right biceps. When he saw the huge man come crashing through the
back door, he cowered back and scooted himself even farther into the corner, his face blanched with fear and amazement.

Wolf quickly shut the door and snarled in Julia's ear. "You say one word and I'll kill the boy, so help me."

Swallowing a scream, Julia semi-collapsed in the desperate rancher's arms, her will to resist broken. Mick thundered down the hall toward the front room, shouting like a man possessed.

Marty followed the barrel by a scant second, diving head-first through the window and rolling to a stop on the floor, his guns out. He looked up into certain death.

Even as George Parrott's chin dropped in surprise at the sight of a barrel and then a man flying through the side window, he stood and aimed at the rolling man, faster than most men could blink. His finger was tightening on the trigger when Mick burst into the room, bellowing like a runaway bull, swinging his rifle toward Big Nose George. Seeing the hated image of the man who had beaten him in the barroom brawl, the mighty outlaw swung his pistol at Mick without first shooting Marty, who was desperately trying to bring his own guns to bear.

Marty's first shot beat Parrott's shot by a fraction of a second. The hastily aimed bullet fortunately hit the outlaw in the right wrist, breaking it and knocking the pistol out of Big Nose George's hand. Marty's second bullet hit George high in the leg, eliciting a scream of pain as it tore into his thigh muscle. Mick's bullet was aimed at Parrott's black heart, but he had twisted under the impact of Marty's bullet and the shot hit him in the shoulder, knocking the massive bully both down to the ground and unconscious.

Waco had to stand up to get a clear shot at Marty, who was still sprawled on the floor. As he did, his side and back were exposed to Paco, who was still hidden behind the water trough. His quick shot put a dozen lead pellets into Waco's side and arm, knocking the gunman flat on the floor as well.

Marty scrambled to his feet and headed for the room where he thought Julia was. Inside he found Johnny screaming in fear and abandonment, but Julia was gone. "She's gone, along with Larkin," he shouted to Mick, who was gazing in awe at the two men moaning and bleeding on the floor of the living room. "Come on, they had to go out the back."

Marty ran out to see Tom standing by the tree, his rifle held in one hand. "He's got Julia," Tom shouted, and pointed toward the barn. "He said he'd kill her if I tried to stop 'im. They went into the barn."

"Quick, Tom. Head around to the back door. You too, Mick. If he tries to ride out, shoot him. If he tries to use Julia as a shield, shoot his horse. Don't let him get away with her."

"Come on, Mick," Tom shouted as he ran for the rear of the barn.

Marty headed back inside to meet Bob and the rest, who were just stepping up onto the porch to enter the house. "Larkin has Julia. They're in the barn. Come on, we've got to get him surrounded."

The men quickly ran out the front door and took up positions around the barn, covering every possible exit. Marty put his back against the rough wooden boards that made up the siding of the barn, next to the closed front double doors.

"Wolf Larkin, you hear me? Let the woman go, and come out with your hands up."

From inside the barn, Wolf answered in a feral scream, more like a cornered animal than a man. "You git away or I'll kill her. I swear, I'll kill her. You back off and let me ride out or I'll kill her. You hear me? I'll kill her!"

Marty motioned to Mick and Bob to join him at the corner of the barn. "Mick, the doors closed in back?"

"As tight as a tick on a houn's back, me bucko."

"I want you to go to the back doors and count to twenty. Then hit 'em with all you've got. Burst through, if you can. When you do, I'll go in the front door and hope Larkin is looking your way."

Marty looked at Bob. "Bob, you and Walt take that piece of head beam laying by the side of the barn there and, at my signal, hit the front door with everything you've got."

"Sure enough, Marty. You'll be awfully exposed once you get in there."

"I know, but we can't wait. Wolf sounds like he's about to lose it."

The two men hurried off. Marty silently made his count. As he reached twenty, he heard a mighty crash from the rear of the barn. He nodded at Bob and Walt, who was holding an eight-foot-long piece of ten-by-ten-inch beam. They ran hard into the entry door built next to the front double doors. It smashed inward and Marty followed, rolling on his shoulder and coming up with both guns in hand. Wolf Larkin was standing halfway back, Julia still secured in his arms, but facing the rear. As Marty came through the front, Larkin swung her around until she was between his body and Marty's six-guns.

Wolf Larkin's face was twisted and desperate. His eyes were as red as those of a man coming off a three-day drunk. He screamed like a wild animal whose paw was caught in a steel trap.

"I'll kill her! I'll kill her! I mean it. Drop your gun or she's dead. You hear me?"

Marty slowly stood, his gun aimed at Larkin. "Give it up, man. You're surrounded and trapped. You can't get away. Let her go. Do the right thing."

Larkin's scream was even louder and more desperate. "You want her dead? I said drop yur guns or I'll blow her head off. I mean it."

Marty slightly lowered his pistols, his face calm and his voice contained. "All right, Wolf. You win. I'm lowering my guns. See?"

Julia put out a hand, seeking to steady herself. She could hear Larkin and Marty talking, but it seemed as if their words were coming from a long distance away. Her hand brushed up against the wall of the barn. Her fingers closed over an iron spike, nearly ten inches long, lying on a cross-beam. It was a spike like those that had been used to nail the barn's crossbeams together. She clutched it firmly in her hand, and as the pressure from Larkin's hand eased on her hair, she swung the nail with all her might into his right leg, just above the knee.

Screaming in pain, Wolf involuntarily reached for his knee, pulling the gun away from Julia's head.

Marty smoothly raised his pistol and shot Wolf Larkin dead between the eyes, right where his heavy dark eyebrows met over the bridge of his nose. Larkin lurched back, his face registering the surprise that was the last emotion he had in his life. His lifeless fingers dropped his handgun. It fell to the dusty floor. He slammed into the wall of the barn and slid down to the ground, his big dreams and evil plans gone like a wisp of smoke in the breeze.

Marty caught Julia in his arms as she fainted, and carried her outside. "Get Pam, quick," he shouted at Wil Horner, who stood on the small rise above the bunkhouse. "Walt, get inside and find Johnny. Bring him to Julia. She'll want to know about him the instant she wakes up."

As soon as Pam began tending to Julia, Marty entered the main house. Dan and Paco had Jimmy Campbell on the sofa, and they worked on the wound to his head. Big Nose George was propped up by the fireplace, next to the bodies of Waco and Frank and the unconscious Sam, still out cold where he'd fallen.

"How's Jimmy?"

Dan answered, "He'll live, I think. The bullet grooved a hunk of skin off his skull, but didn't go too deep. I reckon he'll have a headache fer a few days, but then should be jus' fine."

Big Nose George groaned, his good hand cradling the

busted one. "My hand needs tendin'. So's my laig and shoulder. You fellas gonna let me bleed to death afore you git to me?"

Marty bent down and looked into the big outlaw's beady eyes. "Big Nose, you worthless bastard. I should kill you where you sit, but I've got a better idea. I'm gonna let you live. You'll pay hell fighting again with your right hand as busted up as it is. You're not gonna like prison, I'm thinking, and you're gonna spend a lot of time there for the next few years. So shut up and let us take care of someone worthy of getting the attention."

Chapter 31

A Vow Fulfilled

Marty rode into the yard as Dan and the others walked out of the kitchen following the evening meal. He saw Julia standing in the shade of the porch, savoring the warm rays of sunset on her face.

"Hello, Julia. How are you and Johnny feeling today?"

"We're fine. Thank you. You get Mick, Tom, and Walt on the stage?"

"They're on their way. Walt says he can't wait to try out building railroads and Tom is anxious to get back to Missouri."

"You see Jimmy Campbell?"

"Sure did. Any chance of some chow while we gab?"

"Certainly, come on into the kitchen."

Marty soon was gnawing on a fried chicken leg and sipping hot coffee. Smacking his lips, he continued where they had left off.

"Jimmy's coming along just fine. He says he'll be back at work in a week or so. He let Otis Beecher and Larkin's regular cowboys outa jail. They convinced him that they didn't know anything about Larkin's plan. I told Otis to bring his three best men out tomorrow. Now that we've lost Walt and Tom, we'll need a few replacements. Otis should be a good foreman—he knows the area and how to raise cattle on the land. Jimmy also says the well-driller sent him a note. He'll arrive Monday. We'll have our new wells in a couple of weeks. Next year you should be able to run five hundred cattle or more on the land. The year after that, twice that number."

Julia shuddered. "And that awful man, Big Nose. Is he locked up good and tight?"

"He's in the county jail in Grand Encampment. It's a better jail than what Warm Springs has. As soon as his wounds allow, they'll put him on trial for kidnapping and attempted murder."

Marty toyed with his coffee cup for a few minutes. "I've been thinking, Julia. I think I could stop my searching and perhaps settle down here with you and Johnny. You're a fine woman. I think I could make a go of this place. What would you think of that?"

"Never, Mr. Keller. Never. I loved my Jim. You killed him. I could never lay down with the man who murdered my husband. In fact, I have been thinking of asking you to move on right away. I think Dan has some feelings for me, but he won't say anything as long as you're here. I think everyone would be a lot better off if you just moved on. You've fulfilled your vow to get me and Johnny here and help us get started. We don't need you anymore. You have my thanks and my permission to go. I'm asking you, Mr. Keller. Please, go."

Marty sat in stunned silence for a moment, then fought to quell the rising anger he felt. Swallowing a hasty retort, he nodded and set down the cup. "Fine, I'll leave tomorrow. Please have some supplies packed for me, if it's not too much trouble."

Julia nodded and said no more. Mumbling a good night,

Marty rushed from the kitchen, and stomped around the yard until he had cooled off enough to go into the bunkhouse. He tossed and turned all night long.

The next morning he bid his farewells to the men and rode away. As he reached the front gate, he looked back. Julia had moved over until she was standing close to Dan. Both were watching him and Dan waved as Marty looked back. Gigging Pacer with his spurs, Marty loped down the road to Warm Springs, seething inside. He felt like Julia had failed to appreciate his efforts on her behalf. She also had coldly rejected his offer to settle down with her, a thought he had entertained quite a bit the past few days. "Well, damn her to hell if that's the way she wants it. Come on, Pacer. Let's put some miles behind us."

He stopped in Warm Springs to say farewell to Jimmy and then walked over to the bar in the Wolf Hotel. Fredrick Wolf stood behind the bar, filling in for Jimmy.

"*Guten tag,* Herr Marty."

"Morning, Fredrick. How's business?"

"Very good, *danke.* You haf a minute to answer me one question?"

"Sure."

"Vhat am I to do, now dat Herr Larkin is dead?"

"I'd say you ought just keep on running this place like you have been. Tell Jimmy you want to buy it and run it. I think you'd do a good job and the town needs the hotel and bar, that's for certain. Jimmy'll take care of you, fair and square."

"Good. I vill do it. *Danken,* Herr Marty."

Marty took his leave, his mood brightened by the friendly exchange with the young German. "He'll be good for Warm Springs, Pacer, ole pal," Marty forecast. "Come on, let's mosey on down to Grand Encampment before we quit for the day. What do you say?"

Marty spent the night at a hotel in the town named after the famous Mountain Men Rendezvous that had been held there nearly fifty years earlier. After finishing his breakfast, he walked over to the sheriff's office. The sheriff was a slender man not much older than Marty, his brown mustache long and shaggy. His blue eyes were quick and appraising as Marty stopped in front of his desk.

"Hello, Sheriff." Marty tipped his hat and then took it off. "I was wondering if I could take a look at your stack of wanted posters."

The sheriff looked at Marty, his eyes turning frosty. "I don't cotton to bounty hunters."